Love How You Love Me

Boys of Riverside

Gracie Graham

To all of the readers who read *Love the Way You Lie* and reached out, expressing how much they loved it. YOU are the reason I write. So, thank you!

Writing is a hard and solitary endeavor, and though I love it, in times of doubt, I look back on your kind words and they fuel me.

This book is for you. I only hope you enjoy reading it as much as I enjoyed writing it.

And if you aren't ready to say goodbye to the *Boys of Riverside* yet, don't worry. There's more to come . . .

CHAPTER 1

MACKENZIE

YOU KNOW WHAT'S HARDER than grieving the dead? Being angry with them.

I crouch down in front of the slab of granite, the green grass beneath my feet spongy from the recent rain. My mother's name is carved into the dark stone, along with her birth date and the date of her death, but that's not what draws my attention. I stare at the cluster of white hydrangeas with a frown. I've been coming here once a week since I recovered my memory, trying to find some semblance of peace among my conflicted emotions, and each week, I find fresh flowers. I have no idea who's bringing them. It's not my father—I asked—which leads me to believe they're from Anthony Mancetti, her former lover.

The thought spurs to life the anger hibernating inside me. Like a beast, it rises on its hind legs inside my chest, stretching out and filling me up. I have so many questions for her, but no way to get answers, which leaves behind a kind of despair and frustration I wouldn't wish on anyone.

I think about the weeks and months following the accident often. How I cried for days, wishing I had died in her place. I'd been driving, yet I lived while she didn't. I missed her desperately, and every time I stared into my father's eyes and saw a hint of his own grief, I hated myself for putting it there. There was no end to my self-loathing, the depth of my despair cavernous. But now . . . I can't erase the things I've learned. Like the fact that had my mother remained faithful in her marriage, none of us would've been there that day. The car crash never would have happened.

I stand back up, straightening as I stare down at her grave, wishing I could remember her how I used to. As the mom who played with me at the lake in the summer. The one who took me to the park and bought me ice cream. The woman who stood in line for hours at the fair so I could ride all of the attractions one more time. She taught me how to color inside the lines, brush my teeth, and comb my hair. She taught me how to love myself so that I could love others. I miss her desperately.

But in death she also taught me things. She educated me on the art of deception. Of how to be distrustful and to never take things at face value—that things aren't always as they seem. Most of all, she taught me how to question love.

A breeze ruffles my hair, rustling the fall foliage in the nearby trees when a hint of spice—cinnamon and cardamom—and cedar drifts toward me. A scent I'd know anywhere.

I lift my head in time to catch sight of Atlas cresting the hill.

He pauses when he sees me, and at the same time my gaze drifts to the cluster of white hydrangeas in his hands.

My mouth parts as I take a step back. Several seconds pass before I find my voice. "It's you who's been bringing her flowers?" I ask, my tone ripe with disbelief.

"Mackenzie . . ." He steps forward, eyes pleading with me to stay, because now, nearly every time I see him, I run.

But I no longer listen to liars. "Don't." I hold an arm out to stop him as I take a step back.

"Would you please just talk to me? Hear me out?"

"You have no right to be here," I say, even though it's a ridiculous statement—no one has rights to the dead—but it feels so wrong seeing him here, knowing he's been visiting her.

I take another step back as he takes one forward, and it becomes clear to me I'm the one that needs to leave. I spin on my heel, ignoring the sadness in his eyes and the way my name sounds on his lips as he calls out to me one last time, knowing that if I stay, I might spiral. My emotions are high as it is, and the last thing I want is to break down in front of him.

I head toward the fence of the cemetery and out the metal gate, shutting it behind me. Goliath is exactly where I left him, tied to the metal bench surrounding the property, waiting. His ears perk when he sees me, and he stands.

If only humans were so loyal.

Unlatching his leash, I beckon him forward. We take the sidewalk and start to run while one question dances in my head.

How the hell did he know her favorite flower?

It's only a day after I saw Atlas in the cemetery at my mother's grave, yet I can't shake the sight of him.

My lungs burn from the cold, cheeks stinging with the bite of the wind. The cool autumn weather seemingly gave way to wintry temperatures overnight, and though I'll miss the sunshine, warm afternoons, and crisp leaves scenting the air, I don't mind the cold; I like the discomfort and the chill in my bones. It gives me something else to focus on when I run, other than the relentless thoughts that plague me. Because there are some things I can't seem to outpace no matter how hard I try.

Beside me, Goliath's tongue lolls out of the side of his mouth while my sneakers smack the pavement. The urgency of my breathing increases along with my speed before it evens out again. Muscles warm, I try to push Atlas from my mind and focus on the homes of Pine Grove looming in the distance, but it's no use. The sight of him is too fresh to forget.

Despite avoiding him at all costs, he seems to be everywhere. My thoughts. The halls at school. The football field. Even my mother's grave is no longer sacred. Every time I see him is a painful reminder of our last conversation—that fateful day outside the football field where I finally regained my memory and realized he knew everything and kept it from me.

Sometimes I lie awake at night and imagine a different scenario. One where Atlas is just as shocked as I am to discover his father played a role in my mother's death. But in the end, the truth cannot be amended to meet my desires. There is no happily ever after for me and Atlas, no matter how badly I want there to be. There's no getting over the fact his father is to blame for the headstone at Riverside Cemetery with my mother's name on it. It's like the giant elephant in the room we can't seem to shove back in the closet. No matter how much time passes or how much we love each other, the truth will always be there, wedged between us, the silent death knell of our relationship.

I've come to terms with it. Mostly.

On the other hand, Atlas keeps trying to convince me we stand a fighting chance, no matter how many times I shut him down.

I'm not giving up on you. We're not done yet, not even close.

His words haunt me.

I shouldn't have watched the Rebels interview, and I know it. Every time I see his face, all I think about is how he took me in his father's car, knowing his own flesh and blood used it as a murder weapon, then lied to me about it only to turn around and take advantage of my vulnerability.

He can pledge his love publicly to me all he wants, but it changes nothing. It doesn't erase the betrayal. Just like it does nothing to eradicate the memory of his dark gaze on mine. The soft press of his warm lips igniting me like an inferno—

I stumble. Catching myself, I push back against the image of Atlas in my head, but he's all around me. The wind whips, reminding me of the way his touch sinks into my bones. The whirring of a chainsaw in the distance brings me back to the sound of his raspy voice. The pine tree up ahead stirs up the earthy scent of his skin.

Gritting my teeth, I run faster.

My feet pound. My legs scream. My body vibrates.

I don't want to think about the way his eyes crinkle at the corners when he smiles just for me, or how smooth and tan his skin is. Nor do I want to remember the thick ropes of muscle rippling just beneath the surface. I don't want to think of him at all.

It makes me want things I can't have.

It makes me wish things were different.

A knife twists in my belly when I realize this is how Graham must have felt when I rejected him. This gut-wrenching, stab-bing pain inside is my penance for hurting him. Either that, or karma really is a bitch.

A wave of shame washes over me at the thought of my best friend. Through it all, he's been so loyal, so devoted, and it makes me feel unworthy. It's a miracle he still wants to be my friend at all. I'm not sure I could be the bigger person if the situation were reversed.

A car pulls up beside me and slows down to match my pace. I glance over to see his face and my stride falters. Stumbling, I catch my foot on a massive crack in the sidewalk and yelp. My arms flail at my sides for balance, but it's no use. The sound of my name reaches my ears as I fall backward into a patch of thick brush with unladylike grace.

Oof!

Stunned, I lie there, grateful I saved my head from cracking like a melon on the concrete, when I realize I'm no longer holding Goliath's leash.

I try to sit up, but I'm caught on something, and when I crane my neck for a better look, I see a thicket of burrs tangled in my long hair and groan. "Well, this should be fun," I mumble.

At the sound of my voice, Goliath appears and drags his tongue over the side of my face in a sloppy kiss.

I wince and hold him back. "Where were you a second ago when I lost my balance, huh?"

With a sigh, I reach behind me and do my best to release my hair at the same time I hear a car door close. The heat of a blush rises to my cheeks as I manage to free myself and stand.

"Kenz!" Graham yells among the sound of his heavy footfalls.

Great. As if facing Graham these days isn't humbling enough, he has to witness me biff it. I'm a freaking mess, inside and out, and I have no doubt I look as bad as I feel.

My ankle throbs. I must've twisted it when I fell, but I ignore the pain and hobble forward at the same time Graham reaches me, and I offer him a mortified wave.

Graham ushers me to my bedroom, and I'm infinitely grateful my father isn't home. He and I aren't on the best of terms, and the last thing I want is him hovering and obsessing over the fact that I fell while running when I'm completely fine.

I sink down on the edge of my bed at Graham's urging while he takes a step back and fights a grin. "You should see yourself."

"Ha ha," I deadpan.

"Here, sit on the floor, and I'll help you get the burrs out."

"Are there a lot?" I ask, patting the back of my head to discover what feels like a brambly bird's nest. "It's fine. I can just—"

"Sit." He motions to the spot beneath my bed, his stern gaze leaving little room for argument.

I do as I'm told and sit, crisscross-applesauce as he takes the spot behind me on the edge of my bed. His touch is gentle as he starts to work on my hair, untangling each strand from the burrs that entwine them while I stare at our reflection in the mirror on the closet door across from me.

His sandy hair is longer than it used to be and slightly disheveled. For the life of me, I can't remember the last time he got it cut. It curls around his ears and just above his collar. The length suits him, unlike the fatigue in his once vibrant green eyes, which makes him look older than he is—tired. Dark circles ring them like crescent moons, and when he glances up at our reflection, I notice they're red-rimmed, like he hasn't been sleeping well.

He quickly glances back down to my hair, placing one of the untangled burrs on the bed beside him while guilt gnaws on my insides like vermin.

I wonder if I'm the cause before I tell myself I am. *Of course, I am.*

I bite my lip in an effort to replicate even the slightest bit of the pain I caused him while he removes another burr. His hands move so effortlessly, I barely know he's there—such a stark contrast to the shame stabbing my insides with reckless abandon.

I don't deserve his grace, nor the tenderness he's showing me.

"Graham..." I swallow over the ache in the back of my throat before I can continue. I've apologized to him a million times over in the past few weeks, but it never feels like enough. "I just want to tell you again how sorry—"

"Where's your dad?" he asks, cutting me off. Based on his tone, I know he has zero interest in hearing any more of my apologies.

"At work."

"Are things getting any better between you two?"

I sigh and think about my answer. I've barely spoken a word to my father in weeks, but avoidance seems the best medicine for my anger and loathing. We're like strangers under one roof, with him making all the effort and me ignoring it.

Though it's only been a month since I discovered the happy family I once had was all a lie, it feels like a lifetime.

In my naivete, I thought remembering what happened would solve all my problems, give me closure and allow me to move on, yet it's done none of those things. Somehow, it's only

caused me more heartache and grief than healing.

My nightmares have increased. Flashbacks occur in regular intervals, each one sharper than the next, and my personal life is a wreck. My father is enemy number one. So, no, things have not gotten better between us. If anything, they're worse.

"Have things gotten better between you and *your* father?" I ask.

His mouth presses into a flat line. "Touché."

Graham pulls another burr from my hair, along with a twig and a couple of leaves before he reaches for the brush on my nightstand and begins to run it through my long locks.

I close my eyes as he works, wondering how he can be so gentle when it's obvious he's still angry with me. Not that I blame him. I rejected him for his cousin. All along Graham said Atlas would hurt me, and he did, leaving him to pick up the pieces.

But who's picking up the pieces for Graham?

I want to.

I wish more than anything to be that person for him, but when you're the one who did the hurting, it's kind of hard to do the healing as well.

They say you can't help who you fall in love with, and maybe that's true, but we *can* help what we do about it. Had I heeded

Graham's advice and steered clear of Atlas, I can't help but think we'd all be in a better place right now. Things would be different.

I've wondered a million times in the past month if I chose the wrong boy, knowing it's too late. All of us are already broken.

I open my eyes, watching as he runs the brush down the length of my hair.

Graham says he forgives me, but the dull light in his eyes when he catches me staring and the stiff set of his shoulders say otherwise.

So, I try again. "Graham, I—"

"You have enough on your plate." He shoots me a pointed look, his tone dismissive. "Why don't you try and focus on that, hmm?" When he stands and scoops the burrs into his hand, I know this part of the conversation is over.

I swallow, instantly chastised, before I nod and wait as he returns from my bathroom and takes a seat back on the bed. I sink down beside him, noting the way his hands clench into fists, and I wonder if it's because he's fighting the urge to hold my hand like he used to, or whether he's angry with me.

"So, tell me what's got you all keyed up," he says, his voice soft.

"What makes you think something's wrong?"

He arches a brow. "How well do I know you?"

Sometimes I forget how well.

"Right." I sigh, before I shrug off his concern. "It's nothing much. My father mostly."

"And . . . ?"

I bite the inside of my cheek, reluctant to talk about my problems with him when they involve Atlas.

He nudges my shoulder with his. "Spill."

I groan, knowing he won't let up until I give in. Because that's how Graham is, always pushing me until I crack. "I feel like one giant jumble of emotions, and I can't determine where one feeling ends and another begins. I'm angry with my mother. Like, super angry. I don't understand how she could do what she did, how she could betray us. I thought they were happy—I thought *she* was happy—and I have so many questions. Was it just a fling, lust? Or did she love him? And if she did, when did she stop loving my father?"

I pick at a loose thread on my bedspread as my thoughts darken. "Still, no matter how badly my father was hurting, he let me believe I was responsible for her death. He ignored evidence that could've vindicated my mother and my own pain and suffering all because of . . . what? Shame? Ego?"

I snap my mouth shut and swallow over the ache in the back of my throat as my thoughts drift to Atlas. I know better than to say his name, but so much of this is about him, too.

"Do you know my mother's favorite flower?" I ask, biting my lip as I picture Atlas, a handful of hydrangeas in his fist.

Graham frowns, his hands moving through my hair. "Sunflowers like yours? I don't know. Why?"

"No reason," I say, quickly, brushing off the thought. "I want Lee Scott to pay for driving drunk, then leaving us. Maybe I'd feel better if he did. But jail doesn't seem good enough. And even if it was, I still lose. Because by turning him in, my father and I will get dragged into this mess."

Graham leans back on his arms, staring over at me, his expression earnest. "How so?"

"My father filed the police report. He ignored an eyewitness testimony that indicated a second vehicle. And as angry as I am with him, I don't want him to lose his job. Or worse, get into legal trouble. Riverside is a small town. Gossip will run rampant and before I know it, my family's name will be whispered all over town. My mother's affair will be scandalized. Our reputation will be dragged through the mud. And maybe my father deserves some of that, but I sure as hell don't. Do I really want to deal with the fallout?"

And do I really want Atlas to watch his father go down for murder?

Despite how much he hurt me, I'm not sure I can do that to him.

But I don't say so, because I know it won't go over well.

Instead, I sink my head into my hands as Graham reaches out and runs a hand through my hair before brushing a thumb over my jaw. And just like that, a wave of calm washes through me. His touch is familiar and comforting all at once.

But when I angle my head and look at him, he snatches his hand away, holding it close to his chest as if it's on fire. His throat bobs, and it's a moment before he speaks. "That's . . . a lot," he breathes. "But you don't have to do anything about it if you don't want to. It's not your job to bring my uncle to justice."

"Then if it's not mine, whose?"

"*His.* Your father's. My cousin's," he says between gritted teeth, and my cheeks heat with shame. He can't even say his name. "All of them failed you, and it's up to them to make this right. You did nothing wrong here."

I nod and stare into Graham's solemn gaze, agreeing with him, though it doesn't feel like I'm innocent. It feels like I'm very much culpable. "Maybe you're right."

His fingers grip my chin as he holds my face, keeping my gaze steady on his. "You've already lost your mom. Whether you like it or not, your dad is all you have, and no one will blame you for not wanting to destroy what's left of your family. No one will blame you if you don't want to go through the scrutiny of it all."

I nod. "I thought everything would get easier once I remembered, but it just feels harder."

"Sometimes the truth hurts," Graham says, his tone hard in a way that tells me he's talking about more than just my memory returning. He's talking about us.

"But it's necessary to move on, right?" I try to read his solemn expression and fail. "Because that's what I keep telling myself."

"Then what else do you need to know? What do you need for closure?"

"I need to talk to Anthony Mancetti, the man my mother was having the affair with," I say. "Now that I know the truth, I want to confront him and get some answers about his relationship with my mother. I need to understand why she'd risk our family, our happiness, for whatever it is they had. Because the fact of the matter is if she hadn't been having an affair, neither of us would've been there that day. And none of this would've happened."

I bite my lip, thinking of what I'm about to ask him next. After everything I put him through, I don't deserve his help. But there's no one else I'd want with me.

"Will you take me to speak with him?" I swallow, waiting for his response.

His eyes narrow on my face, his brows pulling together, and for a moment I think he might say no, but then he nods. "Yeah, of course. How about tomorrow?"

CHAPTER 2

ATLAS

WHEN MY PHONE RINGS for the millionth time, I have half a mind to chuck it across the room before I think otherwise and pick it up. No matter how many times I've tried to squash the hope it might be Mackenzie, I can't seem to do it. I'm a fool for thinking there's even a remote possibility of seeing her name on my caller ID, but I'd rather be a fool than give up on her.

She and I, we're better than this—stronger—and I refuse to believe we can't get past what happened between us.

I inhale and glance at the screen, preparing myself for the chance it's her, but it's the same unknown number with the out-of-town area code that's been calling me for days.

Cursing under my breath, I hit ignore and send it to voice mail. Seems my mother can't take a hint.

I have no idea how she got my number, but she's been calling me multiple times a day ever since the Rebels interview when I declared my love for Mackenzie. I couldn't care less about what she has to say, and all she's doing by pestering me is reaffirming my decision to bail on her the second the words "Atlas it's me . . . your mother" left her mouth. Not a single part of me feels sorry for not hearing her out. She's had hundreds of moments before now to get in touch. Birthdays. Christmases. Summer vacations. And a thousand more in between. That ship has sailed.

Right now, my focus is on two things, and two things only: Football and winning Mackenzie back. I have no time for anything else.

Someone knocks on my closed door and I startle at the sound. Lifting my gaze from my phone, I call out, "Come in."

I wait as it pushes open and Uncle Cal steps into the room. His gaze flickers to the large television mounted to the wall across from my bed to see I'm watching game tape to prep for States, and he smiles. "Getting ready for next week?"

I lean back against the headboard, feeling the tension drain from my muscles, relieved to take my mind off my mother and focus on the one thing that seems to be going right in my life. "All day and all night," I say.

"And how about the rest of the team?"

I hesitate, pursing my lips as I mull over my response.

Is the team ready?

Most of us are.

Okay, all of us, with one exception. But I won't call out Graham to his own father. Uncle Cal knows something went on between him, Mackenzie, and me. He just doesn't know what, and seeing as Graham and his father have their own problems, I have zero desire to insert myself in their mess of a relationship.

Besides, even if I wanted to help Graham out, he'd never allow me to, considering he hates my guts. We're lucky we can even stand to be on the same field together without ripping each other's throats out.

So, I shrug in response and mutter a noncommittal, "We'll be okay."

"Graham's struggling."

I say nothing. That much is obvious, so I stare at my uncle, waiting for him to get to the point.

"I can't say I know what to do about it. Nothing gets through to him, and if I didn't know any better, I'd say he's intent on throwing away the whole season. He's doing everything but focusing on these next couple weeks despite the fact that they determine his whole damn future." He shoves his hands in the pockets of his pants, then takes a step closer. "Listen, I don't know what happened between the two of you . . ."

Here we go.

I hold my breath and turn my gaze from his, waiting for him to call me out. Ever since my father was arrested and he took me in, I've been preparing for the other shoe to drop. Waiting for him to realize I'm not worth the effort and boot my ass to the curb.

I can't even say I blame him.

"But I'm worried about *both* of you," he adds. My head jerks to his and I force the surprise from my expression. "You had an amazing season, Atlas. Better than my son's. But there's no denying States can change your life. If you ever had any hope of solidifying recruiter interest, it's next weekend out on that field.

I nod. "Yes, sir."

"Both you and Graham need to be ready, and whatever this is between the two of you"—he motions to me—"needs to be set aside. I think it goes without saying no girl is worth your future." He eyes me pointedly and I fight the urge to shrink under his gaze, because he's only partly right. Football might be my future, but so is Mackenzie.

All I have to do is win her back.

"Right." I clear my throat. "Well, I'll be ready to bring my A game, I promise you that. I might be dealing with some things right now, but I can guarantee you I'm focused on States and I'll do everything I can to get recruited."

"Good." Uncle Cal nods. "At least you have your priorities straight. I wish Graham did." He sighs and tucks his hands in his pockets. "Speaking of my son, do you happen to know where I can find him?"

"No, sir." I shake my head, wishing I could be more of a help, but I haven't a clue. Selfishly, I hope he's not with Mackenzie, but from what I can tell, Graham is hardly ever home these days, and when he is, I've made it a point to make myself scarce in his presence.

Uncle Cal's forehead creases with worry and he reaches up to rub the knot between his brow. "It feels like he's rarely ever here, and when he is, he's sulking, hiding away in his room, refusing to talk to anyone. Half the time, he looks like he hasn't slept in days and sometimes, I catch the hint of booze on his breath."

I swallow. Everything Cal says is true, and I know it. But I don't know how to comfort him. Emotions aren't my strong suit, and I've seen firsthand the cycle of addiction and how it can grip a person by the throat. It runs in our blood. Our genetics are ripe with it, which is why I've never taken so much as a sip of alcohol. But I've witnessed Graham shot-gunning beers faster than he can crack 'em open at a recent party, and his behavior as of late offers little reassurance this is merely a passing phase, the innocent rebellion of a high school senior letting loose before he graduates.

"I'll let you know if I see him," I say because it's all I've got.

He nods, then reaches into his pants pocket and pulls out a small white envelope, then offers it to me. "This came for you today."

When I glance at the return address, I see it's from Rise Rehabilitation and my blood runs cold. "Thanks," I mumble, turning the envelope over in my hands.

"Anything else bothering you?" Uncle Cal asks, hovering by the doorway.

I lift my gaze to find him watching me, a knowing expression in his dark gaze, and my thoughts immediately flicker back to my mother. "What makes you think something else is bothering me?"

He shifts his focus, looking everywhere but me and shrugging a little too casually. "No reason. You just seem . . . burdened."

I slowly shake my head as the muscles in my neck tense. For a moment, I wonder if he knows about my mother showing up a week ago and what that means if he does.

"Nope. Nothing," I say, my tone clipped.

He smiles, but it doesn't reach his eyes. "Okay, just remember I'm here if you need me. Anytime you want to talk or have a problem . . ." He raps his knuckles on the doorframe, lingering, while the suspicion he knows more than he's letting on blooms stronger inside me.

It takes everything in me to fight the urge to interrogate him, but I don't want to seem ungrateful for everything he's done for me, so I simply nod and say, "Sure thing."

I have no choice but to trust he's on my side. Besides, ever since Pops and I moved to Riverside, he's given me no reason to believe otherwise.

He turns and closes the door on his way out, leaving me to myself and I settle back on the bed, envelope in hand. I stare at it a moment longer before placing it on the bed in front of me. I haven't seen my father since the day I visited him in jail, and the last time I spoke to him was the day I asked for his keys—the same day I realized he'd been the one to kill Mackenzie's mother— and I'm not sure I want anything to do with him again.

Trying my best to ignore the letter, I focus back on the television and the game tape in front of me, watching as Crestmont, a team from Cincinnati, plays on the screen. They're our first opponent next weekend at States and their quarterback is amazing, practically untouchable. If we want any chance of beating them, Graham will have to be at his best. Might be nice if he actually acted like he gave a shit. A lot is riding on this one game and the outcome would affect the fates of half our team. Jace, Knox, Teagan . . . a lot of us depend on each and every one of our teammates to give it their all.

Crestmont takes the ball on the screen and lines up. The football snaps and they spring into action, but the plays don't register. The blue and gold uniforms blur as my eyes glaze over, my thoughts and gaze drifting back to the envelope on the bed in front of me like a homing beacon.

I sigh and pick it back up, then tear it open. I always was a curious bastard, and I know I won't be able to focus until I see what's inside.

I slide a little card out and open it to see a note written in an unfamiliar script. I can tell immediately by the loopy scrawl, it's written by Dr. Fatima Smith, my father's therapist. My brow creases as I read it, then rake a hand through my hair and turn my gaze to the window beside my bed.

The trees are almost bare, with only a few leaves clinging to the branches. Soon, there'll be none at all, and then the snow will start. Everything barren, cold, and white, and seemingly dead. Kind of like how I've felt these past few years. Until

Mackenzie came along and sparked everything inside of me to life again.

I wonder what she'd think about my invitation to come visit my father rehab. I wonder what she'd say if she knew they wanted to celebrate his six-week sobriety mark, or that they'd deemed him stable enough for visitors in his recovery while her mother's rotting in her grave.

Fuck that.

I crumple up the card and toss it on the floor while my stomach twists.

I have so many fucked up emotions when it comes to my pops. Despite being a falling down drunk and addict, he was the one person in my life who stuck around. He might have been a shitty role model, but at least he was *there*. I've always been grateful for that, because as long as he stuck around, I could tell myself at least *someone* loved me. At least one person cared enough to stay.

Sometimes I can even fool myself into thinking not all the memories are bad either. Like holidays where he made sure we had a decent meal. Or Sundays watching football. Afternoons where I clung to his every word as he regaled me with stories of his glory days.

My heart thuds painfully in my chest at the memory.

Back then, I listened with awe. That was before I knew better. Before I realized he gave his whole life to bottles and pills.

But for every "happy" memory, there were a million more horrific ones to drown them out. Like cleaning up his puke after a bender, or finding him passed out, drunk. Forgotten holidays, birthdays, and empty cupboards. Evictions and empty promises.

And when I think about these things, the truth hits me like a tidal wave.

He did abandon me. Just in a different way. Because he cared more about getting fucked up then making sure I was fed and clothed and bathed at night. He cared more about his next hit than school functions, homework, and keeping a roof over our heads.

He's taken so many things away from me in the short span I've been on this earth, and now he's taken Mackenzie away from me, too. How long will I pay for the sins of my father?

I was okay dealing with the consequences of his addiction when I thought I was the only one hurting from it.

But he hurt Mackenzie, too.

He killed her mother.

And for that, I'll never forgive him.

I have no idea why Mackenzie hasn't turned him in or why she hasn't gone to the police with what she's remembered.

But I'm done waiting for her to make a move.

I've given her time. Space.

Now my father needs to pay for all the pain he's caused, which is why I need to stop waiting for her to make the first move and turn him in.

I hop to my feet and snatch my jacket from the back of my desk chair, grab my keys, and head for the door.

I need to tell Chief Hart the truth. Now.

Then, maybe, just maybe, Mackenzie might find it in herself to forgive me. Maybe then I can win her back.

I only hope I'm doing the right thing. Because once I do this, there's no turning back.

CHAPTER 3

MACKENZIE

G RAHAM TAKES THE WICKLAND exit and follows the GPS while I try not to think about the last time I came here with Atlas. It was just after the bonfire at Crow's Creek where we kissed for the first time. He'd blown me off at school the following Monday, and I thought for sure his feelings for me were nothing more than a moment of convenience. But then we'd gone to the precinct and got the accident report, went to Mancetti's, and afterward, he kissed me again.

As if sensing the trajectory of my thoughts, Graham glances over at me, but I avoid his gaze as guilt washes through me.

We stop at a light, and I shove the swirling of emotions aside and turn to my friend, whose weary gaze focuses up at the traffic light. Sometimes I curse myself for not making him and I work. For not pushing my heart in his direction instead of allowing myself to fall for Atlas.

But then I remember the truth, that Atlas and I were drawn to each other from the start. Inevitable. Because the heart wants what the heart wants.

When he says nothing, I angle myself toward him, and my chest pinches as I think of all the things I'd do over if I could. Like lying to him about spending time with Atlas. Or playing down my feelings for his cousin, when I knew they were more than I let on. I wouldn't kiss Graham back or hold his hand in the hall. And most of all, I would say no to wearing his jersey.

I sent him all the wrong signals, and being unsure of my own feelings wasn't enough of an excuse.

I love Graham, and I should've protected him. I've always been his priority. I should've put him first, too. Had I done that, our friendship wouldn't be in this awkward limbo, like the aftermath of some kind of messed up love triangle blown to bits with him looking worse for wear.

"What's on your mind?" he asks, bringing me back to the moment.

I force a smile. "Just thinking about you. Worrying about you, actually."

"This again?" He sighs and runs a hand through his hair, then presses the gas and we start to move.

"You just seem to have something on your mind."

He shrugs, the movement stiff. "Why would you think that?"

"I know you, Graham. Sometimes I think you forget just how much. You've been distant and quiet. Teagan tells me you've been talking to Peters a lot, too. Is something going on that—"

"Nothing's going on," he snaps. "Peters just happens to be the only person on the team who despises my cousin as much as me, and it's nice to have someone to talk to who doesn't worship his ass."

"Oh." I fiddle with my seat belt, unsure of what to say next. All I want is for him to talk to me—*really* talk to me—without the tension of what happened crackling between us like the flick of a bullwhip. "Is your father riding you about States?" I try again. "I can only imagine the pressure he's putting on you. I know what he's like during the regular season, let alone a state championship your senior year."

"Cal is being Cal. Nothing out of the ordinary."

"If you need someone to talk to, I'm here." My gaze bores into the side of his face as he comes to another stop, but he says nothing, and I wish for just a moment, he'd lower the shield he's resurrected between us. "Is there a reason you're not hanging with the guys like you were? Jace told me you've skipped the last two field parties at Crow's Creek."

He shrugs. "Nope. Just not feeling it."

I sigh, frustrated. "Graham, come on."

"What?" he asks, his tone hard. "I'm answering your questions, aren't I?"

"Yeah, but you're not really telling me anything, are you? You're giving me these vague, meaningless answers, but when you ask me how I'm doing, I'm supposed to spill my guts to you or you get mad."

He clenches his jaw, averting his gaze, and I can tell I've hit a sore spot.

"I don't know what you're talking about," he says, his tone flat.

"How are you doing, Graham? Like, *really* doing?"

He stares straight ahead, his gaze vacant, saying nothing as his throat bobs, and my heart aches for him. I want to reach out and pull him into my arms, hold him in one of our giant bear hugs and tell him everything's going to be okay. But I'm so afraid of hurting him again, so afraid of sending him the wrong message or leading him on. So instead, I let my frustration and helplessness fuel me as I say, "I realize I'm not the only one hurting, and I know these past few months have been hard on you, but you're distant and sullen. You're not yourself, Graham. Even the guys are starting to notice."

"Oh, I'm sorry." His head snaps back to me, and his hands tighten on the wheel. "I didn't realize you were so damn sick of me trying to recover from you stomping all over my heart. What an inconvenience. Yet here I am, helping you anyway. So maybe you could cut me some slack."

My eyes widen as his words hit their mark.

Swallowing, I try and stifle the pain threatening to twist my features by pressing my mouth into a thin line. "Yeah, you're right," I croak out, because I won't make him feel bad for telling me how he really feels. After all, it's what I wanted, what I asked for. "I'm sorry. I just . . ." My mouth opens and closes as I struggle for words. I glance away from him, so he doesn't have to watch me flounder. "I won't ask again," I say.

It kills me to leave the conversation like this, but I don't expect him to help me out and make things any easier. Not when I'm the one that did the hurting.

We ride the rest of the way in silence, and when we approach Mancetti's house, my skin prickles in anticipation. I sit straighter in my seat and point at the same time the GPS indicates we've arrived. "This is it," I say.

It's the first words I've spoken since he chastised me, and I'm embarrassed at the thickness in my voice, how raw with emotion I am. "You don't have to come in if you don't want to," I add, already wrenching open the car door.

"Of course, I'm coming in," he says, hastily.

I exhale slightly, relieved I won't have to face Mancetti alone, and offer Graham a soft smile and step out of the car.

I make my way over the sidewalk, Graham nipping at my heels while my chest tightens. I wonder how many times my mother came here. A woman emerges next door and I wonder if they ever met her.

She offers me a friendly wave while balancing a covered dish in her arms. I lift my hand to return the greeting, though I'm not feeling particularly friendly, then watch as she turns to lock her door while clumsily bobbling the dish before it slips from her grasp entirely. It lands with a thunderous crash. Shards of glass spray around her feet while she curses loud enough for me to hear, and I freeze, my feet rooted to the cement beneath them.

My eyes glaze and my visions blurs as my breathing turns shallow.

I know what's coming.

Just like I know I'm powerless to stop it.

A whimper escapes my parted lips while I fight to stay grounded to the present, but it's a losing battle. My eyes fall closed, and I scream.

CHAPTER 4

MACKENZIE

THE PRICKLING SENSATION CREEPING up my spine intensifies until my limbs go numb and nausea bubbles from my stomach into my throat. The next thing I know, I'm standing back at Manja, Manja, cold and wet as ice water soaks into my clothing.

A shock rips through me while my heart races.

"I'm so sorry," the waitress says, hands fluttering as if unsure how to help me.

"No. No, it was my fault." I risk a glance over my shoulder and when I do, Mom's eyes lock on mine.

She knows I know.

I dart for the door.

The crisp autumn air hits me the moment I step outside and sprint for my car. Wasting no time, I jump inside and start it, hands trembling as I turn the keys in the ignition.

Mom appears on the sidewalk, searching the lot for me, and when she finds me, she heads my way.

I put the car in drive and press the gas pedal pausing only a moment before I pull out onto the road, but it's just enough time to allow Mom to open the passenger door and jump inside.

"Get out," I scream at her as I pull out of the parking lot.

I'm so mad at her, my chest aches.

How could she do this to me? To my father? To our family?

"Not until you talk to me," she says, her voice thick with emotion.

An engine roars behind me and I check the rearview mirror to find a small blue Ford Fiesta coming dangerously close to my bumper. I flinch, sure they're going to hit me from behind when they go to pass. Something dangles from their rearview mirror, and I try to make out what it is only to realize with disgust that it's a lucky rabbit's foot.

"I don't want to hear anything you have to say," I tell her once my eyes are back on the road.

"Mackenzie, please—"

Before she can finish her sentence, the blue car darts back in our lane too early, cutting us off. Their backend smashes into the front of my car and we careen off the road straight toward a telephone pole.

A scream curdles in my lungs and out of my mouth as I–

"Kenzie! Kenz, wake up!" Graham's voice slices through the memories.

Slowly, I come back down to earth, my body shaking like an earthquake while my heart pounds and my shirt clings to my sweat-dampened back like a second skin.

I gasp for air. I'm a fish out of water, yet my lungs can't seem to get their fill. Every time I have a flashback, the memories become crisper and I remember something new, feel a little more.

Clinging to Graham's arms, I lean into him while he strokes a steady hand down the length of my hair, even while I curse myself for it. Because here I am, once again, falling to pieces in his arms.

"What the hell happened?" he rasps out.

I swallow, allowing my pulse to calm some more and catch my breath before I answer. "I don't know. I was walking when I heard something crash or break or . . . it all came tumbling back," I say, gasping over the words.

Graham leans closer, staring into my eyes with his moss-green gaze. Concern wrinkles brow, his voice calm as he murmurs, "It was just a flashback. You're okay now."

I nod, knowing he's right.

But in the moment, it felt so real. Like I was right back at Manja, Manja, reliving the crash all over again.

"I'm okay," I say with a weak smile.

"Are they always like this?" he asks, his tone laced with fear. He's well apprised on how I've been reliving that day for the past month.

"They've been hitting me more, yeah," I say, avoiding the whole truth. Which is that they're getting worse, not better—both the frequency and the strength of the flashbacks—but they'll go away once I know more. Of that, I'm convinced, because I still need to make a decision on what to do about Atlas's father. He still hasn't been brought to justice, but once he is, and he pays for what he's done and I can understand why my mother tore our family apart, then I'll have the closure I need. I can rest, and the memories will disappear just as quickly as they came.

Or at least that's what I keep telling myself.

I focus back on Graham, noticing for the first time another presence beside him. Anthony Mancetti is crouched down, staring at me like a bug under a microscope.

Animosity prickles under my skin. This man, of all people, who helped destroy my family, has some nerve staring at me like I'm broken when he lit the dynamite.

"You okay?" he asks.

I glance away, jaw tight, unwilling and unable to speak to him over the lump in my throat.

"She's good," Graham answers for me, his tone clipped, for which I'm grateful.

With a nod, Mancetti reaches out and takes one of my arms, helping Graham steady me as I get to my feet. "Why don't you come inside?"

I glance around me and note the woman next door where she's crouched down, cleaning up broken glass off her concrete patio. When she offers me a sympathetic smile, my stomach squeezes.

I quickly glance away.

I probably look insane.

"Just a sec," I mumble, taking a moment to fill my lungs with oxygen and calm my racing heart, willing the heat in my cheeks to disappear. "Okay." I nod through my embarrassment before I follow behind Mancetti, wondering how many others witnessed the episode on his lawn.

Beside me, Graham holds my arm in his vice-like grip, as if at any moment, I might collapse again, hit with another flashback.

"Thanks. I'm good now," I tell him, meeting his eyes, even though I'm not. I'm anything but good.

I try my best to smile in the hope he'll believe me, and it seems to do the trick because the tension leaves his shoulders and he loosens his hold.

Mancetti swings the front door open and when we step inside, I'm brought right back to the day Atlas and I came here, hoping for answers. Yet here I am, months later in the same place, only instead of desperately needing to know *what* happened, I want to know *why*.

He takes us through the foyer, past a quaint living room with plush sofas, and I push down the bile rising in the back of my throat as I avert my gaze. Were they intimate here? Did they watch movies on the large TV above the fireplace?

A million questions tangle together in my head with no answers as he guides us into the kitchen and motions for us to sit at the table.

I follow Graham's lead, taking everything in. I wonder how many meals they shared. If they talked about me or held hands across the table like the day I caught them at Manja, Manja, sharing a bottle of wine. I wonder if she sat in this same chair, traced the grain of the oak with her fingers, ate from his dishes, while staring out the French doors leading to a stone patio outside.

Just the thought makes me ache and springs to life the need for answers to even more important questions.

Was I a burden? Or was it just her marriage?

When did she fall out of love and why?

Was she ever going to tell me the truth or leave me in the dark?

She had this whole second life, a part of herself she kept secret, and it pains me that I'll never be able to ask her about it all or get clarity.

I settle into a chair as Mancetti brings me a glass of water and tells me to drink. Though I'm disinclined to take orders from him, I do so anyway, needing something to soothe my dry and aching throat.

By the time he sits down across from me, I've drained the entire thing and set the glass down on the table while he fiddles with his hands in his lap, clearly nervous. "I've thought a lot about . . ." He trails off, clearing his throat, but I have zero patience to wait for him to collect his thoughts.

"I remember," I blurt, interrupting him.

He straightens in his seat and runs a hand over the dark scruff on his jaw. "What do you remember?"

"Everything."

His eyes lock with mine, and I notice for the first time they're an impossible shade of hazel. Not quite green or brown or gold, but some nebulous shade in between, and though I hate it, I can see how my mother would be drawn to him—the attraction.

"Listen, Mackenzie . . ."

"For the record, if my mother were still alive, I wouldn't be here. But I have questions, and she's not around to answer them, so that leaves you," I say stoically. I'm not rude, but there's a chill to my tone I can't contain.

"Okay." He nods, the gesture matter-of-fact. "Then I'll try to answer them as best I can."

"How did the two of you meet?"

His eyes never leave mine as he answers. "The restaurant. It was a Tuesday, and Laura had a lunch meeting there for work. Her clients were running late, and we got to talking."

I swallow, hating the intimate way her name rolls off his tongue, but his answer also makes sense. My mother was a realtor and lunch meetings with clients weren't uncommon.

"So, what, did she give you her number? Did you ask her out despite the wedding ring on her left hand?" Mancetti flinches. "How did it even start?"

Graham places a hand on my arm, a subtle message to relax and let Mancetti answer, and though his touch soothes me, it does little to ease the knot tightening in my stomach.

"It was . . . gradual. She started showing up more, using the restaurant as her usual spot for meetings. One evening in particular, she had just closed on a house for a client that was a pretty big deal. I guess it was a huge commission, and she stopped by for drinks to celebrate. This was a little less than a year before the accident."

The Byler house; I remember. Mom had been in a tizzy all week, praying nothing fell through with the sale because she was representing both the seller and buyer and stood to make almost fifty-thousand dollars off the single sale. It would be her biggest commission ever.

I swallow as he continues.

"Anyway, we got to talking over drinks, and before we knew it, the restaurant was closing. But neither of us wanted her to go, so she stayed and we talked some more. I'd sensed from previous conversations there was a riff in her marriage and that she wasn't happy. But in this conversation, she confirmed her marriage wasn't just on the rocks, it was over. She wanted a divorce and had approached your father about it, but he wasn't on board and threatened to make things difficult for her if she followed through."

He blows out a breath and leans back in his seat, continuing, while I cling to his every word. "Until then, I'd been attracted to Laura and my feelings over the months of her coming and going had grown. But for me, this is what pushed me over the edge, knowing her marriage was dead and she was leaving. That night, I admitted my feelings, and she reciprocated them. It's also the night we shared our first kiss."

All the air leaves my lungs, and it hurts to breathe. "So, you were seeing each other for . . . ?"

"About nine months," he says, a slight tremor to his voice.

"I found divorce papers. So, she *did* file."

"She had them drawn up by her attorney about seven months in, but Hart," he pauses, seemingly choosing his words carefully, "well, he was staying true to his word, and it didn't seem like he was gonna make things easy on her."

I pause to collect my mounting emotions. I can't imagine my father would let her go that easily. "Did she ever talk about me?" I say, a frog in my throat.

"All the time," he answers quickly—easily—and my eyes fill, my vision blurring with unshed tears as I try and choke them back.

"Was she . . . did she . . ." I try, but my voice cracks and I have to stop.

"She loved you so much." Mancetti leans across the table as if to hold my hand. "You must believe that. She'd be devastated to know you thought otherwise. She was going to tell you. We talked about that a lot before she. . . before . . ." He swallows, his throat bobbing with emotion as if speaking out loud about her death is too much to bear. "Once Christmas was over, she planned on separating from your father. She finally decided it was time to tell you about the divorce the day of the crash. Her plan was to give you time to heal, and then, when the time was right, introduce you to me. We agreed it was best to wait until you were ready."

A bitter laugh bubbles from my throat. *Did she honestly think I'd ever take this in stride?*

"So, she was done with my father, just like that?" I snap my fingers, finding it difficult to contain the anger simmering in my veins. "She was going to give up more than eighteen years of marriage because she met someone new?"

I don't get it, and it's so different from the mother I knew that it's hard to reconcile.

Mancetti shakes his head, and I have to give him credit. He remains unruffled despite my cynicism. "No. It wasn't like that. Your mother loved your father, but she wanted more freedom than he was willing to give. They got married young, when your mother had yet to establish a career, before she knew what she really wanted out of life, and she felt . . . stifled by him. Smothered. Like he was no longer growing with her, but instead, they were headed in two completely different paths, their trajectories opposite of one another. I think, for once in her life, she wanted to choose herself. But never at any point or any time, did she stop loving you or caring about you. Mackenzie, you were always her number one concern. It's why she made things work for so long. It's why she stayed as long as she did."

I glance away from him, unable to look at him any longer because I don't like what he's implying, and it doesn't sit well with me that my mother might have sacrificed her happiness for my sake.

"Do you think she was happy? Before she died?" I ask after a moment.

He reaches across the table and places a hand over mine, and this time I let him. Mostly, because I don't have the energy to pull away. I feel as vulnerable as a sheet of glass and every bit as prone to breaking. "Yes. She was very happy," he says.

"Did you love her?" I whisper.

"Very much so," he says with conviction. "Laura was the love of my life." His eyes glisten with emotion, and his words hit a tender note inside.

A balloon swells in my chest while the fresh press of tears stings the back of my eyes. I can't hear anything else without completely falling apart. I'm done. Drained. "I think I'm ready to go now," I say, hating the way my voice shakes.

Graham nods and we both stand while he places a hand on my arm to steady me.

"Can I ask you something?" Mancetti's voice breaks through the frantic beat of the pulse in my ears, and I nod.

"Did you ever look into the other vehicle, the one I said hit you?"

I stiffen, unsure of where this is heading. "I did."

"And did you find anything?"

My heart stutters in my chest. I didn't just find anything; I know who killed her.

But something makes me hesitate. "I might've remembered some details about the other car that can help."

"Oh, thank God." Mancetti covers his face with his hands for a moment, and when he lifts his head again, his red-rimmed eyes are filled with pain. "You have to tell someone at the precinct, someone other than your father. You need to—"

"You realize that if they determine my father ignored eyewitness testimony, he'll be fired, or worse, charged."

"We need justice for Laura. We need the truth," he says, his expression earnest.

"And I want that, I do. But he's also my father, my only—"

"You know something else, don't you?" His eyes narrow as he grabs my arm. "What do you know? Tell me," he barks.

I yelp and yank my arm from his grip.

"Hey!" Graham comes between us, one hand on Anthony's chest, while his stony gaze stares him down. "She's had enough for one day, and the only one who deserves anything in this scenario, the only truly innocent person here, is Mackenzie. Don't forget that."

He places his hand on the small of my back and guides me out of the kitchen, down the hallway, and to the front door while my heart races. Opening the car door for me, he helps me get inside on shaky limbs.

Silence stretches between us as he turns the ignition and the engine roars to life, then pulls back out onto the road. It's not until several miles later that I break the quiet. "What if he's right? My mother deserves justice, but I'm not so sure my father deserves grace. What if I'm doing the wrong thing by waiting?"

Graham is quiet for a moment, staring at the road while the muscle in his jaw flickers, which is how I know he's thinking about my questions. "You're the one here, not your mom, and even if they had more evidence against my uncle and arrested him, it won't help her now. He's in rehab. He won't be hurting anyone anytime soon, which gives you time. Throwing your life into further chaos doesn't have to be the answer. You're doing the right thing by waiting until you're sure."

I swallow and my eyes tear. "Thanks."

He glances over at me and nods, his mouth a thin line before he focuses back on the road. A few minutes later, he slows down as he approaches my house and curses.

I follow the trajectory of his gaze and my eyes home in on the black Harley sitting in the driveway, and like throwing kerosene on a fire, anger ignites my veins.

CHAPTER 5

ATLAS

Nerves jump in my stomach and doubt creeps into my veins as I stand in front of the Hart residence, fist raised, ready to knock on their door. Maybe I'm doing the wrong thing by telling him what I know. Or maybe I should go straight to the precinct and avoid Hart altogether.

After all, I'm the last person on the face of the planet Chief Hart wants to see standing on his doorstep. The last time we saw each other was only a few days after Mackenzie recovered her memory. Determined to win her back, I camped out on her doorstep, refusing to leave until she gave me a chance to explain when Hart's cruiser pulled into the driveway and he stepped out, making his purpose very clear when he pulled his cuffs from his gun belt.

Needless to say, I left before things escalated. I might be a fool, but I'm not stupid enough to get my ass arrested for a chance to talk to a girl who had so little desire to speak with me, she'd rather call her father and have me arrested.

I shake my head at the memory. I'm overthinking; this means more. Standing face-to-face with Doll's father, the spouse of my father's victim—a man who also despises me—is a hell of a lot harder than giving my statement to some faceless, nameless cop.

Call it atonement, but I can only hope it sends the message to Mackenzie that I'm willing to do just about anything to win her back.

I swallow and muster my courage as I rap my knuckles against the door, wondering if Mackenzie is home, and what she'll think of me turning in my own father. If she'll feel even an ounce of sympathy for me—maybe even something more—or whether it will change nothing, and she'll still despise me.

The sound of footsteps approaches, and when the door swings open, I'm both relieved and disappointed to see Chief Hart standing there. "Good afternoon, sir," I say, nodding in greeting.

His expression morphs, his brown eyes narrowing while the rest of him hardens like stone. "I don't know what you're doing here, but you have two seconds to get off my property."

"I just want to talk." I hold my hands up in surrender. "I have some—"

"I have zero interest in anything you have to say," he bites out, then turns and starts to slam the door in my face, but I'm faster. I catch the door before it closes, slamming it back open, and step inside after him as he swings back around with fire in his eyes.

Maybe it's a death wish, but I stand my ground. I didn't come here to get turned away before he even hears what I have to say. I'm doing this for Mackenzie, and nothing will stop me from my mission. Not even him.

"What the hell do you think you're doing?" he yells.

Palms out, I say, "I'm not leaving until you hear me out."

"The hell you aren't."

"I have information I think you'd like to hear," I start, but he cuts me off.

"I don't know what you did to my daughter, seeing as how she won't talk to me about it," he says, pointing a finger into my chest like Kenzie's animosity toward him is somehow my fault. "But I was right. I warned her against you. She didn't listen, and now look at her. She's broken again. Just like before."

My stomach clenches at his words, and I take a step forward. "What do you mean, she's broken like before? Is Mackenzie okay? Is she—"

"Don't ever utter her name again." He stabs a finger in my chest. "Do you hear me? You stay away from her or I swear to God I'll have you arrested."

"All I ever wanted was her happiness."

"Sure seems like it," he snaps.

"If you just tell me what's going on I'll—"

"It's none of your damn business."

I growl, sinking my head into my hands, digging my fingertips into my skull. Frustration doesn't even begin to describe the churning, sinking feeling raging inside me.

But I've gotten off track.

I need to remember why I came.

It's the only chance I have to right my father's wrongs and find my way back to her.

"Listen"—I lift my head, desperate for him to hear me out—"I know you don't like me. I get it. But before she ended things with me, Mackenzie and I spoke with the witness to the car crash, and he told us—"

"Anthony Mancetti is a liar and a cheat." Hart's face turns red and a vein in his forehead begins to pulse. "He'll say anything to get attention, and you have no right digging around in our business. You need to back off," he says through gritted teeth.

"I don't know the dude, okay? That's not . . . I'm not defending him." I grind out, frustrated he won't let me get a coherent thought across. "That's not even what this is about. It's about the fact that I know who—"

The front door bursts open, missing me by inches, and crashes into the wall behind it. Startled, I swivel around on my feet toward the sound, only to come face-to-face with the girl who haunts me, the one who occupies my every waking thought.

And she's standing next to my cousin.

I suck in a breath, rattled by her sudden appearance. "Mackenzie . . ."

"What the hell are you doing here?" she snaps as she glances from me to her father.

I take a step closer and away from her father, lowering my voice to a whisper as I say, "Are you and Graham . . .?"

Her blue eyes turn glacial. "Yeah." She shrugs, then makes a move to brush past me as she murmurs under her breath, "Not that it's any of your business."

My stomach sinks as if a weight has been pushed into it, and I wonder if she knows how much her words gut me.

I grab her arm and spin her around to face me at the same time her father steps forward. "Keep your hands off my daughter," he booms.

"Can we have a second?" I ask, my tone earnest.

"Are you out of your—"

"Dad . . ." Mackenzie scowls at him as she holds a hand out, effectively shutting him up, and I wonder who she loathes more: him or me. "You shouldn't be here," she says to me, eyeing the hand still on her arm. "I don't want to see you."

Her words strike me like a clenched fist and I drop my hand. "Actually, I came to talk to your father."

"Why?" Her eyes search mine, brow creased, as if I'm a puzzle she can't solve.

"I came to set things right," I say, my meaning clear. "About that day . . ."

"No." She shakes her head.

"I only waited because I figured you told him. I wanted to let you make the first move, but so much time has passed, I thought—"

"You thought wrong." She glares at me and takes a step closer. "Just go."

I blink over at her, trying to understand. "I want to do the right thing."

A throat clears behind us. "I think she told you to leave," Graham says.

I glance his way, noting the tight jaw and clenched fists. Clearly he hates me, but the loathing goes both ways, and I'm not about to take orders from my cousin.

I'm about to tell him just that when Mackenzie says, "It's too little, too late." My gaze flickers back to her. "Just save your breath and let me decide what the right thing is."

So, she doesn't want me to tell her father the truth?

Out of the corner of my eye, I see him watching us like a hawk.

"Mackenzie, I'm sorry, okay? Would you please just hear me out?" She turns her back to me and starts down the hall, but it doesn't stop me from following after her. "I never should've kept it from you, but I didn't know how to tell you. I thought you'd hate me, and as selfish as it is, I didn't want my father taking something else from me."

She spins around on her heel, catching me off guard. "And what about what he took from me?" Her words cut deep, her tone sharp as a blade.

"That's why I'm here. It's why—"

"I don't want to hear any more," she says, covering her ears with her hands.

I take a step back, getting a good look at her for the first time since she burst through the door. Dirt stains the knees of her jeans, and her eyes are red-rimmed as if she's been crying. It doesn't take a genius to see the exhaustion in her wary expression or the way her shoulders slump in defeat.

"Just go," she says, her tone firm.

"You heard her," Hart chimes in. "Or so help me, I'll arrest you myself. Right here, right now."

I swallow, my hands fisting at my sides in an effort to restrain myself from pulling her into my arms like I want to. Everything inside me yearns to hold her, to press my lips against hers to see if she'll melt.

Because I know she's not over me.

The kind of connection we had can't be broken.

But I can do none of those things with Hart and Graham standing here, staring at me like I'm an explosive ready to detonate and take his daughter out.

So I debate options, with the sinking realization I have none. It's clear Chief Hart has zero interest in anything I have to say. He wouldn't let me get more than a word out, and he probably won't believe a thing that comes out of my mouth anyway.

Just like he didn't believe Anthony Mancetti.

And as much as it stings, Mackenzie wants me to leave, too. If it's not already abundantly clear my presence here is unwanted, Graham steps toward me from behind, murmuring, "You've got some nerve coming here like this."

I pivot on my feet to face him, hating the bite of jealousy sinking its teeth into my skin. Even more, I hate that she wants him here, and not me. "I'll go," I say to no one in particular before I start for the door.

I step over the threshold, pausing to glance over my shoulder where I meet Mackenzie's eyes. "You can push me away all you want, but you're it for me, doll. I'm not giving up on us. And that's a promise."

MACKENZIE

My heart is pounding like a jackrabbit as the door closes behind Atlas.

My eyes flutter shut as I press my palm over the aching spot in my chest.

"I thought you weren't seeing him anymore." My father's voice breaks through the heartache, springing to life the anger from seconds ago.

I snap my eyes open and shrug. "I'm not."

"Really? Because from where I was standing, it seemed like, for two people who no longer care, there are a lot of secrets and things you're not saying to each other."

A mirthless laugh bubbles in the back of my throat because he's right. There is a lot we're not saying. I only wish I no longer cared. "Well, if anyone knows what secrets look like, it's you, right, Dad?"

"Um, maybe I should go," Graham murmurs from behind me.

I turn to face him, hating that he has to deal with my drama. I don't blame him for wanting to bail; I would, too. "Call you later?" he asks, and I simply nod before he makes his exit, forcing me to face my father alone.

"Where were you?" he snaps, eyes narrowed on my face.

"Visiting my new friend, Anthony Mancetti," I say with a sneer.

The blood from his face drains and his eyes widen. "You *what*?"

"I had some questions I needed answers to." I shrug.

"You're not to go there again. Do you understand me?"

"Why, Dad? Afraid I'll find something out you won't like?" His face twists in pain, but I'm so full of anger and resentment, I can't help but plunge the knife a little further. "Too late," I deadpan.

"Since when are you even allowed out of my house without my permission? I think you're forgetting your position, young lady." He stabs a finger into his chest, the vein in his forehead pulsing. "You answer to *me*. You do as *I* say. You know nothing about this man. The only thing we do know for sure about him is that he has questionable character. He's an adulterer. And yet you went to his house alone? Without even consulting me? And then that trailer trash shows up here, telling me I need to listen to what he says—"

"He has a name," I snap, but he plows right over me, continuing his tirade.

"—and proclaims his undying love for you, and I'm just supposed to believe the two of you haven't been talking behind my back? I won't have it." He points a finger at me. "From here on out, you're not to step foot out that door without my permission. Not even with Goliath. Is that clear?"

"You've got to be kidding me!"

"I'm dead serious."

"You know, I get it now," I say. My arms shake by my side as I try and restrain the resentment rising inside of me. "I never saw it before because I've always made excuses for you. I told myself you were just scared because you cared so much, that you only want what's best for me, but now I'm not so sure. You only want to control everything and everyone around me, even if it means hurting them. As long as you have what you want, you don't care if I'm miserable as a result."

The vein pulses some more, but I don't relent.

"You probably did the same with Mom. Is that why she turned to someone else? Because you smothered her? Finally, after a hard year, I returned to school and made friends. I even fell in love. I'm spreading my wings, Dad, I'm ready to fly but you keep blocking my path. Did you clip Mom's wings, too?"

The slap of his hand cracks across my cheek, followed by a wringing in my ears and a searing pain.

My mouth drops open, and I suck in a breath as I bring a hand to the throbbing in my cheek. Never in my seventeen years has he ever laid a hand on me. And maybe I had it coming. But the truth knows no bounds, and I'm not about to censor it just because he doesn't like it.

"I won't have you speak to me like that in my house," he says, his tone firm but calmer than it was a few seconds ago.

"I turn eighteen in a few months," I say, my voice shaking. "Then I graduate in May. You can't hold the reins forever."

"You're right, I can't," he concedes. "Which is why I've decided to send you to boarding school in Virginia. It will be good for you, a change of pace."

"But I only have six months left!" I yell.

"They said they'd take you for the second half of the year, no problem."

"You can't do this." My mind spins, and I see red. Reaching out, I place a hand against the wall, afraid for a moment I might have another episode. I can feel myself spiraling as my vision blurs. Back sweating. Heart racing. Blood pounding in my ears.

"I've been contemplating it for a while now, but you're right. The truth is I kept you here for selfish reasons. I didn't want to see you go. But I think this is for the best, even if you can't see that yourself. You've made a series of bad and unsafe decisions since you returned to school, making it abundantly clear you don't have your own best interests at heart. But I do."

"So, you're gonna just, what, stay here? While I'm all the way in Virginia?"

He says nothing, just stares back at me with fire in his eyes.

"I won't go," I spit out.

"You don't have a choice."

I hold his gaze while my mind makes quick work of the situation, desperate to find a way out. I refuse to leave Riverside. Not when I only have six months to turn things around for myself and make things right with Graham. I need to find a way to get him past the rough patch he's going through, just like he did for me. Besides, with the flashbacks coming at me more and more, the thought of being alone in a new city and a new school when one of them hits scares me more than anything.

But I can't explain any of that to him. He's completely unreasonable, especially when he's not in the mood to listen. He's inflexible, his authority and decisions unwavering as he comes at me with his iron fist.

But I do have something up my sleeve; a wild card worth playing.

My mind flashes to Lee Scott. This whole time, I've been struggling with the decision of turning him in because it could hurt my father. But the lingering burn in my cheek makes it perfectly clear he has no problem hurting me.

My lips curve at the corners, my smile serpentine. "You know, when I spoke with Mancetti, he had a lot to say about you. And now that my memory has returned, and I know someone else was involved, I can corroborate his eyewitness testimony. I remember the blue car, Dad. I remember getting struck."

I tilt my head, eyes narrowed on his face as what I'm saying registers and his mouth parts.

"I wonder what your fellow officers will say when I tell them you buried information about the car crash? I wonder what they'd say"—I take a step forward, until we're standing toe-to-toe—"if I told them all about Mom's sordid affair, and how she was going to leave you for him. That you favored your pride for justice."

His throat bobs, his eyes wide. "You wouldn't," he says, searching my gaze.

"If you send me away, I would." I tilt my head and stare at the ceiling like I'm deep in thought. "Do you think you'd just lose your job? Or do you think they'd prosecute you, too?"

"You'd really destroy our name in this town, our whole family, everything—"

"No, Dad. You and Mom already did that and I had no part in it. I'd just be doing the one thing no one seems to want to do around here." I stand on my tiptoes and my lips curl in disgust as I whisper, "I'd be telling the truth."

"Are you threatening me?" he asks, a quaver to his voice that fills me with equal parts guilt and elation.

I shake my head, feeling in control of my life for the first time in a long time. "No. I'm simply informing you that if you send me away to boarding school, I won't go quietly," I say before I turn down the hall and run up the stairs, taking them two at a time until I get to the top and make a beeline for my room.

I enter my bathroom and take one look at the angry red skin over the spot where he struck me and hiss. Without thinking, I pluck the phone from my back pocket, shoot a text to Anastasia, then book an Uber.

By the time I pack a bag and return back downstairs, at least thirty minutes have passed, but I find my father standing in the same spot as I left him. His hands clench and release at his sides, his forehead is wrinkled, and his eyes lost in thought. It's not until I take the last riser and step onto the landing that he turns to the sound of my footsteps.

His gaze shifts from my face to the bag in my hands and his eyes darken. "Where are you going?"

I brush past him, head for the door, and place my hand on the knob as I say, "Anastasia's house. I'm going to stay there for a few days. She already said I could if I needed to."

"You can't just leave. This is your home."

"Is it?" I ask, my brow raised. "Because a minute ago, you were trying to ship me off to boarding school." I open the door, turning to back out the door, and say, "Don't bother calling or coming after me. If you care about me at all, if you want me in your life in any way, you'll holster your weapon and leave me be. Give me time. Otherwise," I say, feeling the familiar prick of moisture in my eyes, "you'll push me away entirely. Just like you pushed Mom away."

CHAPTER 6

GRAHAM

I TAKE THE STAIRS two at a time and slam the door to my room closed. Finding my bed, I sink down onto the edge of it and hang my head, clasping the back of my neck with my hands.

I feel like shit.

My head pounds like waves on the shoreline, and my throat is as dry as sandpaper. Both are products of the hangover I'm still sporting from last night, which made today with Kenzie all the more difficult. Ever since the day I carried her off Riverside's football field, her flashbacks have been getting worse. I don't need a fucking PhD in psychology to know she's suffering with symptoms of post-traumatic stress. It's as if when her memory returned, it did so with a vengeance.

Every time I see her, it gets harder instead of easier, and today was no exception. I'm still angry and reeling from rejection while trying to deny the simple fact that I'm still in love with her and always will be. I know I need space and time to heal, but she's also my best friend, and she needs me. As it is, I lie awake at night while my stomach turns to knots, wondering if she's going to spiral back into the dark abyss I pulled her out of just after the accident. I think of the day her memory returned over and over in my head until I'm sick. Seeing her suffering and in pain kills me.

I'm in the worst fucking catch twenty-two situation when it comes to her: I desperately want to help her, yet it's excruciating to be around her.

My relationship with her in the last few months has been one giant emotional whiplash.

I pinch the bridge of my nose and straighten as her interaction with Atlas yesterday plays in my mind, and I clench my jaw until my teeth ache.

A seed of bitterness sprouts to life inside my chest every time I think about how she chose him over me. He hurt her just like I thought he would. He lied to her, and because of those lies, she fell to pieces.

But I lied, too. I said I wouldn't be here to put her back together again. Yet here I am, still by her side, bandaging wounds I had no part in creating at every turn while my heart withers and dies inside my chest.

I'm tormented by the sight of her, at the thought of what could have been.

Those soft lips. The dark hair that spills down her back. Eyes like polar ice caps.

When I'm around her, all I can think about is how it felt to kiss her. To taste her on my tongue. To feel the hope inside me swell like a monsoon, inflate my chest and lungs and heart until bursting.

I'd be lying if I said I didn't want to feel that again—if I pretended I didn't hope that once she heals, she'll come to her senses and realize what she wants is right in front of her. It always has been. Because Mackenzie is sure as hell the only thing I've ever needed. And without her, I'm flailing. Coasting through life without a purpose. A ship lost at sea with no compass. I so badly want to find my way back to her, I'd do just about anything. I'll even put myself through the fucking torture of watching her try and get over my cousin while dealing with all her other demons.

But it feels impossible.

For Mackenzie and I to be together, she needs to stop loving him and start loving me as more than her best friend, and I have to somehow find my way through the resentment resting in the pit of my stomach like a pit of vipers ready to strike.

But if the way she reacted to Atlas today is any indication, she's not there yet.

And maybe I'm not either.

Because for every ounce of me that still worships her and wants her back, there are equal parts of me still angry and hurt over the fact she chose him over me.

My gaze drifts to my closed bedroom door and I hurt all over. I have no idea where Atlas went after school today. All I know is he's not here, and as comforting as that usually is, I still don't want to be here either.

I'm restless. My arms and legs twitch with the desire to move, to get the hell out of here, but as much as I don't want to be here, there's nowhere for me to go. Lately, I don't find solace in much. I hate being at school where I have to see Mackenzie and Atlas in the halls every damn day, reminding me of everything that happened. My heart breaks a little more each time I catch sight of Kenzie's sweet smile or her icy gaze. And worse of all is the way Atlas looks at her. Like he's drowning and she's his life raft.

I don't want to fucking see it.

Yet I hate being at home. Every time Atlas and I cross paths, all I want to do is rearrange his face. And, oblivious to my perilous mental state, my father continues to remind me of all my shortcomings.

Football sucks, too. Not only because of Atlas, but my playing has only gotten worse since the beginning of the season. It's like when my heart broke, my arm went with it. My drive is waning, and my performance on the field is simply another reminder of how I've let everyone down. Which is why most of my free time this past month has been spent either partying with Peters or hanging out with Jace and Teagan. All of it has been to avoid any possible interactions with Atlas and drowning my woes in a bottle of booze or a twelve pack of beer. Even now,

I feel myself wanting something—anything—to take my mind off the shit day I've had. To numb the pain and thoughts that consume me.

I reach onto my nightstand and grab the remote, then turn on the TV. I should stream some game tape to prepare for States next week. Either that or review the new plays Coach gave us. These games mean everything. They could mean the difference between getting an offer to play college ball or not. Others, like Atlas, have multiple schools who've made their interest known, whereas I need to fight for scout interest. Winning States would sure as hell help.

With a sigh, I find the game tape Coach emailed us and stream it to my TV, doing my best to analyze the footage before me, but I can't focus for shit. I last twenty minutes before my vision blurs and the players on the screen turn into a moving watercolor.

Scrubbing a hand down my face, I pick my phone back up and go over the new plays, but it's no use. The next thing I know, I'm on my feet and pacing my room.

I need to get out of here.

I need to take my mind off Mackenzie, my father, and football. They're like a fucking trifecta, playing games with my head and my heart.

I storm across the room toward my dresser and yank the top drawer open, easily finding the bottle of Jameson wedged between my folded shirts and take it out.

The amber liquid beckons me; it promises to solve all my problems.

My fingers twitch to open it, but on second thought, I shove it back inside and slam the drawer closed. Dragging a hand over the back of my neck, I snatch my phone back off the bed and open my contacts, texting some of the guys from the team to see if there's a party I can crash when my phone buzzes with an incoming call.

I frown at the number I don't recognize.

"Hello?" I answer, pressing it to my ear.

"Graham!" a shrill voice yells over the line.

I wince and hold my phone out, unable to recognize the voice. "Who is this?"

"It's Stasia."

"Who?" I frown.

She sighs, her tone impatient as she answers, "Anastasia."

"Oh." Though Anastasia's a cheerleader, she rarely attends bonfires at Crow's Creek, and she and I have never really spoken, but it seems Mackenzie and her have been spending more and more time together this past month. "Is everything okay?" I ask.

"It's Mackenzie . . ."

She pauses, and the bottom drops out from beneath my feet.

I clench the phone in my hand until my knuckles ache. "What happened?"

"I know she's been having problems with her dad, so I offered for her to stay with me for a few days. After school today, she begged me to take her driving. She was adamant. Said she'd never be free of her father until she got back behind the wheel. I wasn't sure what to do, so I took her."

I close my eyes as the air leaves my lungs, because I know what's coming next. "She had an attack, didn't she?"

"She told me she'd been having flashbacks, but it's so much worse than I expected," she says, her voice thick with tears. "It's like she just completely froze and went off the road. We're fine. The car isn't damaged or anything, but it's stuck in a ditch and, Graham, she's freaking the fuck out. I can't get through to her. I can't calm her down. Nothing I say helps. We're on this Podunk back road in the middle of nowhere, and I can't even convince her to get back in the car."

"Shit." I run a hand through my hair while my mind races. It must be really bad for Anastasia to be as freaked out as she is.

"I'm sorry, but I didn't know what to do or who else to call. I knew she'd kill me if I called her father. You're the only person I thought who might be able to get through to her."

I hesitate, contemplating whether I should tell her to find someone else—anyone else. I can't be her knight in shining armor every time she's in trouble. I just can't. It hurts too much. Being around her is like rubbing salt in a wound. Or worse. It's like taking a fucking cheese grater to my heart.

Mackenzie and I are in a vicious cycle. She needs me, and I run to her.

But what about *my* needs? How the hell am I supposed to be her best friend without killing myself in the process?

I open my mouth to speak—to tell her to find someone else—but my throat swells closed and my voice won't work. I can't seem to do it, and I curse myself for being so weak as I imagine Mackenzie in the middle of nowhere, curled up into a ball on the ground. Crying. Moaning. Screaming as she relives her mother's death over and over again. I just can't do it. I can't say no.

Because I'm Superman, and she's my kryptonite.

The red sedan appears in the distance, sitting cockeyed with its front end buried in the ditch on the side of the road.

I pull over and park a safe distance behind it and get out when Anastasia appears beside me. She grabs my arm, tugging me past her car and to the front where I find Mackenzie, and immediately I see it's so much worse than I imagined. Worse than the one she had yesterday afternoon on Mancetti's lawn.

Mackenzie is curled into a ball in the damp grass. Leaves and sticks are matted in her hair. Dirt covers her clothes as she rocks back and forth, sobbing, with her forehead pressed to her knees. She looks like she's been on the losing end of a war, but more concerning is where she's lying. All it would take is for one vehicle to veer off the road and strike her and she'd be gone.

When I approach, she doesn't look up, so I sink to my knees in front of her. My stomach twists as I place a hand on her clammy cheek. "Mackenzie?"

Her body stills at the sound of my voice, so I stroke her cheek some more and say her name over and over again until she lifts her head and her gaze finds mine. Blinking up at me as if I'm a mirage, a sob escapes her throat before she launches herself into my arms.

I rake one hand into her hair while the other one presses firmly into her back, holding her against me. I shush her, soothing her with soft, whispered words until her crying subsides and she buries her tear-dampened cheek into the crook of my neck. "Graham, you have to forgive me," she says, her voice cracking. "Please. You have to."

My heart stutters.

I know how sorry Mackenzie is for breaking my heart. She's told me at every turn, and I can see the remorse in her eyes when she looks at me. But it's not until this moment, as I hold her in my arms, that I realize whatever guilt she clings to might be making her panic attacks worse. It only adds to her mounting anxiety. And despite the tiny part of me that still resents her and wants her to feel as broken as I do, I can't live with myself knowing I might be even the tiniest bit responsible for her pain.

I press my lips to the top of her head, taking in her sweet scent as she melts into me. "It's okay, Kenz. I'll be fine. We're good, I promise." I try to calm her down—I *lie* to calm her down—and then I scoop her up into my arms and off the cool damp earth.

I press her into my chest as I carry her to the safety of my car. Once I have her inside, I say goodbye to Anastasia, who insists on waiting for a tow, and we drive for a few miles until Mackenzie's breathing evens out and her shaking subsides.

Satisfied she's not going to fall apart again, I pull into the parking lot of a shopping center and turn to her, eyeing her closely. Color has returned to her cheeks and sanity to her expression. "Do you wanna talk about it?" I ask.

Her throat bobs before she turns her gaze to mine, and with a slight shake of the head, she answers. "I'm sorry you had to come and get me."

"It's okay." I reach out and squeeze her hand, trying to warm her icy fingers in mine.

"No. It's really not." Her gaze falls to our interlocked fingers and she pulls away. "I can't keep expecting you to rescue me. It's not fair. Had I been coherent, I never would've let Stasia call you."

"I'm glad she did."

She jerks her head toward me. "Why?"

Fuck if I know.

I exhale a breath and reach out, tucking a lock of hair behind her ear as I evade her question because I have no answers. "I don't think you should stay with her."

"I can't go home. Not now." Her hands ball into fists in her lap. "I'm so mad at him." She speaks through gritted teeth and her voice shakes. "Yesterday, after you left, he threatened to send me to some boarding school in Virginia. It's insane. And I won't—"

"Stay with me." The words are out of my mouth before I can think them through, and though I should regret them, I don't.

"You can't be serious?" Her eyes widen as she waits for my response.

It's probably the worst idea in the world, I know this, yet I can't seem to help myself. So, I say it again.

"Come stay at my house."

CHAPTER 7

MACKENZIE

I stare at Graham, my chest tight. I'm so exhausted, I think I've misheard him. Every single bone in my body aches. My muscles scream for sleep, for a reprieve from the memories that plague me and the burden of the decisions that follow.

Seeing Atlas yesterday in my home speaking with my father reminded me that I need to make a decision. Time is ticking and so is my sanity. The fate of three men lies solely with me. Atlas, my father, Lee Scott—their lives will be forever changed if I decide to come forward with the truth, and the weight of this knowledge crushes me.

I blink over at Graham, my body numb as I wait for an explanation that doesn't come, some sign he's saying something else I'm simply unable to comprehend through the fog of fatigue.

"Come stay at my house," he says, confirming I heard him right. "That way, I'm there if you need me. When you have another attack, I'll already be there."

"But . . ." How could he possibly want me in his home after I broke his heart? "I can't do that," I say, shaking my head. "Your family shouldn't have to be burdened because of my problems."

"They won't be. My parents won't mind, I promise."

His steady green gaze locks with mine. He's serious.

It would be a relief, I think, having someone nearby who understands me.

But then my thoughts flicker to Atlas. I can't stay under the same roof as him. My heart aches just thinking about it. Maybe I wouldn't be a burden, but what would Mr. and Mrs. Scott think? I took two cousins and ripped them apart, turned them into enemies. Accepting his offer would be beyond selfish. "Graham, you know I—"

"I'm not taking no for an answer, Kenzie."

"I can't do that to you." I swallow and shake my head. "When you said I stomped all over your heart and—"

"I was wrong." Graham pinches the bridge of his nose and exhales. "I mean, that's true, yes. But I was wrong to say that. Yeah, I'm hurting. It completely gutted me when you chose him." His voice cracks, and I hate myself all over again for hurting him. "But I made a promise to you that I'd always be there for you no matter what, no matter who you chose, and I need to honor that."

"You don't need to honor anything, Graham. Our friendship isn't a contract. I'll be okay. The last couple of days have been hard. Tomorrow will be better." I bite my lips, contemplating. "If you take me to Anastasia's, I promise not to drive again or do anything foolish. I should've known better."

"You see, I can't do that." He offers me a sad smile that makes my belly clench. "Because I need to know you're safe. I *need* to see with my own two eyes that you're okay."

My shoulders slump forward and I sigh, my eyes locked on those warm, green orbs. With each passing second, my insides twist with uncertainty. I no longer know what the right thing is. My head tells me I should go home, but my heart wants to listen to Graham. My heart wants to go with him, to believe he'll be okay if I do because he's my safety net when I fall. The only one in my life who has the ability to keep me from shattering to pieces.

But reality is a bitch, and I know I can't be around Atlas. "I want to, but I can't be around him," I say, unable to utter his name.

"Atlas is hardly ever home. When he's not at practice, he's working or reviewing plays and game tape in his room. Besides, you can stay in the pool house. There's a guest room and bathroom. It's everything you need, and it has a back door that leads to a gate in the fence. You can come and go without anyone ever noticing."

"I don't know." I toy with my hands in my lap.

"My parents love you," he says, but my mind drifts to the conversation I overheard months ago between him and his father, and I'm not so sure. "It's just for a couple days, until you feel more stable."

My gaze searches his expression for a reason to say no, but I find none. I want my best friend. I want to fall back into our old ways, when it was Graham and me against the world. Everything felt possible then. Everything seemed brighter, rather than this hopeless, desperate feeling settling in the pit of my stomach. And maybe I'm selfish because I want to weather this storm together, to get past the awkwardness in our friendship, so, I sigh and say, "Okay. But just for a couple of days."

CHAPTER 8

MACKENZIE

THE CAR IS QUIET on the way to Graham's house, both of us lost in thought with a tense silence stretching the air between us. My thoughts drift, and I wonder if I made the right choice, why does it feel so awkward?

The beam of his headlights bounces off the Scott's home as he pulls into the driveway and continues around the side of the house, where he parks in front of the garage and motions toward the backyard. "Come on."

We step out into the rapidly cooling autumn air and make our way past the pool, which is covered and closed for the season. Rounding the pool house, he points to a little stone path that runs behind a massive hedgerow of forsythia and leads to a gate in the fence. "It's not impossible to spot from the front but it's not easy either, so you should be safe from view."

So Atlas won't see me.

"Thanks," I say as he guides me back to the main door. He enters and I follow, walking through the small sitting area that smells faintly of chlorine, to the bedroom in the back. A queen-size bed sits in the middle of the brightly lit room with a white pine dresser set along the wall. It's feels like forever since I've been inside, but it's warm and welcoming, and everything I need.

"It doesn't have a TV," he says, flipping a switch and flooding the room with light.

"It's perfect," I say, sinking down onto the edge of the bed.

"Bathroom is off to the right." He jerks his thumb toward a closed door. "Inside, you'll see another door, which leads back out to the sitting area. Might wanna keep it locked just in case, but no one usually comes out here this time of year."

"Thank you," I say, filled with gratitude.

"Is your bag still at Anastasia's."

"Crap." I bite my lip. "I didn't even think about that."

"It's no problem. Settle in and I'll be right back," he says.

Five minutes later, he returns with an oversized T-shirt, a pair of old sweats, and a packaged toothbrush. Crossing the room, he sits them down on the nightstand, then joins me on the bed. "These might be a little big on you, but they should do."

I smile in response, but it mustn't reach my eyes because he lightly taps the side of my head with his finger. "What's going on in here?" he asks.

I swallow, thinking of everything that happened the last few day. I had two major panic attacks, spoke with my mother's former lover, found Atlas in my home, and had a blowout fight with my father, where he slapped me and threatened to send me to boarding school.

My life doesn't even feel like my own any more, and all I want is for things to be easy, like they used to be. "Do you think I'll ever be normal again?"

"You are normal."

I shake my head, because nothing in my life is normal right now, especially not me. Graham and I haven't been our usual selves with each other since everything fell apart. My heart threatens to riot every time I see Atlas in the halls, or if I hear someone utter his name. I'm contemplating seeking justice for my mother's death, but to do so, means ending my father's reputation, or worse, sending him to jail. And, on top of it all, I'm losing my mind.

Because that's how it feels when I have one of my episodes.

With a sigh, I lean my head on his shoulder, staring up at him as I take him in. My best friend with the warm, moss-green eyes, sharp jaw, and shaggy hair. When he smiles down at me, it's soft and kind, exactly how he used to look at me before—no longer the boy whose heart I broke. It makes me feel safe and comfortable, like I can tell him anything and he'll understand.

"All I wanted for so long was to remember. And now that I do, all I want is to forget."

He brushes a lock of hair off my forehead. "It'll get easier."

"Will it?"

"Of course."

I want to believe him.

A shuddering breath escapes my chest at the same time he brings his arms around my shoulders. "You need to see a professional."

"I know," I whisper. "I've looked into it."

"Will you call them this week?"

I nod. I know I can't do this alone, even if part of me is afraid they'll tell me what I already know: that I'm broken, and nothing and no one will ever be able to put me back together again.

"What if this is the new normal?"

Graham stays silent for a moment, as if contemplating my question. "Now that you remember, maybe you can get the closure you need. You just need to figure out how."

I mull this over. Yesterday gave me some insight into why my mother and father fell apart and how she turned to Mancetti, but it doesn't make it any more palatable. I'm not sure anything ever will, yet I can't help but feel that closure might come when I deal with Lee Scott. The knowledge his fate lies partially in my hands is of little solace when I know making him pay means hurting my family. As much as I despise my father right now, he's the only family I have left.

"Can I tell you something?" I ask.

"Anything."

"Yesterday, when we were at Mancetti's house, for a split second, I hated her."

Graham's arms stiffen. "Who?"

"My mother." I lean up so I can look at him and meet his eyes. "She's not here to defend herself or explain. And though I can partly understand what she did and why, I'm angry. I'm so mad at her for doing this to us. Because had she not been there that day, had she not been seeing him, I wouldn't have followed her . . ." I swallow, my breath coming faster, harder, as I work through what I'm trying to say, the feelings festering inside me like an infected wound. "I can feel my memories of her turning sour, decaying like a piece of rotten fruit, and I don't know how to reverse it. Without her here, I don't know how to turn this around."

"Fuck if I know, Kenz." He reaches out and pulls me toward him, pressing me into his chest where I let the tears fall, ones I thought had dried up long ago. "I'm not exactly the poster child for healthy emotions where my parents are concerned."

The soft material of his shirt dampens beneath my face as I try and get a grip, but his mumbled words of reassurance only make me cry harder.

I spill my heart to him, telling him all my fears—everything I'm afraid to admit out loud, the things that keep me up at night. It's so much like old times, he and I talking and bouncing things off one another, I almost forget everything that happened between us these last few months.

I sniff and lift a hand to wipe my dampened cheeks, turning my head in the crook of his neck before wrapping my arms around him in one of the giant bear hugs I miss so much. He presses his cheek against mine in response. Calmer now, I slowly turn my gaze to meet his, so I can thank him for always being there for me when I so desperately need it.

I pull back slightly and our eyes lock.

We're so close, I can see the pulse jumping in his throat.

His hand stills on my lower back, pressing into me as if drawing me closer, and when his breathing quickens, my brain starts firing warnings at me like a car alarm.

Another inch and our lips will touch.

We're in dangerous territory. The quicksand of my bubbling emotions is threatening to swallow me whole. I need to wade carefully so no one gets hurt. Graham is not where my heart lies, and I've already caused him enough pain to last a lifetime.

I place my hands on either side of his face and lick my lips, ready to thank him for being such a good *friend*, but he must read me wrong.

His eyes widen; the breath catches in the back of his throat before he jerks away from me, as if remembering he can't have me before the words can ever leave my mouth.

He jumps to his feet, his brow pinched. "What the hell, Kenz?" His eyes flash with anger, darkening to pine in the fading light as my mouth drops open to defend myself.

"I wasn't—"

"You can't do that shit," he snaps.

"Graham, I swear, I wasn't—"

"Don't." He holds a trembling hand out, eyes closed, mouth in a flat line. "Just, fucking don't."

And then he turns and leaves before I can explain I wasn't going to kiss him. Before I can even defend myself.

ATLAS

My mind spins as I drive the darkened back roads just outside Riverside, headed toward a new job. With autumn comes less daylight, and the darkness at six p.m. isn't helping my sullen mood. I need to stop thinking about Mackenzie, but I can't.

I keep replaying yesterday afternoon in my mind like a film strip. The way anger turned her irises to flames when she burst through the front door and saw me standing there, talking to her father. Her biting tone and refusal to listen. The way Graham hovered protectively nearby.

The sight of them together gutted me.

I rarely see them with each other in the halls at school, so it's been easy to tell myself Graham hasn't picked up where I left off, but now I'm not so sure.

Clearly, I'd made a mistake going there. Chief Hart wouldn't stop for even a second to listen to what I had to say, and it seemed Mackenzie didn't want him knowing the truth, either. My entire reasoning for turning my father in was to right his wrongs, to prove to Mackenzie I know just how much I fucked up and I'm sorry.

But if she doesn't want me to tell anyone, then I have no choice but to leave the ball in her court and continue to be patient. After all, she's the one that's hurting, and though I'm desperate to prove to her how much I love her and win her back, it's going to take time.

I stop at a red light and throttle the engine of my Harley. I'm not sure how much longer I'll be able to drive my bike before it becomes reckless. It's already the third of November and the weather has turned cold. The first snowfall is right around the corner, and soon, the roads will be icy in the morning. It won't be worth the risk, but I also have no idea what I'll do for transportation once I put it away for the winter considering driving my father's car isn't an option anymore.

With a sigh, I take off when the light turns green and make the next turn into a quaint suburban neighborhood. I pull over to the curb once I reach my destination, shut off my bike, and yank my helmet off.

The house is a small yellow two-story with pale blue shutters and a fence out back, nothing lavish or extravagant. Not exactly the clientele I'm used to serving. Typically, the women who utilize my services have more money than they know what to do with, but I'm fine taking jobs for working-class families as long as they can pay. One of my regulars, Katherine McMillan, set this up, so I trust it. Besides, when you come from nothing, your wallet doesn't discriminate, and ever since I moved into Uncle

Cal's place, I've been able to save a lot of my earnings since I no longer need it for necessities like food. At the rate I'm going, I'll have a nice little nest egg built up before college next year.

I adjust the backpack over my shoulders and head toward the front door, unsure of what to expect. All I know about this client is that she recently moved to town and needs me to help her get the house live-in ready, whatever that means.

I knock and wait as the sound of footsteps echo from within. A minute later, when the door swings open, I blink in shock. It takes several seconds for my mind to compute who I'm looking at. But then it registers and anger spikes in my veins. Every muscle in my body coils, prepared for a fight.

My mother stands before me, her smile tentative, her big brown eyes cautious.

"No fucking way." I whirl around, cutting straight through the grass toward my bike as her voice calls after me.

"Atlas, wait!"

I shake my head, lifting my hand as I give her the middle finger because words aren't needed to express how I feel.

"Just let me explain," she cries as I sidle up next to my Harley.

I quickly grab my helmet off the back when a hand reaches around me and snatches it from my hands. Pivoting, I stare at my mother wide-eyed, hands fisting as my temper takes hold. She opens her mouth to speak again, but this time I don't let her. I beat her to it because I have a million things to say, a thousand questions bouncing around in my mind with no answers. "You live here?" I jerk my head toward the house.

"For now," she says, her tone soft.

"I thought I told you to go back to wherever the hell you came from?"

A ragged breath escapes her lips, but I feel no sympathy as she replies. "If you'd just let me explain . . ."

"How exactly did you find me, anyway? How'd you know where to look, who to contact? And how'd you get in contact with one of my clients?"

She opens and closes her mouth, clearly at a loss for words, and her hesitation is all I need to be certain I don't want to hear the answer. I lunge forward and reach for the helmet in her hands, but she pivots, holding it away from me while my pulse pounds furiously in my eardrums.

"I found out about your father's arrest and his rehab stay a few weeks ago. I came as soon as I could. I wanted to be here for you."

I bark out a laugh but it's a bitter sound, ripe with resentment. "You left me fourteen years ago. I was just a kid, practically a baby. Why the hell would you think I need you now?"

She flinches as if my words hurt, but her pain only fuels me further. She has no right to pain when it comes to leaving me. No right to make me feel bad for my cutting words when the pain is all mine. "I needed you *then*."

I step closer, spitting words at her like daggers. "When Dad was so strung out, he forgot to fill the fridge. Or when, at fucking six years old, I had no clean clothes or shoes without holes, and had to figure out how to do laundry and mend them.

I could've used you when we lost our house and had to live in the van for months on end. Not now"—I stab a finger at her—"not when I'm nearly eighteen, already a man, and making it on my own. So, you can take your sorry ass and whatever the hell you came here to say, and shove it. I'm not interested in your pathetic excuse for an explanation." I flick my head toward the helmet in her hands. "Just keep it. I don't need it. Just like I don't need you."

"Atlas, I . . ." She pauses and her eyes flutter closed. "I had to go, but I thought you would be okay. I thought I'd made sure of it. I didn't know until recently how awful things had gotten with your father. When I left, I was assured you'd be cared for. I had no idea you weren't."

"What a joke." I shake my head, unable to hear any more. When I turn for my bike, her voice calls out.

"I'm not leaving until you talk to me."

"Then I guess you'll be here a while," I call over my shoulder.

"You're being childish."

I pause, rolling my head on my shoulders to release the tension before I snap, because God help whoever is in my way when I do.

Turning, I narrow my eyes at her and hold my head high, hoping she gets the message that she's beneath me. "First, you show up at the Rebels press conference, and now you're stalking my clients, lying to them, and tricking me into meeting you. You have no right—"

"No *right?*" She steps toward me, her whole body trembling with emotion as she holds her hands out, my bike helmet still dangling in her grip. "No *right*? Maybe I made mistakes, but I still gave birth to you. I carried you in my womb for nine months, then gave you life and held you in my arms. I nursed you, nourished you with my body. Spent more sleepless nights than I can count rocking you to sleep in my arms." She straightens, her voice firm. "I'm still your mother."

"Yeah," I laugh bitterly. "Some mother. You left your only son to be raised by a drunk and an addict. Hang on, let me get you an award." I reach behind my back, then whip my hand back around, waving my middle finger in the air.

"Real mature," she snaps.

I roll my eyes. "Well, I had a shitty example of maturity, considering my one and only parental figure was passed out on the couch in a puddle of his own drool half the time."

"You have no idea how much I wish I could go back. I'd do everything differently."

I scoff and shake my head as my mind races.

Why the hell is she really here? Why go to all this effort to track me down after all this time?

I can't handle this. Not now.

All I want—all I need—is Mackenzie, and if I can't have her, then all I want is to be left alone.

Why can't she just fucking leave me alone?

"The reasons for why I left, they're complicated," she continues in my silence. "It's not so cut and dry. When I said I believed you'd be taken care of, I meant it. I had no idea things had gotten as bad as they were. Had I known, I would've found you sooner."

I raise a hand for her to stop. I can't hear any more. I can't stand here for one more fucking second and listen to her excuses, because the truth is none of them are good enough. None of them will ever be enough to explain why she abandoned her own child.

Surprisingly, she listens. Her mouth mashes into a thin line as she falls silent. I unclench my fist and run both of my hands over my face, suddenly tired—worn thin like a piece of parchment. Even the slightest breeze threatens to tear through me.

I drop my hands and raise my head to her once more before I turn to leave, when the door behind her opens. Startling, I realize we're not alone as a boy steps out. He's young, maybe ten, with shaggy dark hair the same shade as mine and my mother's, and almond-shaped eyes so similar to my own, I think I must be dreaming.

Only I'm not.

A creeping sensation crawls up my spine as I freeze in place, rooted to the sidewalk as the boy takes one cautious step forward and calls out.

"Mom?"

CHAPTER 9

ATLAS

THE WORD "MOM" SINKS into my bones like an electric current, and I stumble back. Eyes wide, I blink as realization hits.

If she's his mother, then that means . . .

In one swift movement, I rip the helmet from my mother's hands while she steps forward, pleading with me to stop and listen. "Atlas, wait . . ." she calls out. "Please."

"This was an ambush!" I shout, motioning between her and the front door with my helmet before I shove it on. "And I want nothing to do with whatever Machiavellian scheme you have going. Nothing," I grind out. "Do you hear me? Leave me the hell alone!"

My parting words echo in the air between us as I slide onto my bike and hit the throttle, bringing the engine roaring to life before I peel out onto the road.

My traitorous eyes drift to my mirror and I catch sight of the young boy, staring after me, mouth parted. Maybe it's my imagination, but his face brightens with hope; it practically beams with it, and I spend the rest of the drive trying to forget that expression.

I fly on the highway and into town as if my wheels have wings. I take the bends too fast, the curves too sharp. It's a miracle I arrive back at Uncle Cal's alive.

I pull into the driveway and park my bike. Leaves skitter on the pavement around my feet as I step down, cursing the throbbing pulse of emotion in the back of my throat. All the years of pain, resentment, rejection, and sadness combine like a toxic pool inside my gut. One I refuse to acknowledge.

I make my way around the back of the house, needing a moment alone and some time to breathe before going inside. Uncle Cal is home and I can't risk seeing him, or anyone else, right now. I'm in no position to speak, let alone act like everything is normal.

I wander through the gate, into the fenced backyard and past the pool, trying to ignore the heaviness in my chest for fear it might crush me if I do.

Fourteen years have passed since my mother left, yet she still looks exactly as I remember. Her scent is still the same, too—brown sugar and vanilla. It's a scent that somehow comforts me still to this day. It's also a fact that angers me as I stand here, trying not to fall apart.

I stare up at the night sky. Only the stars and a crescent moon brighten the blackness above. A soft breeze ruffles everything around me to life. The rose bushes and forsythia dance, and the mostly bare tree branches creek around me.

I shove my hands in my pockets, warding off the cold as I try and steer my train of thought away from my mother but fail.

The destructive self-monologue that I'm not good enough rears its ugly head, and though I try to smother it, the roots of abandonment grow deep. It's hard not to feel unworthy, to have the self-worth of a pea. The knowledge she left me has always hurt, but my ignorance saved me. As long as I had no idea where she was or what she was doing, I could convince myself that she had her reasons. That maybe it wasn't me. But the truth stared me straight in the face today, because not only did she start a new and better life for herself, she had another child. One she kept.

I grind my teeth, trying not to picture the boy with the almond-shaped eyes—the one that called her *Mom*. There's too much significance in that title. Too much weight in that single word.

But it's no use.

The fact is obvious. She moved on to greener pastures, while I struggled just to get through a single damned day unscathed. For all I know, she has a whole damn family I know nothing about.

"Why?" I ask into the silence. "Why did she leave and why the fuck is she back?"

I spin in a circle expecting an answer but find none.

My hands clench until my knuckles turn white. Until I shake with rage, and my entire body itches to destroy something. I need an outlet, some way to release the frustration bubbling inside me, threatening to erupt like a volcano and turn everything in its wake to ash.

I imagine flipping the lounge chairs into the pool. Shattering the glass coffee table. Busting the stone fountain. I picture taking a sledgehammer to the slate fireplace and large TV screen under the patio. Mowing over the landscaping, knocking down the fence, and destroying the lush hedges surrounding it.

Tearing everything around me down might somehow distract from the fact it feels like everything is crumbling inside me.

But I only clench my hands tighter because there's no place for destruction here. If my past has taught me anything, it's that acting out won't solve my problems. It won't erase the past or make my father ten years sober. It won't send my mother back to where she came from or put Mackenzie in my arms. It won't help a damned thing in my life make more sense, despite how desperately I want it to.

Still, I want my mother to hurt.

I want her to feel the pain I felt as a child, the agony I feel now.

I want her to feel empty and helpless and lonely like I did.

I want to make her pay.

This must be how Mackenzie feels about my father.

The revelation hits me like a right hook. Because there's no coming back from that, there's no making amends.

I reach up to my chest and fist a hand over the spot where the aching won't quit, then wrench it away again nearly tearing the soft material of my shirt as I do. Raking my hands into my hair, I take my frustration out on myself, scraping my scalp with my fingers and tugging at the roots until I feel them rip. Without thinking, I curl my fists and smash them into the stone fountain next to the pool, over and over and over. I keep going until my skin busts open and blood coats my knuckles, warm and sticky, it's coppery scent lingering in the air. Until all my suffering drains away.

The breath wheezes from my lungs as I drop my arms to the side. My hands throb, but I ignore the pain as I tilt my head back to the sky, blinking back the tears clogging the back of my throat.

Fuck.

I won't cry.

I won't fucking give her the privilege.

Instead, I let out a guttural moan—an animalistic sound that perfectly encapsulates how I feel in this moment.

Desperate. Hopeless. Unworthy. *Alone.*

And so fucking angry I don't know what to do with myself.

I clench my jaw, the bone locking with muscle until I think it might pop when I hear a soft voice call out.

"Atlas?"

Mackenzie.

My heart leaps in my chest, beating to life with the sound of her voice.

I glance around me wildly, until I can just make out her silhouette on the far end of the pool, and my heart rate picks up. I squint to see her better in the darkness: The soft slope of her nose. Sharp cheekbones. Lush lips and perfect cupid's bow. I know that profile by heart. I've traced those lips with my own, tasted that mouth, and pressed my palm over the smooth angle of her jaw. When she takes another step closer, a halo of light surrounds her, illuminated by the stars above. She looks like an angel, which is fitting, because that's exactly what she is to me—supernatural, heavenly in her beauty, perfect in every way.

"Mackenzie . . ." I trail off, certain my eyes are playing tricks on me, because there's no way she's really here, saying my name with concern laced in her voice, rather than the malice I've grown accustomed to. And just when I'm convinced she's nothing more than a mirage brought on by the stressful events of the day, she moves closer, until I can make out her ice-blue eyes the moment before they drop to my fists.

Her forehead pinches in concern as she gasps. "Atlas, your hands."

In my mind, I straighten, play it cool and act like the blood dripping from my hands is normal. Like I'm in no pain at all. Nothing fazes me. I'm stone, a brick wall. Indestructible.

But in reality, I break.

The dam holding back the ocean of tears welling inside of me crumbles. I stagger forward, drunk on emotion. I need to be closer to her, to know she's real.

Tears track down my face, unrestrained and silvery under the moonlight while I spill. I tell her about everything that's happened since the day her memory returned. I explain how my mother surprised me at the press conference. How she tracked me down and, after I refused to speak with her, how she's been calling me nonstop. I detail how she tricked me into going to her house today, thinking I was headed to work. And I confess how she looks just as I remember—pretty, seemingly happy, and well-adjusted. The years appear to have been kind to her while they've been cruel to me.

And she has a son. A half brother I knew nothing about. One that looks just like me.

My body shakes like an earthquake when she places a hand on my arm, and I have to fist my hands inside the pockets of my coat in an effort not to reach and pull her to me.

I hate myself for falling apart, especially in front of her. I'm supposed to be strong, my hard outer shell invincible, a man devoid of emotion. But from the moment I met Mackenzie, she had a way of bringing all my raw emotions to the surface. She cracked straight through all my defenses. Formed a fissure in the wall around my hardened heart that can never be repaired.

When I finish, she takes a step back and releases my arm, and I instantly mourn her touch. I'm a man lost at sea without her, bobbing in the surf while he watches his life raft float just out of reach. Unmoored and untethered in a storm.

A war wages in her eyes, and as she stares at me, her brow creases, and I can tell a decision is being made. Then she reaches out and pulls my hands from my pocket and I'm found again.

"Come on, let's get you cleaned up." She tilts her head toward the pool house, beckoning me to follow.

CHAPTER 10

ATLAS

MACKENZIE LEADS ME INTO the pool house bathroom and directs me to sit on the ledge of the soaker tub while she searches for bandages.

I do as instructed, waiting as she turns and opens the large cupboard across from me, and try not to stare. Outside, when I spilled my guts to her, she looked at me with kindness in her eyes for the first time since she ended things, and it gave me hope. Just when I thought there was none left—no chance of reconciliation—she's given me something to cling to.

Maybe she does still care. Maybe not all is lost.

That's enough for me. For now.

I watch as she retrieves a white metal case off the shelf and turns to me, eyeing my knuckles as she steps forward. She snaps open the lid and takes out a dark brown bottle, along with some gauze and bandages to wrap my hands, laying everything out beside me. Uncapping the astringent, she dampens the gauze and begins to dab the knuckles of my right hand.

I stiffen at the sudden burn of the cleanser, and a hiss escapes my parted lips as she murmurs her disapproval. "You really did a number on these. For future reference, I don't recommend picking a fight with a stone fountain." She arches her brow, and I can't help but laugh. The sound is so foreign coming from my own lips, I'm not sure it's mine.

"I needed to hit something," I say with a small shrug. "It was the closest thing available."

"Boys and their fists." She sighs. "You always think it's the best way to solve your problems."

Graham immediately comes to mind, in particular, our fight at Crow's Creek. I wonder if she's thinking about it, too, maybe even referring to it.

I shake off the thought as she moves to my other hand. My split knuckles hurt like a bitch, so I distract myself, focusing on her touch instead of the pain and the way it sends an electric jolt to my bones. It's been far too long since I've felt the soft press of her skin against mine or the warmth of her hands, and I have no idea when I'll feel them again, so I savor it.

Her fingers slide over mine, her touch featherlight, as she gently cleans away the evidence of my despair. I can't help but notice the normally pale blue of her eyes darkens to cerulean underneath the soft vanity lights, creasing in the corners with her concentration while she applies the ointment. Grabbing the bandages, she begins to wrap my right hand while I watch her work with the knowledge it will end far too soon. Yet I'm grateful for the chance to be close to her again, even if it's temporary.

"I can't imagine what I'd do if I were in your shoes," she says after a moment.

It's the first thing she's said about everything I just told her, and I nod, appreciating her honesty. "It's . . . a lot," I say, feeling my cheeks heat as I remember the way I fell apart outside. I should be humiliated at my outburst, ashamed. But somehow, I'm not.

She sighs, securing the last of the bandages before she meets my eyes and takes a deep breath.

"Thank you," I murmur, afraid that now she's done, she'll bolt.

My pulse hammers in my chest as a thick and impenetrable silence settles between us, when it hits me. "What were you doing out here, anyway?"

Please don't say it's because of Graham.

I stiffen as I wait for her answer, even though I can most certainly guarantee she was with him, and that's how she found me. As pathetic as I am, I hope I'm wrong, that maybe she came to see me.

"It doesn't matter," she says, her tone clipped.

She begins to clean up the first-aid supplies, gathering and shoving them back in the container before she snaps the lid with efficient movements, then stows it back in the cupboard. Once she finishes, she comes to stand in front of me. Her arms hang at her sides, her hands and fingers twitching as if we're in some kind of duel and she's waiting for me to make my move.

"I'm surprised you even decided to help me," I say, lifting a bandaged hand.

"I've seen you upset before. Seen you angry and hopeless." Her lush lips part on an exhale before she glances away from me. "But I've never seen you look like *that*."

I swallow. "Like what?" I ask, not sure I want to know.

"Like . . ." She shakes her head, staring at nothing as her throat bobs. "Like you were drowning."

My chest squeezes at her words. "I always feel like I'm drowning without you."

"Atlas. Don't." Her eyes flutter closed for a moment, and I want to take her in my arms and shake her. Make her see how much I love her. How good we are together. How the past means nothing if it means we have no future.

Instead, I drink her in and verbalize another truth. "I'm surprised you still care."

"Of course I still care," she says, her tone sharp as her eyes meet mine once more.

The unexpected display of emotion emboldens me, and I push to my feet, until we're standing only inches apart. Her breathing hitches but does little to stop the pull between us, the one that tugs me closer. The tether connecting us—the invisible force that draws us together—is as strong as it's ever been. Whatever magic we had still remains, and the way her eyes widen, the black of her pupils eviscerating the icy blue, tells me she feels it, too.

My hands ache to hold her, to reach out and cup her face, bring her lips toward mine. But I'm afraid of ruining the moment—maybe more afraid than I've ever been of anything in my whole life—as the air between us thickens and fills with the sound of her heavy breathing.

Unable to wait any longer, I take another step toward her. I lean down and press my forehead against hers while I pull air into my lungs like a dying man.

She smells like spring—apple blossoms and sunshine—and I wince at the pain caused by the restraint of holding back. I want so badly to press my lips to hers, it hurts. But she hasn't pushed me away yet, and I don't want her to.

"Doll . . ." I murmur, and she flinches.

Taking a step back, I watch as the blood drains from her face, leaching the tenderness from her gaze.

And just like that, the moment is lost.

I said the wrong thing.

I fucking ruined it.

Only a foot separates us, yet it might as well be as deep and vast as the ocean when her words cleave me in two.

"I should go," she says, then turns and leaves me standing there with nothing more than loss and regret.

MACKENZIE

I wedge myself behind the back of the pool house, between the shrubbery and the private gate Graham showed me earlier, when a crashing sound erupts from inside. I shrink further into the shadows as I hear Atlas curse. A moment later, I hear the front door of the pool house open and snap shut again. I hold my breath, afraid he'll somehow sense my presence, but after a few minutes, I gather my courage and peek around the corner to see he's gone.

With a sigh of relief, I stare up into the night sky while my heart races at the memory of my nickname on his tongue and how it brought everything back. Every emotion. Every ounce of longing and heartbreak and betrayal.

Finally, I head into the pool house once more and stare at the bed, wondering how long I'll be able to stay here with Atlas and Graham both yards away. It's a recipe for disaster, and I never should've agreed to it, even if I was falling apart and if Graham insisted.

Tomorrow, I'll go home.

As much as I've come to resent my father, it's the safest place for me with everything going on.

I crawl under the covers of my bed and pull the blankets up to my chin, not even bothering to change out of my street clothes and into the clothes Graham brought me earlier. I don't have the energy.

I need sleep. Distance from my thoughts.

I close my eyes, but I can't push Atlas from my head. I keep coming back to the sight of him falling to pieces in front of me, his bloodied hands, and the feel of his skin hot against my own. These memories blot everything else out. For once, instead of fighting them, I allow them to take over and something surprising happens. My demons vanish. My heartache and all my fears disappear, and I can sleep.

GRAHAM

I'm three whiskeys deep and finally starting to feel the warmth of the alcohol in my limbs. At least, I think it's three whiskeys. It's hard to say since I'm drinking straight from the bottle. Either way, no beer for me tonight. I need the hard stuff, something strong enough to numb the memory of Mackenzie in my arms and how my heart fluttered to life at the thought she might kiss me. The anger that followed was so hot and bright, it threatened to swallow me whole.

It wasn't until after I tore out of the driveway that I started to question whether she was actually trying to kiss me or if my subconscious went into overdrive. Was I making something out of nothing? Did I overreact?

I lift the bottle to my lips and take another sip. The burn of the booze in my throat helps me not give a shit.

"Slow down, Scott. We haven't even gotten there yet and you've drank a third of the bottle," Peters says, eyeing the amber liquid with a scowl.

He takes a turn too quickly and my body hits the passenger door of his car. "You're a shit driver," I say with a laugh. "The last thing *you* need is more to drink."

Peters rolls his eyes, but focuses back on the road.

Normally, Jace and Teagan are my go-to, but after I left my house, I went straight to Peters. He's the only one who won't see my sullen mood and immediately tie it to Kenzie or Atlas. Our friendship is surface level. It never goes beyond whatever we're drinking or doing at the moment. It suits me well because lately, I don't want to think or talk about the past or my feelings or my father. All I want to do is forget everything around me.

"Where the hell are we going anyway?" I ask, taking another sip from the bottle.

"Dude, I told you before we left and you said you were down. Were you not listening?"

I shrug. "Tell me again."

He sighs and rolls his eyes. "We're going to this dude's place. He runs poker parties."

I nod, vaguely recalling it, but I'd been too busy thinking about Mackenzie when he'd suggested it. "Oooh, like *underground* poker parties?" I ask, guffawing like a buffoon.

"Something like that, but I'm starting to rethink my decision to bring you. He takes this shit serious. It's not fucking family game night."

"Aw, come on, man. I can be serious," I say, fighting a smile and failing.

"I can see that." He shoots me a glare, then turns back to the road. "He had a couple of guys drop out. Thought I might know someone who wants in, so when you called, I told him we'd check it out."

"Have *you* ever played poker with these dudes?" I ask, my interest piqued. It sure as hell beats sitting in my bedroom, dreaming about Mackenzie.

"Sure. A time or two. It's intense."

I snicker, because it's a card game. How intense can it get? My imagination conjures an image of a bunch of nerds sitting around a dining room table, a bowl of chips between them, and a tally sheet to keep score.

"What's so funny?" he asks as he pulls over to a house I've never seen before. Then again, we've been driving for thirty minutes and I haven't been paying attention, so I have no clue where we're even at. Probably not in Riverside.

"Where the hell are we?" I ask, eyeing the neighborhood like we're in Skid Row, although nothing about it looks sketchy.

"Listen," he says, his expression serious, "before we go in, you need to know these games are no joke. The stakes are high, and they take it seriously. These guys don't mess around. You feel me?"

I sober; suddenly the little card party I'm about to crash got a lot more interesting. "I feel you," I say.

"Okay, so you in?"

I hesitate for a moment, wondering what all this entails. But I've played poker before, and it might be a great way to forget my problems. Besides, right now, I give zero fucks about whether I lose or win. At this point, I'm used to losing. It's all I ever do. So, I don't overthink it. Instead, I nod my head and say, "I'm in."

CHAPTER 11

GRAHAM

I NSTEAD OF ENTERING THROUGH the front, we round the house and push open a back door, which leads to a stairwell. It's dark with very little lighting, and the walls are the color of an inky sky. We take the stairs down into the basement where we step into a dimly lit room. A bar sits to my right with an impressive display of liquor bottles behind it, but the focal point is a felt-covered table. Pendant lights hang from the tall ceilings, illuminating the cards spread out before the men seated around it. I watch as they each flip their cards and the dealer takes them, adding them to the house's hand.

A tall man, who looks to be in his twenties, with a buzz cut and a sharp gaze, lifts his eyes to Peters and stands. He's dressed in a gray suit and a white button-down with several gold chains around his neck. Black dress shoes top off the ensemble. I know nothing about this guy, but he screams money and power—this whole place does.

Buttoning the jacket of his suit, he closes the distance between us. He reaches out, shaking Peters's hand while a gold Rolex glints under the lamplight. "Jamie, so glad you could make it. And your friend is . . . ?" he asks, turning to me.

Peters nods toward me. "This is Graham Scott."

The man's brows draw together as he shakes my hand. "Scott," he murmurs. "Peters has mentioned you before. You're Cal Scott's son, right?"

I glance at Peters, unsure whether I like the fact this guy knows anything about me or my family. "That's right," I say as I drop the handshake.

"I'm Darrell Crenshaw," he says before he spreads his arms out. "Welcome to the Play Room. There's an open bar. Feel free to help yourself. Our bartender, Frankie, will make you anything you want. There's a twenty-dollar play fee, but drinks are on the house."

The burly man behind the counter waves and I nod to him with a slight lift of the chin; I have a feeling he and I are about to become well-acquainted.

"Have you ever played poker before?" Darrell asks, pulling me from my thoughts.

I shrug. "A little." But it looked nothing like this.

"Why don't you grab yourself a drink and come join us. We're about to start a new hand." He reaches into his pocket and pulls out a wad of cash. Counting the twenties, he hands them to me.

"Here," he says. "Just to start you off, until you get the hang of it."

"Seriously?" I ask, eyeing the money.

"Consider it a welcome gift." He winks, then turns and heads to the table while I stare slack jawed at what has to be nearly three hundred bucks piled in the middle of it. Hell, I could just take the money and walk.

I glance at Peters, and he grins. Leaning into me, he whispers, "I told ya, man. This place is the shit. Just take it easy, okay?" He slaps a hand over my shoulder. "And go slow with the drinks. There's a reason they're free." He eyes me meaningfully, and I nod.

A few minutes later, with a Jack and Coke in hand, we join everyone at the poker table. There are five men, not including Darrell and the dealer. Most of them are young—twenties if I had to guess—but older than us by a mile.

"Okay, so here's the skinny." Darrell nods toward the table. "Each player is dealt two pocket or hole cards, then the dealer reveals five community cards. Players must make the best poker hand combination between their hole cards and the five community cards. For ease, first bids are called at three community cards, then the fourth, and fifth. Hole cards obviously stay face down and private to the owner until the bet is called, and one by one the dealer will ask each player to reveal their hand. Highest hand wins. Blind bets start at twenty bucks. Make sense?"

I nod, getting most of what he said as I take a sip of my drink and the dealer starts to hand out cards. Now I see why he gave me three hundred bucks. If I have to pay twenty before the cards are even dealt, the pot will rise fast, and all I have in my wallet is a twenty.

The call for blind bets starts and I place a twenty in the pot, then wait as the cards are dealt. Once the dealer finishes, I peek at my hole cards to see I have two jacks.

I curl my lip. *Not bad.*

I check three community cards that are turned face up: an ace of clubs, a three of clubs, and a jack of spades.

Bets go in, rising another five bucks a person. I stay in, confident in what I have.

Another community card is revealed—a ten of hearts.

Shit.

I call and bet another five, and the fifth community card is dealt—a jack of hearts, giving me four jacks.

Fuck, yes!

I smother my smile as bets go around, and I raise, throwing in another twenty. Two men drop out, including Peters—the pussy—but three stay in. The dealer reveals their cards one by one while my heart pounds in my chest. First hand is three of a kind. *Jackass.* Second hand, which belongs to Darrell, is a full house. The third man has two pair. *Even bigger jackass.*

When I turn over my cards and the dealer takes them, he announces, "Jack of diamonds and a jack of clubs makes four of a kind, jack high. Four jacks takes the pot."

With a grin, I rake the pile of money toward me, mentally calculating it in my head. I won nearly three hundred bucks, including my bids.

"Ah!" Darrell claps, a lazy smile on his face as he watches me. "Is this beginner's luck, or do we have a novice on our hands? I'm excited to find out."

I wink at Peters who glances over at me with an arched brow. For once, it feels good to actually win something instead of coming in second.

A sense of calm washes over me as blind bets are placed. *Suddenly, this night is looking up.*

The next forty minutes go much the same way. I only fold a few hands, but for most of them, I stay in and win the majority of the hands I play. The stack of money in front of me has grown tenfold. It's actually ridiculous how well I'm doing, and I can't help but feel like I've found my calling, something I'm naturally good at other than football. And a hell of a lot more profitable, too, with the side benefit of my father's absence.

Peters is out of money, and as the dealer shuffles the cards, he eyes me. "You wanna share?"

"Hell no. So you can lose it all?"

He crosses his arms over his chest and grumbles something about bringing me here when the dealer calls blind bet and I add a twenty to the pot.

I check my cards—a three and five of spades.

Then I check the dealer's community cards. He turns over a ten of clubs, six of spades, and four of hearts.

All I need is a seven and I have a straight. It's worth the bet, so when it's called at ten bucks, I ante up.

The dealer slowly turns the fourth community card. "Seven of spades" he announces.

Bingo. My lips twitch, and when it's my turn I add another ten to the pot.

Dealer turns the fifth and final community card. "Four of spades."

Holy shit.

My stomach clenches as a shiver of anticipation creeps up my spine. I have a straight flush. With a solemn expression plastered to my face, I raise at forty bucks. One of the men drops out while Darrell eyes me warily, then calls.

One by one, each player reveals their hand. A straight. Full house, king high, four-of-a-kind aces. And then the dealer gets to me and I turn my cards over, meeting Darrell's dark eyes with a smile.

"Three of spades and five of spades," the dealer announces, adding them to the community cards, "makes a straight flush, the winning hand."

My smile splits my face in two, my heart threatening to beat out of my chest as I gather the cash from the center of the table. Two of the other men say they're out for the night, so Darrell calls the game.

I fucking shut the house down, and it's my first time playing. Who knows what could have happened if I had all night, or if the bids were even higher.

I gather my mountain of cash in front of me, just barely refraining from counting it right here, right now, when Darrell hands me a velvet pouch. "For your winnings," he says, motioning toward it. "That was quite a lucky streak you had there."

"Nothing lucky about it," I say, feeling a little cocky. But in all honesty, it's been a long time since I felt *this* good at something, like I was made for playing poker and not chucking a ball on a field. All football has ever brought me is grief from my father, but tonight helped me forget all of my problems. For a short time, I truly enjoyed myself. I let go of the past and lived in the moment. It was refreshing. Exhilarating.

I want to do it again.

"I stand corrected." Darrell grins, then leans forward and whispers in my ear, "I have an exclusive group that joins us on weeknights. It's only for men like you, though. Men who are serious about winning big. Maybe you could join us some time …?"

I glance beside me where Peters is sucking up the last dregs of his drink, the best part of his night, and I nod because I need this. I need to win at something like I did tonight. So, I say, "Yeah, I'd like that. Count me in."

CHAPTER 12

MACKENZIE

ALMOST A WEEK HAS passed since Graham rescued me on the side of the road and took me to the pool house. I only spent two nights there. I couldn't bear any more than that, not after Graham got pissed at me and things got awkward. Not to mention the fact I couldn't stop thinking about Atlas. Everywhere I looked, I saw him. I heard the thickness in his voice as he told me everything that happened with his mom. I smelled the spicy scent of his cologne lingering in the bathroom where I doctored his hands. Felt the warmth of his touch. Heard the sound of my nickname rolling off his tongue.

It was too much.

And now things are once again tense between Graham and I since our little misunderstanding. He picked me up on Monday morning barely saying a word. Ever since, we've ridden to school in silence, and though I hate the distance between us, I can't help but feel that whatever is going on with Graham is bigger than me. He's been distant and sullen. The guys have been complaining that he comes to football practice late, some days smelling of booze. He's tired and cranky most of the time, like he stays out too late, and when I ask him about it, he shuts down.

Between Atlas, my increasing panic attacks, and the looming decision on what to do about Lee Scott, I'm ready to crack.

Graham pulls into the student lot and turns off the ignition and sits there, staring ahead at our classmates as they make their way into the building, while I try and read his mind. When I can't, I give up and sink back into my own seat, content to sit beside him in silence.

The truth is I don't want to go inside.

I don't want to plaster a smile on my face and force myself to focus on classes when my mind is elsewhere.

I almost suggest we skip. Take off and do something carefree and reckless. But when I turn to him, I notice the dark circles beneath his eyes are more prominent than usual. Stubble covers his jaw, and his hair is disheveled. "You look tired today," I blurt.

He glances at me and blinks, as if he forgot I was there. "Ah, yeah." He clears his throat and scratches a hand over the scruff on his face. "I've had a couple of late nights, I guess."

I nod, wondering where exactly he goes in the evenings. After he left me in the pool house the other night, his car disappeared. Was he hanging out with Peters? Or the guys? And was he drinking? He seems to do a lot of that these days, and it worries me.

My stomach twists at the thought. All I want is to have my best friend back. "Listen, I know things have been strained between us for weeks now, but the other night, in the pool house—"

"No," he says, his tone firm. "That was all on me. I totally overreacted. I just . . . being that close to you, I guess I got triggered . . ." His throat bobs. "Anyway, I'm sorry. I feel like an idiot. We good?"

"Of course, we're good," I say, smiling for the first time in days. Relief floods through me and I can see it reflected in his eyes. I don't want to be right. I just want to be a good friend, and for that reason alone, I'm glad he realizes I wasn't trying to put a move on him or toy with his emotions. And next time, I'll keep my distance. I won't make the mistake of getting too close. Things are different now. We can't be like we were before, as much as it saddens me.

When he grins back, the tension between us disappears. Like popping the top off a Coke, the air has thinned, the pressure gone.

He glances back to the windshield one more time, then nods to himself as if he's making his mind up about something, and turns back to me. "Fall Fest is tomorrow. I know we have to be there for the parade, but why don't we go early and enjoy it?"

Graham and I always go together, but things are different this year, and with everything that's happened, I figured it was off the table. So, I'm hesitant to agree, even though he's just told me things are good between us.

"Come on, we can't not go," he says when I don't answer him. He stares at me for a moment before he cocks his head and catches my gaze, as if he can sense what I'm thinking: that things are weird between us and I don't want to make them worse.

"Let's say screw it. Forget everything that's happened, even if only for a day, and just have fun. Forget the past. What do you say?"

My eyes brighten as I stare at him. I'd love more than anything to forget the mistakes I've made, and I desperately want my best friend back without the awkwardness that's been lurking around. "Really?"

When he nods, my thoughts drift briefly to Atlas. He'll be there, too, for the Rebels float and MVP award announcement. I do almost anything to avoid him these days. But if I go with Graham tomorrow, he'll certainly see us together, and I'm not sure I can handle another confrontation after the other night at the pool house.

But I also don't want to say no to Graham, because the idea of going back to the way things were, if only for a moment, is too enticing to pass up.

"Okay, yeah. Let's do it," I say. Then I cross my fingers and say a little prayer because where the Scott cousins are concerned, nothing ever seems to go according to plan.

ATLAS

Today is Fall Fest, and I'm supposed to be getting ready, but I can't stop thinking about Mackenzie. She's occupied my thoughts all week, and today is no exception. I lie in bed, staring at the ceiling while I recall the way she listened to me spill my guts outside the pool house. The way she looked into my eyes as she cleaned my knuckles and the heat of her touch is seared into my memory. We shared something in that moment that felt a hell of a lot like it did before my life went to shit.

Until I called her "doll" and ruined it.

I sigh into the silence. Everyone is gone already. Graham left hours ago, and I can't help but wonder if he's taking Mackenzie today.

Groaning, I run my hands over my face. According to Jace, they're not together, but it sure as hell seems like they are, and the reminder that she once chose *me* does little to ease the pain that I went and fucked everything up.

No thanks to my pops.

Then again, maybe this is the universe's way of righting itself. I have no doubt she and Graham would probably be an item right now if I'd never transferred to Riverside.

Shit, I can't even blame her. Graham was the smart choice all along.

Throwing the blankets off me, I launch myself to my feet, grab my football jersey and joggers, then throw them on. The stairs creak in the quiet as I make my way to the first floor and into the kitchen, glad no one is around to witness my shitty mood. I grab a box of cereal and set it on the counter, then open the fridge and remove the milk and fill a bowl. Taking a seat at the island, I dig in, when the intrusive thoughts return. Except this time, they're about my father. He left me a message just last night about visiting next week—said he hoped I came. He's sober, a miracle in and of itself, but I just can't bring myself to face him. Not knowing what I know. Not after it destroyed the one good thing in my life other than football.

The cereal turns to paste in my mouth, thickening to concrete when I swallow. I shove the bowl away from me, no longer hungry.

Like it or not, I better head to Fall Fest if I'm to make the parade. Besides, I have an ace up my sleeve. With any luck, I'll get my moment alone with her.

MACKENZIE

I smile as carnival music floats through the gates. "I'm glad we decided to do this."

Graham glances over at me, his expression warm. "Yeah, me too."

"All right, then. Let's do this thing," I say, bumping his arm with mine as we make our way through the gates. Despite the chill in the air, a flush of warmth floods through me as I take in the familiar sites. The pumpkin carving booth. Candy and caramel apples sitting on display along with bags of brightly colored cotton candy. The lemon shake stand. Ring toss. Balloon darts. The sight of the Ferris wheel looming in the distance, towering over everything to the backdrop of the tinkling music.

"Remember the time my mother roped us into working the information booth in exchange for free ride passes?" Graham asks, arching a brow.

"Um, yeah. Everyone was asking questions we had zero answers to."

"There were a lot of lost people that day." He shakes his head with a laugh and I'm reminded of all the memories we share on these fairgrounds: the years we came here together, riding the Ferris wheel into the night, spending ridiculous amounts of money trying to win prizes, and eating junk food until our bellies ached.

They were simple times. Carefree. The source of some of my favorite memories.

I glance up at him and his green eyes tell me he knows exactly what I'm thinking. "Where to?" I ask.

"Do you really have to ask?" He grabs my hand and tugs me past the saltwater taffy booth, around the peanut stand, and I instantly know where we're headed. I can smell the cinnamon and sugar in the air before we even get there.

The line for Cindy's Cinnamon Buns is long but it moves fast as we take our place, and before long, we're at the front and Graham is ordering for us. "Two rolls, please," he says.

A moment later, he hands me a clamshell full of the warm cinnamon-coated dough, oozing with butter. It's happiness on a plate, and I moan as I take my first bite.

"God, that's good," he murmurs in agreement.

"If taste buds can harbor memories, it's definitely in these rolls," I say as another flood of memories hits me. Except these ones are from my childhood, my mother and I prowling the festival while my father worked the Riverside PD booth when he was just a street cop, and not the chief of police. A time when they were happy. Or so I thought.

The dark turn in my thoughts threatens to wreck my mood, so I quickly change the subject, along with the direction of my thoughts. "Is your mom here?" I ask.

"Probably in the fair office," he says, motioning in that direction.

"And your dad?" I peer up at him through the sun.

"He'll be here later, for the float and award." He rolls his eyes, which tells me everything I need to know about how he's feeling about the Rebels football festivities today. "You sure you don't want to join us?"

"Um, no." Some of the girls from the squad participate each year. They ride the float with the boys and help present the

MVP award, but seeing as how there's tension between myself and two particular Rebels, I felt it best to sit this one out. "I know we initially signed up to walk together behind the float, but if it's okay with you, I'll be cheering for you on the sidelines. You deserve all the accolades coming your way and more," I say, meaning it. Graham's had a hard year where football is concerned, so it would be nice for him to be awarded the title of Rebels MVP.

I take another bite of my roll, then lick the cinnamon from my lips, drawing Graham's gaze. The green of his eyes intensifies, and it reminds me of the way he looked at me the day he kissed me in his bedroom. "You've always been my biggest cheerleader," he says, his voice soft. "I don't know what I would've done all these years without you."

I swallow and quickly glance away, feeling the heat of a blush creeping up my neck. Clearing my throat, I grab his free hand and tug him forward. "Come on, let's get our ride tickets before there's a line."

Two hours later, the fairground is packed with people and our pockets are stuffed with ride tickets. We've gone through several of the big barns and outbuildings filled with crafts and vendors. We've bobbed for apples, voted for the best pie, watched a sheep shearing demonstration, and played a rather competitive game of ski ball.

Walking side by side, we head toward the Ferris wheel, passing the old-fashioned photo booth when I pause.

Following my gaze, Graham glances at the sign and groans.

"Come on," I plead. "It's tradition."

"The question is *why*?"

My mouth drops open in mock offense and I lightly smack his arm. "You like taking these photos, and you know it."

"I want to dress up in old musty western wear for a black-and-white photo about as much as I want an enema."

I fight back a laugh as I clasp my hands together and pout. "*Please . . .?*"

"*Fine,*" he says on a sigh. I squeal and clap my hands as his deep laughter rumbles behind me and into the booth where we begin to pick through the old wardrobe chest to find our outfits.

Once I exchange my cheer uniform for a Victorian dress, complete with a parasol and hat, and he trades his jersey for a western vest and dust jacket, we pose for the photographs. We laugh until our stomachs ache, making silly faces for the camera and standing in dramatic poses. After we finish, I pay for the photographs and the older woman running the booth hands us our sepia proofs.

Holding in a laugh, I wave one in front of him where he's twirling a ridiculous handlebar mustache. "These might be the best ones yet."

"These should be burned," he says, swiping it from me. But his smile says otherwise, and it feels just like old times. Like it's just Kenzie and Graham again, best friends for life.

"Such a cute couple," the woman running the booth says, and I freeze. Lifting my eyes to Graham, I watch as his smile begins to fade and his expression darkens. But then, it's as if someone flips a switch. He clears his throat and turns to me, a mischievous glint in his eye as he says, "Last one to the Ferris wheel buys lunch!"

He takes off, a maniacal cackle trailing after him, while I scramble to catch up, awash with relief the moment isn't ruined. "Cheater!" I yell at his back.

An hour later, we're stuck at the top of the Ferris wheel on what might be our fiftieth time around. We stare down at the fairground below us, packed with people, while the sounds of the nearby carousel float to us on the breeze.

I lean over the side of our car, staring at the buzz of activity around us. "Look! The taffy booth is finally open. We have to get a bag of watermelon."

Graham scoffs. "Everyone knows cinnamon is the superior flavor."

"What?" I yell, jerking my head up and straightening. "No way."

"Yes, way." Graham's hands squeeze the bar in front of him while he speaks through clenched teeth and I remember he hates when the cars jostle. "But if you rock this thing again, they'll be scraping us off the ground."

"*Ooh*," I taunt. "Oh, my."

"What?"

"I forgot how nervous you get when these things move." My lips instantly curl into an evil grin. "You hate it when I do *this*." I shift my body forward, then back again, rocking our car so furiously it's a miracle the hinges don't fall off.

"Mackenzie!" Graham's eyes widen and he braces his hands on the sides of the car, his knuckles turning white with his death grip. "I'll never ride this blasted thing with you again, I swear."

"I don't believe it," I say, having far too much fun with this.

"When we get off this thing, you're a dead woman," he snaps, but his threat only makes me laugh harder until we start to move again. As my gaze catches the Rebels float by the grandstand, I realize it's almost time for us to meet up with the team. I instantly sober at the thought, hating that our fun is about to end, because whenever his father and Atlas are involved with anything these days, it puts him in a sour mood and things go south.

Shielding the sun from my eyes with my hand, I glance over at him again, so I can read his expression. "We should probably get off this time around so you can get ready for the parade."

He groans and loosens his grip on the sides of the cart. "Maybe I should just skip it."

"You're their quarterback, Graham. You need to go, and I want to cheer you on. You've earned it."

A sandy brow lifts. "Have I? Because twenty bucks says Atlas gets all the recognition today for making it to States."

I swallow. "Since when are you the betting type?" I say, trying and failing to bring some levity to the conversation.

He shrugs, but something I don't recognize passes through his eyes. "It just seems to be the way things go lately. Atlas wins, and I lose."

"Graham . . ." I say, at a loss for words. I can only apologize so many times until it becomes meaningless. But I also know this is about more than me. It's about his father, too. "This is our last year," I say, changing the trajectory of the conversation. "States is a big accomplishment. The team—Jace, Knox, and Teagan—you've been with them since middle school. Don't miss out on something great on account of anyone else."

He licks his lips and glances down at his hands, as if he's afraid to voice his feelings out loud. "The truth is my heart's not in it like it once was. Lately, it's like I'm simply going through the motions. Everything feels like an obligation. A chore." He lifts his eyes to mine once more. "Trust me. If I don't go, I'm not missing out. If anything, going is just one more thing I have to do, and I'm kind of done trying to please everyone else."

By everyone, he means his father.

"*Okay*," I say, slowly. "If you don't want to go, then I won't either. We'll both skip out on it. Just be sure because you don't want to have regrets."

If anyone knows about regrets, it's me. If I could rewind and change the last couple of months I would. If I could go back and never follow my mother to Manja, Manja that day, I'd change the course of time.

We near the bottom of the Ferris wheel and get off without speaking, but a moment later, Graham breaks the silence. "Is it hard seeing him?"

I know without asking who he's talking about and his question surprises me only because he and I rarely discuss Atlas where I'm concerned. It's like an unspoken rule. Don't address the elephant in the room and it doesn't exist. "Yes," I say.

I imagine it's every bit as hard for Graham to be around me after rejecting him. Yet here he is.

"Do you think you'll ever forgive him for keeping the truth from you?"

My throat bobs and I kick a rock across the pavement as we walk. "Even if I did, I'm not sure I could ever get past the fact his father was behind that wheel. It's too much, you know?"

He nods. "And then he took you for a driving lesson in the same car." He shakes his head, his mouth pressed into a thin line, making my stomach clench.

I press a hand to my belly, suddenly nauseous, and I'm about to tell Graham I feel like I might be sick when a body pushes between us, draping his muscular arms over both of our shoulders. I glance up into the aqua eyes of Jace Taggart.

My eyes widen and I meet Graham's gaze. If we had any chance of skipping out on the float, it just passed us by.

"Hey, kids," he says, grinning from ear to ear. "It's about time you joined the party. The float is this way," he says, nodding up ahead and pulling us in the direction of the grandstand where the float waits.

"Actually—" I start, but Jace interrupts me.

"You weren't thinking of skipping now, were you? I mean, we can't possibly have a parade without the king and queen of football."

"I think we're gonna sit this one out," Graham says.

"Riiiiiight." Jace rolls his eyes. "Like I'm gonna let you. Not just because your father will beat my ass if he knows I found you and let you play hooky, but because the captain of the football team is not going to skip the parade and MVP award. Dude, you know you're gonna win, right?"

Graham hesitates, saying nothing as his gaze makes quick work of the float and all of his teammates piled around Jace's truck, which is decked out in Rebels colors, streamers, balloons, and football paraphernalia—the whole works. "I'm not holding my breath."

"Naw, it's in the bag," Teagan says, joining us and overhearing our conversation. "I heard Coach talking. Apparently, it was a close race, but your father was the tiebreaker."

"So, he'll vote for me," Graham murmurs, almost to himself.

Teagan claps him on the back. "You deserve it, man."

Graham's gaze drifts to mine, his demeanor noticeably brighter. Shoulders back, chin up, he eyes the float once more. "I guess we can spare some time. Do you mind?" he asks.

"Of course not," I say, though the tightening in my gut says otherwise. "Let's do this."

"You still single, Hart?" Jace asks with a wink.

"Back the fuck off." Graham glares, which makes Jace tip his head back in laughter.

"Still territorial, I see," he says, his tone amused. "Glad to see some things never change."

"Always stirring the pot," Teagan mutters with a shake of the head, and I can't help but grin as we sidle up to the truck.

"All right, listen up!" Jace cups his hands around his mouth. "Mascot and QB are on the float. Everyone else is walking behind. The lineup is on here." He grabs a clipboard off the bed of his truck and waves it in the air. "Everyone get in your places as marked. We leave in ten!"

"Wait," I say when he drops the clipboard and turns back to us. "Graham and I were supposed to walk together."

Jace frowns and stares down at the papers. "Nope. This says he's supposed to ride on the float with the mascot and pass out candy. Two lucky winners get a free trip and tickets to State."

I shake my head and snatch the clipboard from his hands. "That can't be right. They had us paired . . ." I drift off as I make quick work of the list. Finding my name, my eyes zero in on my partner and my stomach drops. Beside my name, written in bold ink, is "Atlas Scott."

I shove the clipboard back into Jace's chest. "This can't be right. Change it."

"What's the problem?" Graham asks as he takes a look for himself. The minute he sees my pairing, his eyes harden. "We'll switch."

"Hell, no." Jace grabs the clipboard off him and chucks it inside the window of his truck. "I was given explicit instructions not to fuck with it and that *you*, the Rebels's golden boy, are supposed to be throwing candy. No one else."

"Then Kenz can come on the float with me," he says, grabbing my hand.

"Is there a problem?" The deep rumble of Atlas's voice creeps up my spine.

I turn to face him, and his eyes shift to my hand enveloped inside Graham's.

"Yeah. Someone must've screwed something up with the lineup," Graham says, his voice tight.

Atlas smirks. "Gee. Wonder how that happened? I mean, sign-up sheets were initially recorded in pencil. Strange . . ."

My jaw drops, mouth open as Graham's expression turns to stone.

"All righty, then"—Jace claps his hands, tone bright—"now that we have this settled, and you've met with your partner, Kenz, time to get this show on the road." Jace pushes on Graham's shoulders, guiding him toward the float while he reaches out to me, arguing the entire way.

Teagan joins them and gives him a nudge in the back. "Let it go, man. Deal with it later."

They continue to bicker as they guide Graham further away, and I turn toward Atlas, my gaze weaponized.

He shrugs, grinning. "What?"

With a grunt of frustration, I cross my arms over my chest and storm away. He follows on my heels but says nothing as I head toward the lineup, finding our place in the back.

"I had to find some way to talk to you, didn't I?" he says, moving beside me.

My stomach roils as I try to ignore his presence beside me, but he's so close I can feel the heat of his skin. The spicy scent of his cologne drifts toward me and I risk a glance out of the corner of my eye, hating that he's so gorgeous. Thick, dark hair above equally dark eyes. A square jawline with a hint of dark stubble. Full mouth. A football jersey that clings to his muscles. Tattoos covering his arm in a swirl of black ink.

When his lips twitch, I know I've been caught looking and curse myself for poor restraint.

Fine. He wants to play games, I'll keep my mouth shut the entire time. I won't say a word.

I stare straight ahead, smashing my lips together, as he clears his throat and shifts on his feet. His arm brushes mine, sending a swarm of butterflies rioting in my chest.

He rubs his hands together as if to ward off the chilly autumn air, or maybe it's to draw attention to his biceps, I'm not sure. The muscle pops with the movement. I catch sight of his still-bandaged hands, and try to ignore the press of memories from the other night. Nothing good will come of remembering the way it felt to touch him again, to look into his eyes and feel something other than betrayal.

Up ahead, Coach Clancy starts to give instructions. We're to walk from the grandstand, around the fairground, into downtown Riverside, and back, where they'll present the MVP award.

I focus as the line starts to slowly move and Atlas drifts closer. He drops his hand, and his fingers brush mine. Once. Twice. A third time, and the breath catches in my throat.

He's doing this on purpose, I'm sure of it, and when we take our first steps and begin to move, the slightest graze of his hip against my own brings my nerve endings to life.

This is going to be the longest march of my life.

CHAPTER 13

ATLAS

I REACH ACROSS MACKENZIE, offering a fist bump to a little Rebels's fan who runs to me from the crowd, and my forearm brushes her breasts.

A groan threatens to bubble from the back of my throat.

I've been nonchalantly touching her for the past twenty minutes, and I'm driving myself fucking crazy. But if the rapid rise and fall of her chest and the way her throat bobs every time we touch is any indication, I'm driving her every bit as insane. Which is enough for me. For now.

"Would you please stop?" she asks through gritted teeth when my hand brushes her bare arm.

"Waving to fans?" I ask, my tone innocent.

She turns her fiery gaze on mine. "I know what you're doing."

"What?" I shrug, but a grin curls the corners of my lips. I can't help myself. A pissed and sexually frustrated Mackenzie might be my favorite.

"Touching me," she hisses.

"I've been touching you?" I ask, and when she lets out a low growl of frustration, it takes everything in me not to lean forward and take her pouty lower lip between my teeth.

Pleased with myself, we go another minute before I lean closer, until her floral scent makes me dizzy with want, and I ask the question that's been plaguing me all week. "So, are you two together now?" I manage to keep my tone casual despite my clenched jaw.

I probably don't want to hear the answer, but I need to know what I'm up against.

"What? Who?" she asks, her tone defensive.

I roll my eyes and stare down at her. "You and Golden Boy." I jerk my head toward the front of the lineup, where Graham sits on the float throwing candy to the crowd.

"No. We're just—"

"Friends?" I shake my head. I'm not sure if she and Graham were ever only friends, but I'm also not sure she knows it. Then again, maybe those feelings really did only run one-way. At least, that's my hope.

I feel her gaze on me. "Why can't you just let it go?"

"What? You and Graham?" I ask.

She shakes her head no. "Us."

My stomach clenches, and I meet her eyes. "Never."

"Why?"

"Because you and me, doll, we're meant to be together, and the sooner you realize it and stop fighting your feelings for me, the better."

She scoffs, and I admire her fire, even if it is directed my way. "The better for who? You?"

"And you. And Graham. The team. All of humankind." I grin. Maybe it's wishful thinking, but I swear I see the hint of a smile beneath her scowl.

"You're incorrigible," she says, tearing her eyes from mine.

"I've been called worse things."

She snorts. "Some from my own mouth."

"So, you admit you talk about me when I'm not around?"

Her head snaps up and she glares. "That wasn't a compliment."

"Still, it means you think about me."

"All bad thoughts, maybe."

"*Ooh*, like naughty ones?" I wink.

She opens her mouth to speak, but chokes instead.

"Is that a yes?"

"You wish." Her eyes turn to blue flames.

"I do. I really do."

She lightly punches me in the arm but this time, when she turns away, I see her smile.

The parade ends far too soon for my liking. The instant we arrive back at the grandstand and Graham comes down from his throne and joins Mackenzie, the moment is broken. The team and cheerleaders are ushered to the stage facing the grandstand filled with fans, parents, and students. Graham and Mackenzie head across from me, opposite the podium where Uncle Cal and Coach Clancy wait to begin the ceremony.

A few minutes later, Coach Clancy introduces himself, and speaks for a moment on the football program at Riverside before acknowledging the senior players by name and handing the mic off to Uncle Cal.

He stares out at the crowd, looking sharp as always in a charcoal suit which earns him several catcalls. Smiling, he offers the perpetrators a wave. Uncle Cal is probably the biggest thing to ever happen to Riverside. In fact, they probably have him to thank for the top-tier football program. His influence helped make it what it is.

Leaning into the microphone, he says, "Next Saturday, the Riverside Rebels will compete for the state championship. It's been an honor to get to know the young men that grace our field throughout the years. I'm always proud of our boys, but this year holds a little more significance than the others. As some of you may know, I have a personal stake in the outcome next week. My son, Graham Scott . . ." He motions to his left, waving for Graham to step forward, who is standing beside Kenzie with his arms crossed over his chest, looking pissed. I can see the flicker of muscle in his jaw as his father murmurs into the microphone. "Come on, son, don't be shy. Step forward."

Graham does as he says, moving closer to the podium as Uncle Cal turns my way and stretches an arm toward me. "And my nephew, Atlas Scott." He waves me forward, and I come to a stand beside Graham, both of us tensing from the close proximity. Other than our time on the field, we're hardly ever in the same room.

"These boys, along with their team will be competing at States, and I have every confidence they will *win* this Saturday!" he yells, bringing his fist down over the podium like a gavel while the crowd roars in response.

"As you know, every year, it's tradition to announce a senior as Rebel MVP. This year's vote was close. The athletic department, along with the coaches and players, vote for the most valuable player, and this year's race was so tight, a tiebreaker was necessary."

I tense as I glance over at Graham. Suddenly, it's a lot more obvious why Uncle Cal called us out. The tie was between us. Ironic, considering it's not the only thing we've been competing for these last few months.

Graham meets my gaze, his green eyes ripe with anger. I can't say I blame him for being mad because if I hadn't moved to Riverside, none of this would be happening. He'd have team MVP in the bag. And the girl, too.

Turning my gaze back to the crowd, I swallow over my nerves, listening as Uncle Cal continues to talk us up, wondering who got the tiebreaking vote. For some reason, I suspect it was him.

"As you may know, the winner of the Riverside Rebels MVP award will receive a five-thousand-dollar scholarship toward the college of their choice, along with a spot on the Rebels's wall of fame—"

It's stupid to want something so much. Just a silly high school award. It means nothing. Yet suddenly, it means everything to me. I want it so bad I can taste it.

"—so, it's my honor to announce this year's Riverside Rebels's MVP . . ."

Uncle Cal begins to open the envelope in his hands. Nearby, Coach clutches a gold medal in his fist.

I close my eyes, heart jumping in my throat. The crowd quietens with anticipation, and the only sound is the rustling of the paper in Uncle Cal's hands as he moves closer to the microphone. You can hear his exhalation of breath before the sound of his voice. "And the award goes to . . ." He pauses. "Atlas Scott!"

My eyes snap open. Several people rap me on the back. A frog jumps in my throat as I turn toward Uncle Cal, who's staring at me with affection—the kind of affection a father shows his son. The kind I've wanted, craved, my whole life.

I stumble forward on numb legs, stopping in front of Coach who places the medal around my neck, then shakes my hand, offering me his congratulations before I turn to face Uncle Cal again. He claps one hand on my back while he draws me into a hug with the other.

"Congratulations, Atlas. You've earned it."

My chest swells with pride while gratitude fills me up. Though Uncle Cal hasn't always been there for me, he's been present in some of the moments that have counted the most. During these last few months he's mentored me, given me a roof over my head, and a chance at a future beyond high school.

He believes in me.

Which is more than I can say for my own father.

When he releases me, my gaze drifts to Graham. His eyes shift wildly, flickering between us.

A stab of sympathy works its way into my conscience as Mackenzie leans forward, whispering something to him I can't hear but wish I could.

Whatever she says mustn't be enough to ease his anger because he turns and storms off the stage, punching a Rebels mascot display on his way and knocking the head off. A cacophonous gasp ripples through the crowd before he kicks a second one and sends it flying with an ominous crash before he's gone.

CHAPTER 14

ATLAS

I WANDER THROUGH THE crowd of people, searching for Mackenzie. After Graham made a scene, Uncle Cal and Coach did their best to downplay the commotion from his early departure, then dismissed the team. Even though I know I should head home, I can't. Not without seeing her before I go.

After searching for thirty minutes with no luck, I amble toward the animal barns. They sit just in front of the wood line. The only other thing here is a small outbuilding with restrooms, otherwise, it's mostly abandoned. I'm about to cut my losses when movement catches my eye.

I draw closer, rounding the barns, when I'm struck with the sight of Graham, his head bowed, while Mackenzie places her hands on either side of his face.

My muscles stiffen and my hands fist. The bitter taste of jealousy rises to the back of my throat like bile as she murmurs something to him I can't hear.

He nods, then lifts his eyes, but instead of meeting hers, they clash with mine. A cruel smile twists his lips as he straightens. "Well, well, if it isn't the prodigal son."

Mackenzie whips around, eyes wide as she takes me in, but I can't bear to look at her. For someone who claims she and Graham are just friends, they sure look a hell of a lot like a couple. Which, I suspect, is exactly how Graham wants it.

I wonder if she even sees it, or if she really is that oblivious.

I glance away from them for a moment, not because Graham's words hurt, but because my heart is fucking breaking at the thought she'll eventually decide he's the one she wants.

I swallow, regaining my composure. Any sympathy I felt for Graham moments ago when I won MVP disappears as he directs his rage my way. "You're not done with your temper tantrum, I see."

He laughs, but it's full of bitterness. "You do realize it was probably just a sympathy vote. You know, because you don't have a mother and your father's an addict, so they wanted to give you a win."

Mackenzie turns to him, mouth gaping. "Graham . . ."

I shake off the sting of his words, emboldened by the look of disgust twisting Mackenzie's features. I rock back on my heels, my gaze traveling over him. "You know, jealousy looks bad on you."

"You should know," he quips, with a smirk.

This time, Mackenzie takes a step away from him.

Go ahead, act like an ass. See how far it gets you.

I move closer, my jaw locking as I do. Graham is so full of rage, he'll hang himself where Mackenzie is concerned if I let him keep talking. And I'll gladly hand him the noose.

"You're right," I say, meaningfully. I meet Mackenzie's gaze, my eyes burning into hers. "Maybe I am jealous."

"What was the plan anyway?" Graham asks, stepping around her, blocking her from view. "You couldn't get your own father to give a shit about you, so you thought you'd steal mine?"

I laugh and shake my head. "I never went to your father," I say. "I've never asked him for a damn thing. He came to *me.*"

Surprise brightens the green of Graham's eyes, and I wonder if someone told him otherwise and, if so, why. Regardless, I continue, unable to resist poking the bear. "Oh, you didn't know? How he used to come to some of my games at Shaker? How he came to me during conditioning this past summer and told me he was going to get me a spot at Riverside? Practically begged me to join the team. I think his exact phrasing was, 'They need all the help they can get.'"

I grin as my words hang in the air between us. The latter is a lie—at the very least, a stretch of the truth—but the rest is exactly as it happened. Either way, I'm so damned sick of Graham acting like he's the only one that deserves anything good in his life. The second everything stopped being handed to him and he had to actually work for it, he blamed everyone else for his shortcomings.

Graham takes another step closer, his posture rigid. The tension is so thick it's hard to breathe, and just when I think I'm going to get the fight I crave, Mackenzie steps between us. "Stop it." She glances from me to him. "You two are acting like children. And until you grow up, I'm done with both of you."

She pushes past both of us, and I turn to follow, calling after her at the same time Graham does when we hear the rustling of something behind us, followed by the murmur of raised voices, one I distinctly recognize as—

"My father," Graham murmurs beside me with a frown.

I scowl, and without saying anything we head toward the sound, skirting the bathrooms entirely until we face the woods.

"Right there." Mackenzie points to the trees where Uncle Cal stands, grasping a woman who is not Aunt Sheila by her arms, an intense look in his eyes.

"What the hell?" Graham scowls, reading my thoughts.

Uncle Cal glances up, frowning at the sound of Graham's voice as the three of us scramble to duck back behind the building for cover.

He searches his surroundings for a minute, too distracted to see us before he turns his attention back to the woman. I sigh in relief, but the feeling is momentary because the second Cal drops his hands from the woman's arms, she turns, and I get a better view.

"Who is that?" Mackenzie murmurs.

Busty. Dark hair and eyes. Tanned skin.

My stomach drops out from under me.

I can't breathe.

Because I know who she is.

"It's my mother."

I can feel Mackenzie's gaze on me while chills palpate my spine. I glance over at Graham and motion for them to keep quiet before the three of us turn our attention back to the woods where Uncle Cal faces my mother in what must be some kind of confrontation.

"What the hell are you doing here, Marie?" he hisses. "This isn't the place for you right now."

My mother barks out a laugh. "Where exactly is my place, Cal?"

"When you came to town, you promised me you wouldn't push. Then you promised me you'd back off if I gave you his number and he wanted nothing to do with you." He waves his arms angrily. "Yet you've done the exact opposite since you got here."

I swallow. I guess my instincts were right. Uncle Cal *did* know about my mother's return. Not only did he know she was in town, but, apparently, the lying fuck is the one who told her where to find me and gave her my phone number. *But why?*

Betrayal settles in the pit of my stomach, warring with the part of me that feels an allegiance to him for giving me a home when I had none. For being the father figure I've never had, even if only for a short time.

Ever since he helped me, I've been waiting for the other shoe to drop.

Maybe this is it, the moment I discover his true motives. However, if it involves my mother, I'm not sure I wanna know what his angle is.

"I had to promise those things," my mother spits out. "You never would've allowed me near him otherwise, and we both know it."

"For good reason. He doesn't want to see you." He pokes a finger at her. "I told you he—"

"I don't give a shit what you told me," she snaps, her tone shrill. "He doesn't know what's good for him."

Anger fists in my chest, hot and sharp. I have half a mind to storm over to where they're standing and give her a piece of my mind, tell her exactly what I think of her. But before I can, Cal snaps back.

"And you do?" he asks, his tone bitter. "You've been gone a long time."

A shock of pain distorts my mother's features before she lunges at him, fists out in front of her as if she might strike. "And whose fault is that?" she asks, her voice low and menacing.

"So, this is all my fault now? You're going to act like you had no part in leaving?"

What the hell are they talking about? My mind spins as I try to figure out exactly what my mother is accusing him of, but I can't compute. My hard drive is busted. There's something they're not saying, both of them dancing circles around it.

"You can't be here. You need to leave." Cal lifts his chin, towering over her, but she doesn't even so much as blink.

"I'm not leaving until I talk to him and explain."

"This isn't a joke, Marie," he says, his voice deathly calm despite the vein pulsing in his forehead. "My wife could find us at any moment. This is a public place, for fuck's sake. You need to leave. Now."

A laugh spurts from my mother's lips, but there's nothing happy in the sound. "Leave the festival? Or Riverside? Because the latter isn't happening." She sneers, eyeing him in disdain. "You treat us like trash, Cal. I never should've let you pay me off to leave. I should've been stronger. I should've stayed, instead of having faith Lee would get his shit together and take responsibility for our son."

I take a step back on legs so numb it's a miracle I don't fall.

I never should've let you pay me off to leave . . .

She steps closer, until they're nose to nose, Uncle Cal looking down on her as she murmurs, "But maybe my biggest mistake was trusting *you* to look after them. Seems to me he would've been fine without me, but it's *you* that dropped the ball."

Silence descends between them and I swallow, unable to believe what I'm hearing, what I'm seeing.

Uncle Cal paid her to leave? But why?

None of it makes sense.

My heart pounds in my chest, a lonely staccato as I try to come to terms with what I've just heard. I can feel someone watching me, gauging my reaction, and I know it's Mackenzie because I've memorized the heat of her gaze just like I've memorized the taste of her mouth. But I don't glance her way. I can't. I'm too horrified by the scene unfolding in front of me to shift my attention for even a moment.

"I did my best," Cal starts, his voice thick.

My mother's gaze hardens, her dark eyes cold. "You and I both know your best isn't good enough."

She turns away from him, giving him her back for a moment as if collecting her thoughts. She leans against a tall oak, speaking to its branches as she says, "Don't worry, Cal. I'll keep some of your secrets, but I made a mistake fourteen years ago, and I plan on righting those wrongs. Not only that, but Storm loves football."

Storm . . . the boy . . . my brother.

"Just like his daddy," she says, spinning around to face him.

My eyes widen as her words sink in, and I stumble back on leaden legs while the aftershocks of them ripple through me.

Uncle Cal is Storm's father. My mother and Uncle Cal . . .

My stomach squeezes, and my knees threaten to buckle under the weight of this revelation. Seeking purchase on the side of the building next to me, I struggle to keep my balance. It's like a nightmare, only I can't wake up.

My mother and Uncle were having an affair, so he paid her to leave. And she agreed based on the condition that he look after me. But somehow, they must've gotten back together again because she got pregnant with another son—his son—in the interim.

I close my eyes and spin around, dizzy but unable to hear anymore, when a hand settles over my shoulder, followed by the voice I hear every night in my dreams.

"Atlas . . ." Mackenzie says, but I shrug her off, my desire to flee stronger than my need for comfort.

I blink my eyes open and I stumble into Graham. His face is pale, his eyes wide, but I don't have time to contemplate what this means for him. How this might affect him. I'm too busy thinking about how it was all a lie. Uncle Cal never gave a shit about me. All of the help he's given me, the advice, the roof over my head, it was all for show. A debt he owed my mother for keeping their dirty little secret.

My hands shake as I rip the MVP medal from my neck. Stepping around Graham, I let it fall from my fingers to the ground with a thud.

CHAPTER 15

GRAHAM

MARIE—ATLAS'S MOTHER—FACES MY FATHER, her words resonating in the air between them long after they're spoken, hitting the three of us like a death knell.

I'm frozen, my feet rooted to the ground beneath me as I replay their conversation over and over in my mind until it makes sense.

But I'm not sure it ever will.

Because my father is a cheating son of a bitch. And I have a brother.

My stomach pitches, and for a moment, I fear I might be sick when Atlas pushes past us, looking both crestfallen and angrier than I've ever seen him. The medal I wanted so badly is ripped from his chest and thrown at my feet as he storms off like a walking thundercloud.

My heart thumps in my chest as Mackenzie turns to me, mouth agape, clearly every bit as stunned as I am.

As if we haven't already seen and heard enough, Marie continues before I even have time to react. "I'm done running, Cal. It's time to make things right for both of my sons, and Storm deserves to know who his father is. He deserves to know his brothers. I thought . . ." She trails off, her voice tight with emotion. "I thought you'd be proud he's following after your footsteps, and he deserves every opportunity you can afford him. Which includes playing football at a great school like Riverside."

He deserves to know his brothers . . .

I bring my hands up to my hair where I pull at the roots, releasing a bitter bubble of laughter. This can't be happening.

"What in the actual fuck?" I yell.

My father whips his head in our direction, where Mackenzie and I are no longer hiding from view, and the anger in his expression morphs as the color drains from his face. Beside him, Marie—his ex-lover, Atlas's mom, gold digger, whoever the hell she is—won't meet my eyes. I have to give Atlas credit, he may be a prick, but he's no coward. I wonder where he gets it from.

I watch as she smooths a hand down her blouse and clears her throat. "I better get going," she says before she makes her exit, gracefully leaving the canopy of trees to head back toward the fairground.

My jaw hardens as I stare at my father. I've never hated him as much as I do in this moment.

He takes a tentative step toward me, as if he's unsure, wobbly on his feet like a newborn fawn. I'm not sure I recall a time I've ever seen him so shaken, but I feel zero sympathy where he's concerned. I give zero fucks if he's ashamed. He should be.

"Graham, I—"

"Save it." My voice is lethal as a poison dart as my gaze bores into him, cutting him like a knife.

I take two steps back, ready to retreat, both satisfied and furious when he opens his mouth but nothing comes out.

He's speechless, as he should be.

He clasps his hands in front of himself as if in prayer. "I can explain. Please . . ."

It's the first time my father's ever pleaded with me for anything.

But I'm not down for bargaining.

Shaking my head, I take one last look at him before I spit on the ground by his feet. "I don't want to hear one thing that comes out of your mouth." I tell him.

MACKENZIE

My heart flutters in panic as I try to catch Graham's arm as he leaves, but my hand grasps nothing but air as he skirts past me, making his exit. Unsure of what to do with myself, I stand there, cheeks red, my hands opening and closing uselessly at my side.

My mind reels with everything I just witnessed and what it means for both Graham and Atlas. I hate the fact they both left the way they did. But if I can't make heads or tails of it, how can I expect either of them to stand by and process how they're feeling about it?

I swallow, shifting my gaze back to Cal where his forehead creases in defeat and his eyes darken with the weight of his sins. He looks twice his age in this moment, with his shoulders slumping and his mouth pressing into a thin line. And though I don't particularly care for him, mostly on account of the way he treats Graham, for some reason, I can't seem to move my feet. I can't leave him.

"You have to understand," he reasons, shoving his hands into his pockets as he takes a step closer, "before Graham and Atlas were even conceived, Marie and I had a kind of a flirtation, but we never acted on it because of Lee. I knew they were together, so I tried to move on, but it got harder and harder. We had a fling the night before I married Sheila. After, I remained faithful, but it was hard on Marie, seeing me with her after being together. Then, one night we had a close call. Lee was using and Marie turned to me for support. She'd been drinking more and more, and needed to get away. If she stayed, she was either going to get caught up in his world or we were going to slip up."

"You don't have to explain . . ." I raise a hand, taking a step back, because I don't want to hear this. It's none of my business, and I have enough of my own baggage to carry around without stowing his, too.

"No, I do. I need you to understand none of this was done in malice. It . . ." He swallows, then continues. "It's Marie's place to explain her reasons because it's not all like she made it seem. I didn't just pay her."

"But you went back to her, right?" I asked, uninterested in his excuses. "You got her pregnant years later."

"About eight years ago, Sheila and I hit a rough spot, and my brother was at an all-time low. I knew his drug use had escalated so I sought Marie out. I went to her with the intention of telling her how bad it had gotten. But in a moment of weakness, we spent one night together."

The contents of my stomach curdle. I don't want to hear this.

"By the time she told me she was pregnant, Sheila and I had fixed our issues and our relationship was solid. My career was still going strong, and I knew the scandal of fathering a child to my brother's girl would ruin not only my marriage but my remaining time in the NFL. So, I paid her to stay away. I chose Sheila and Graham over her and the baby, and I don't regret it. My relationship with my son is rocky as it is. Had he known . . . Well, we might not have a relationship at all."

"You also chose Graham and your wife over Atlas, too. Not just the new baby. He needed you," I say, my voice thick. "He needed someone to intervene and help him. Instead, you let all these years go by, knowing why she left and you never told him?"

"Yes, but I couldn't—"

"You do realize he thinks no one wanted him, right? He thinks he's unworthy." I point at his chest, angry for both Atlas and Graham. "And your silence confirms this belief. You let him live out of a freaking car with his junkie father!" I blink as tears fill my eyes and clog my throat. Tears for the boy who's never had a single person in his life put him first. He may have hurt me and betrayed my trust, but no one deserves what he's been through.

"What good would that have done anyone?" he shouts.

Is he freaking kidding me?

I bark out a laugh, dumbfounded he could be so stupid. "You could've told her how bad things had become for him. How strung out Lee was all the time. He needed help. He was just a kid, for crying out loud. He needed a parent, someone to put him first."

Cal's throat bobs. "I might have known Lee was using, but I thought he was still working. I hadn't realized how bad he'd gotten. By the time I realized it, I'd already cut ties and needed to keep it that way. I had my own family to worry about"—he pounds his chest with his fist—"my own mess to clean up, and I couldn't risk anyone finding out about the baby. I changed my number. We moved and built this house. We started over again."

Unbelievable.

I shake my head while the last remaining shred of respect I had for Cal Scott vanishes. "So, you built a life raft for yourself while leaving Atlas to drown."

"It's not like that!" he snaps, spittle flying from his mouth. "I made mistakes, sure, but I did what I thought was best at the time to rectify them. And if anyone can understand loving two people at once, it's *you*," he says with a sneer.

I flinch, his words a sharp blow as my mouth parts. I drag a shaky breath into my lungs before I manage to speak. "Don't you dare compare me to you."

Cal purses his lips, his expression so haughty I want to punch him in the face. "You're right. I'm sorry. Look"—he holds his hands out—"I don't know what all went on between the three of you. But I'm worried about Graham as it is, and with Atlas's mother back in town badgering him . . ." He draws closer, until he comes to a stop directly in front of me, and it takes everything inside me to stand my ground and not shrink at his proximity. "No matter what you or anybody thinks of me, I care about them both. I'm worried about the direction Graham is headed. I'm worried Atlas might spiral now that his mother is back. If you care about them at all . . ."

"Of course, I care!" I bark out.

I'm not the one that hurt them, I almost say, before I realize it's not entirely true. I did hurt Graham. And though I had no part in what happened between me and Atlas, I know he's hurting just the same.

"Good." He nods. "Then talk to them for me."

I scoff, eyes wide as I search his face. *The audacity of this man!* "And why would I do that?"

He runs a shaky hand through his hair, his gaze on the grass beneath his feet. "I don't know what this is going to do to my marriage." He pauses and stares off into the distance as if he's mulling over the collateral damage his past is about to cause. "My family as I know it might be ruined. My NFL career is already over, but I don't know what this will do to my endorsement deals and ongoing sponsorships. Regardless, Marie's return will change all of our lives for better or worse. Mostly worse," he mumbles.

His rambling reminds me of my father. Maybe my mother was the cheater, but he's never taken responsibility for his actions or how he played a part in pushing her away, and then he lied about everything. Not once did he stop to think about how his actions might hurt everyone else. Instead, he just covered everything up. And Cal has zero intention of taking responsibility for this, too. It's Marie's fault for returning. For outing him and telling him the truth.

I'm so sick and tired of liars, I can't see straight.

I clench my teeth, every bit as furious with the man in front of me as my own parents—my mother for her affair and my father for his selfish dishonesty. The only difference here is that Cal hurt a hell of a lot more people than just his son. The ripple effect of his actions will continue to spread for years to come.

And I'll be damned if I do his bidding.

He huffs out a breath and places his hands on his hips and turns to me, seemingly unfazed by the murderous look I'm throwing his way. "You'll do this for me. I know you will," he says confidently.

"And how can you be so sure?" I ask between gritted teeth.

"Because they're hurting. And if there's one person who can make them understand, it's you."

CHAPTER 16

ATLAS

I DRIVE THROUGH RIVERSIDE with no destination in mind, my head a mess. I have no idea where to go. All I know is I sure as hell don't want to go back to my uncle's house, and I can't run to Mackenzie, so after a while I wind up at the only place I have left.

My feet crunch on the gravel driveway as I make my way onto the sagging porch of the double-wide I shared with my father when we first moved to town. Normally, I avoid it here. There are too many depressing memories: My father passed out on the couch while I play the best games of my life. His arrest. The sight of his car parked in the driveway. All of these are reason enough to stay away.

But today is different. Today, I want to remember.

I let myself inside. It's not locked—there's nothing worth stealing—and upon entering, my first thought is how different it looks than when I left it. The upturned trash can, rotting food, and dirty dishes have been replaced with sparkling counters, an empty sink, and mopped floors. It's no secret Cal has been paying our rent since the day we arrived, and it isn't hard to deduce he must've sent his housekeepers to clean up.

I should owe him a debt of gratitude, but I don't.

Everything good Uncle Cal ever did for me was all a lie.

All the times he helped me, coached me, praised me, and treated me like his own son were out of obligation, some debt he owed my mother. Not because he cared. Not because he actually wanted to see me succeed.

He knocked her up, then made damn sure she stayed away.

I shake my head awash with anger.

I should've known.

Guys like him have a history of throwing their money and social status around to get what they want. Which usually means guys like me lose.

I wander through each room like a ghost, banging around in the kitchen, checking the cupboards to see the clean dishes neatly stacked in their proper place. My old toothbrush sits in the glass cup on the bathroom sink, and my bedroom looks exactly as I left it—bed made, an old pair of sneakers sitting in the corner, a tattered copy of a Stephen King novel on the nightstand.

I amble back out into the living room where I sink down into the couch and place my head in my hands. Next Friday I turn eighteen, and I'll finally be old enough to legally take care of myself.

I'll move out, I think. Return here and get out from under Uncle Cal's thumb.

No. Fuck that.

I'll move out before it's official. With everything Cal has done and all the shit he's pulled, he won't dare to try and stop me. If he does, I'll make for damned sure I blow this whole thing up. Throw everything in his face. Go to the media. Sell the story. He may no longer be in the NFL, but his career is fresh enough and his endorsements are ongoing, so people would want to hear what I have to say. And though I hate that he's still paying for the place, I'll let him. There's not enough money in the world to atone for what he's done, but I have little recourse. If I spend my savings on rent and food, I won't have any left for expenses at college. Even with a full ride at a Single A school, I'll need cash for books, supplies, a meal plan, maybe even housing, depending on what kind of scholarship I get. Until I sign in February, I won't know how much cash I have to spare.

I shift my body and kick my legs up on the couch, lying back and settling in because I have no intention of going back to my uncle's house. Ever.

My thoughts drift to Storm. I found out he existed before Graham, but I never would've guessed Cal fathered him. Which means Graham and I are bound by yet another thing. A brother. Hell, it practically makes us siblings ourselves. How fucked up is that? It's like our lives are turning into some kind of deranged episode of *Days of our Lives*. At any moment, Mackenzie's mother will come back from the fucking dead and say she somehow escaped the crash.

The thought sobers me. It's a shitty thing to think and is a joke in poor taste, but this whole situation is so messed up, I can't help but laugh about it because anything seems feasible at this point.

My head begins to throb as the exhaustion of the last month presses down on me with the weight of a thousand tons. I close my eyes, willing away the oncoming headache when the crunching of tires on gravel draws my attention.

My eyes snap open once more, my head automatically swinging toward the window. My whole body stiffens, my muscles tense. I'm not sure who I want to see less at the moment, Cal, Graham, or my mother. My guess is whoever's coming to visit is one of them.

Lucky me.

When I don't recognize the car coming to a stop at the end of the driveway, I assume it's my mother, and I tense, ready for a fight.

But then the door pushes open and it's not her gracing my doorstep; it's Mackenzie.

My heart kicks, coming to life inside my chest, as I get to my feet and head toward the door and open it, bracing one arm above the frame while I watch her. Pink lips curved into a frown. Long, lean legs clad in dark denim, a change from the cheer uniform she wore earlier. Her dark hair hanging like a silk curtain around her face.

"Hey," she says when her eyes meet mine and she starts up the stairs.

The nerves inside my body flicker to life as I watch her approach. "Hey."

"Can I come in?" Her pale blue eyes blink up at me, reaching out and gripping onto my soul with two hands.

"Sure." *As if she even needs to ask.*

I take a small step back and wave her in, but I don't give her much space. Instead, I continue leaning with one arm on the door frame, while she skirts past. Her body brushes mine as the scent of apple blossom clings to the air in her wake, a scent I crave. One I dream about.

I fight the urge to close my eyes and breathe her in as she glances around her, taking in her surroundings. I know what she's thinking; it looks a lot different than the last time she was here. I don't say anything, though. Instead, I wait as she takes a seat in the chair beside the couch before I sit down across from her.

It's obvious why she's here. To talk about the shit show the three of us witnessed. But what's not clear to me is why she isn't with Graham. Why me?

"What are you doing here?" I ask, my voice soft.

"Cal wanted me to talk to you." I crack my knuckles, waiting for the punchline while my pulse begins to race. Just when I'm about to jump to my feet and show her the door, she rushes to add, "But I don't give a shit what he wants. I'm not here for him."

"Then who are you here for?"

"Who do you think?" she murmurs as her eyes search my face.

My chest tightens, making it hard to breathe. Suddenly, there are a million things I want to say. But I keep my mouth closed, unable to get the words out through the lump in the back of my throat.

"Besides, I had to check on you," she says. "We can't have Riverside's star receiver beating up any more stone fountains now, can we?"

A startled laugh bubbles from my chest. "Only you."

"What?"

"Only you can make me laugh right now."

"Well, those hands are pretty talented," she says, eyeing them with a smirk, and I know she's talking about football, but I can't help but think of all the other things my hands are good at. All the other things I'd like to show her.

My gaze shifts from her mouth, down her body, and back. By the time I reach her face again, her cheeks are bright red, burning up from the cutest fucking blush I've ever seen.

A devilish smile curls the corners of my lips in victory, because no one else can make her feel like I do. No one else can make her skin flush with a simple glance.

She clears her throat and glances away from me, her breath heavy in her chest. "I came to see if you're okay."

And just like that, the moment is fucked.

I exhale, then lean back into the couch as I contemplate my answer.

Am I okay? *Fuck, no. But I'm sort of used to being dealt a crap hand, and after this, nothing will surprise me anymore.*

"Yes. No," I answer with a shake of my head. "I don't know. If I'm being honest, I don't think I've been okay for a long time."

She turns her eyes back to mine, and I drink in all that endless blue.

"It hurts," I say, surprised at my brutal honesty. Then again, Doll has always been able to make me crack. "To know that Cal's part of the reason she left. That he fucking paid her to leave, and he never so much as said a word to me about it. This whole time, he's acted like he cares. He's taken me in. Treated me like a son. Helped me. Coached me. And I fell for all of it."

Hell, I was so damn proud today when he presented me with that stupid award. I felt like he chose me in that moment. Someone saw me and said, "you're good enough."

I swallow and stare down at my hands. "Turns out, it was all for nothing. Everything he did was out of guilt. A debt he owed to my mother for screwing me over when I was just a kid. I mean, what the hell am I supposed to do with that?" My jaw tightens as I relive their conversation, and the heat of anger flares to life inside my chest like a stick of dynamite. "If they had never been unfaithful and if she hadn't gotten pregnant years later, maybe she would've stayed. Maybe my whole life would be different."

"I know . . . It's unfathomable." Mackenzie sighs as she says, "But maybe you should hear her out?"

My eyes widen, my nostrils flaring with the thought of listening to anything that woman has to say. "You can't be serious?"

"Maybe there's more to it. I don't know." She shakes her head. "But what have you got to lose?"

"My fucking pride, for one," I snap, then rake a hand through my hair as I close my eyes, trying to maintain my composure.

"What about your brother?"

"Half brother." My lids flutter open as I picture the young boy with doe eyes and hair the color of an oil slick.

"He's innocent in all this, Atlas." She leans forward, her expression earnest. "Look, all I'm saying is he didn't do anything to deserve this mess any more than you did. And, yeah, he's had your mother this whole time, but he also knows what it's like to go without a father. Cal didn't want him. Instead of owning up to his mistakes and accepting him, he paid to have him sent away. If anyone knows what that kind of abandonment feels like, it's you."

I release a ragged breath, hating that she's right. I don't want to think about him. Because I can't even begin to imagine a world in which anything good could come of all of this.

"What are you suggesting?" I ask, swallowing over the lump in my throat.

"Talk to him. Get to know him. Consider at least giving *him* a chance, even if it means facing your mother first. Not for her, but for him. For you."

For me?

I hang my head as an emotion I don't recognize claws inside my chest like a caged animal.

She pushes to her feet and for a moment, I'm petrified she's leaving. Until she closes the gap between us and stops just in front of me.

I suck in a breath when she places a hand on my shoulder, her touch burning through the fabric of my shirt. I don't so much as breathe for fear she'll withdraw. I'm scared to death of ruining the moment and never getting it back again.

"You've been on your own for so long," she says, her voice low. "Who doesn't want a family?"

"I'm used to being on my own," I croak, my voice thick.

"But what if you don't have to be?"

I tip my head, my gaze colliding with hers. The only time in my life where I haven't felt completely and utterly alone was when we were together. All I want is that feeling back again.

I want her back.

"I don't need a brother," I say, my voice pained. *I need you,* I want to scream.

"But what if he does?"

I press my lips together when her hand slides to the side of my face. No one was there for me when I needed them. Why should I care about someone I never even knew existed in the first place?

Then again, if I ignore him, doesn't that make me just as bad as Cal?

"Wouldn't it be nice if something good came out of all of this?" she murmurs, as if sensing I'm about to crack.

Something good out of everything awful.

It seems impossible.

But I'd do just about anything Mackenzie asks of me. "I'll think about it."

"Good." She swallows, then drops her hand away. "That's good," she says again as she begins to turn and head for the door.

I shoot to my feet. I'll be damned if she leaves before I say my piece. "You said I should at least hear my mother out," I blurt.

She glances over her shoulder and tilts her head, wariness creeping into her eyes. "I did . . ."

I close the distance between us, getting in her face as I say, "Then, if I'm to hear my mother out after everything she did, shouldn't you at least hear me out?"

The darks of her eyes widen. "Atlas, I—"

"Please," I say, my expression earnest. "Just give me five minutes."

I can see the hesitation in her eyes. "*Okay,*" she drawls. "Then talk."

"I fucked up," I say, my tone fierce. "I know I did. When I found out the truth, I had every intention of telling you. All I was trying to do was figure out *how.* That day you tried to relearn how to drive—"

"In the car that killed my mother?" she bites out. "The one you knew struck us and left her for dead?"

I swallow. "I tried to get around driving the car, but you were so insistent, and I hadn't figured out a way to tell you yet without destroying us."

"I still had a right to know the truth. Do you know how sick and twisted it is that you had me try and get over my fear of driving in the car that killed her?"

"I know." I steeple my hands out in front of me, praying she won't leave before I can finish. "It's inexcusable, and I almost told you so many times."

"But you didn't," she snaps, her ice blue eyes flaring to life with anger.

"I didn't," I agree. "And then you found out about your father's lies, and you were so upset. I tried to tell you again, but when you said you'd never forgive him for hiding the truth, I was so damn petrified you wouldn't forgive me either. Even if I hadn't hidden it from you, how do you get over that? How does someone just forget the fact that their boyfriend's father almost killed them and sent their mother to an early grave. I could barely wrap my head around it myself."

"That was for me to decide!" She stabs a finger in her chest. "For me to figure out. But you didn't even give me a choice." Her eyes fill with tears, and I want to drown in them. I deserve no less than a watery death to her grief. "And then we . . ." Her voice cracks, and she brings a hand to her trembling mouth before she tries again. "We slept together with you *knowing* the truth. Knowing how upset I was about my father's lies."

She starts to turn away, her hand on the door, but I stop her. I wrap my hand around her forearm and she stills. My heart pounds in my chest as I step closer, until her back is pressed against me. Until I'm dizzy with the scent of her skin. "If I could do it all over again," I whisper into her hair, "I would. In a heartbeat. I would tell you the second I found out. Let the cards fall where they may and take my chances. But I can't."

She slowly turns in my arms, her chest rising with her breath.

I reach out and grasp a lock of her hair, feeling the silky strands between my fingers. "I still love you. I think maybe I've loved you from the moment I laid eyes on you in that field. It's why I was such a prick. Because I was so damned mad anyone could make me feel that way."

Her gaze drops to my mouth, and my stomach clenches. I want so badly to claim her lips with mine, but I can't, not until I know she wants it. Not until the hate in her heart turns to something else.

"What do you want from me?" she whispers.

"Your forgiveness."

She glances away from me, her gaze staring off into the distance, and just when I think she's going to push away from me and tell me to go to hell, she says, "I forgive you, Atlas. But that doesn't mean I've forgotten."

"Tell me what you want," I say, my tone fierce. "Tell me what I can do to make it up to you."

"All right." Her gaze snaps to mine, a light in her eyes. "Maybe there is something."

"Anything."

"Take me to see your father."

I frown, my brow creasing as my pulse races. It feels like a trap. "My father . . . Why?"

Anger darkens her features, mistaking my confusion for reluctance. "I want to confront him, tell him I know. I want to see the look on his face when I do. You say he's changed?"

The nerves at the base of my spine twist. "I mean, I haven't seen him, and I don't know how much one man can change in a couple of months, but . . . yeah."

Her jaw clenches, her blue gaze turning hard as steel. "Good. Because I want to see the moment that the guilt and grief tear into him."

I blink down at her, surprised by her admission.

"And if they don't?" I ask, because as much as I want to believe he's different, he's still the same man who bought himself a bottle of Jack for Christmas one year while neglecting to leave anything under the tree for me.

"Then maybe I'll have some answers."

CHAPTER 17

GRAHAM

I SLIDE THE KEYS of my car into the ignition and rev the engine, then peel out of the parking lot. I need to get as far away from here as possible, and I'm not gonna lie, part of me was relieved when Mackenzie texted me and offered to find a ride home because I'm not in shape to be around actual people at the moment—especially one that broke my heart. Not when my world feels like it's falling to fucking pieces.

My whole life is a lie.

Or at least that's what it feels like.

When Mackenzie told me about her mother's affair and her parent's pending divorce, I was sympathetic. I tried to understand but couldn't quite grasp the pain she was going through, because no matter how hard you try to put yourself in someone else's shoes, at the end of the day, it's fucking impossible to know how it feels until it happens to you.

My father cheated. With Atlas's mother, of all people. Then he fathered a child and paid them to stay away. It's so unconscionable, my head spins.

I always knew my father was a bastard, but this . . . this is a whole new level of fucked up, even for him, and now I'm questioning everything. He and my mother always seemed so in love. But I guess it was all a lie, at least where he's concerned.

My knuckles clench the steering wheel tighter, until the skin whitens and my bones ache. Turns out my father didn't choose Atlas over me. He's not the son he wished he had but a bargaining tool to get what he wanted—his mistress's silence. It should make me feel better, but it doesn't.

I drive the streets aimlessly, not knowing where to go or what to do with my anger. I'm nearly vibrating with it, and if I don't find a release soon, I might implode. It's not yet evening, and I don't want to go home, but the guys are all still back at Fall Fest, which leaves me little in way of choices.

I pull into the parking lot of a nearby convenience store and park, then pick up my phone and scroll through my contacts, pausing on Peters's name, then give him a call. He's the one person I can always count on for a good time. The one person who hates Atlas as much as I do, ever since the latter replaced him on the team.

When he answers on the first ring, I relax back in my seat.

"What's up, bro? I was wondering if you've got a party or anything on your radar tonight?"

"Dude, it's early yet and everybody in this small-ass town is at that stupid festival. I ain't got shit. Where are you, anyway?"

I pinch the bridge of my nose with my fingers. That's not what I was hoping to hear. "Nowhere. I just need something to take my mind off some stuff."

"You want some grass?"

"Hell, no," I snap. "You know I don't touch drugs."

Peters snorts. "Okay, but you'll drink a fifth of fucking whiskey. Got it."

"Whatever, man." I stare out the driver's side window as a thought hits me. "Hey, what about your buddy? Does he have any games going?"

I think about my win a few weeks back, and I feel lighter. Though Darrell mentioned my return, he hasn't been in touch.

"Crenshaw?" Peters asks like he's not sure what I'm talking about.

"Yeah."

He snickers. "Crenshaw always has something going on at the tables."

"You wanna hit a game?" I ask him.

"I heard you were hanging with the quarterback princess. She gonna let you off that leash?"

Mackenzie. I roll my eyes and grit my teeth. "Nah. I'm over that."

"Are you now?"

"Fuck you, dude," I snap, sick of his shit. "You wanna go or not?"

He laughs. "Chill. I'm just messing with you. I can't go any-where tonight. My parents are home and they've been watching me like a hawk all day. I'm one grade away from failing Phi-losophy, so I have to finish this damn paper. I can give you his number if you want? Hook you up?"

How the hell do you flunk Philosophy?

I sigh, but maybe it's better I'm not with Peters. He sucked ass at poker the last time we played and kept giving me shit when I went in on the higher bets. "Yeah, fine. That sounds good," I say. "Just shoot me over his number."

I hang up and wait for his text. When my phone pings, I add Crenshaw to my contacts and send him a text.

Graham: Hey, man. This is Graham, the dude that was with Peters the other night? I was just wondering if you had a game with an open spot tonight?

Crenshaw: For you?

"Yeah, dumbass," I mutter to myself.

Graham: For me.

Crenshaw: We have a game at seven, but maybe you should sit this one out.

Like hell . . .

Graham: What? Why? Afraid I'll clean you out?

A grin thins my lips as I think about how I raked the coals with everyone last time. Of course, he doesn't want me to go. Probably thinks I'll show everyone up again.

Crenshaw: *This game is for high rollers only.*

I purse my lips, debating before I type.

Graham: *How high?*

Crenshaw: *Opening bets start at three hundred.*

My eyes widen and I whistle.

Shit, that's a lot of money. The kitty probably goes from anywhere between a thousand bucks to five grand.

I purse my lips, and stare out into the empty parking lot, debating on whether I'm up for it. Thanks to my father, I have enough to play, but a few thousand in my checking account won't get me far. Still, if I clean up like I did the other night, I won't even need all of it.

Hell, I stand to make a hell of a lot more than my current account balance if I perform like I did in our little poker game where opening wagers started at twenty bucks.

Smiling, I can already feel the surge of adrenaline in my blood as I reply.

Graham: *All right. I'm in.*

It's getting late by the time I make my way to the back of Jace's house, let myself inside, then head to the game room. His parents are spending a couple of weeks in Florida before winter creeps in, so he has the place to himself, which makes me a jealous prick. What I wouldn't give to have my father leave for a couple of weeks right now. Maybe even an eternity.

Shit. I don't mean that.

Or do I?

Truth is, I don't even know how to feel anymore.

The moment I enter the game room and spot Jace and Teagan at the pool table stacking balls, I breathe a sigh of relief.

Jace lifts his head and straightens, leaning on his pool stick. "Well, you sure do know how to make an exit." When I flip him the middle finger, he laughs and moves closer, slapping me on the arm. "Glad you called to hang out, seeing as how we didn't your ugly mug again after you left. I mean, even if you are a sore loser."

I shake my head. "You're never gonna let me live this down, are you?"

"Nope," Teagan says from behind him, the hint of a grin making his dimples pop.

"Wanna play?" Jace holds out his stick, and I take it.

Leaning over the table, I break. The colorful balls scatter, and a solid orange hits the right corner pocket, then bounces off.

"Where've you been?" Teagan asks, taking his shot. "We got back here after the festival at nine and couldn't reach you. Looked all over for you after the awards, too. Tried calling, and nothing."

"Sorry. I, uh—" I exhale and scratch the top of my head, unsure of how to tell them what happened today when I think, fuck it. "I found out I have a brother I never knew about," I blurt out.

"*Shiiiit.*" Jace's eyes widen.

"Whoa. You serious, bro?" Teagan's forehead knots as I nod, and he comes around the table to sit on the edge of it. "I guess I can understand why you might need some headspace."

"Yeah, you could say that." I huff out a laugh and hold up the bottle of whiskey in my hands. Seeing as how poker didn't help, I need something else.

I think about the games tonight and how much money I owe. I never should've gone to The Play House with my mind so fucked.

"Shit. I guess so. I hope you don't mind, but when you called and said you wanted to hang, I invited some of the others. I had no idea . . ." Jace trails off.

"No. It's all good. Hanging out with everyone will be a welcome distraction."

As long as Atlas doesn't come.

But then Atlas never comes to these things.

Jace nods, his expression sober as he says, "Tell us what happened."

Jace can be the biggest jackass sometimes, but when it comes down to it, he's a pretty good friend. He's there when it counts and never lets you take yourself too seriously.

So, I fill them in on my day, starting with how Mackenzie and I spent the afternoon together. Then I tell them that we saw my father sneaking around with Marie—Atlas's mother—and I recount the conversation we overheard. How he went to see her seven years after she left. How she got pregnant and tried to come back, but he paid her to stay away. The only part I leave out is where I've been the last couple of hours. How I went to Crenshaw's, gambled, and lost.

I take a pull on the whiskey bottle and hiss at the thought. Because, damn, I'm an idiot.

I'd been so eager when I arrived at his place that I didn't take the time to assess my opponents at the table. Of course, they were going to be more skilled poker players—the stakes were higher. Instead, I jumped right in, feeling a surge of victory when I won the first two rounds. But then it went downhill from there, and I was like a domino unable to stop all the pieces from falling as I played and lost hand after hand, never regaining my momentum.

I take another sip of whiskey, hoping to numb the sting of loss.

It's not that big of a deal, I tell myself. I already gave Crenshaw a thousand bucks from my checking. All I have to do is find a way to get the extra thousand from my college savings. No biggie. Crenshaw was generous enough to give me two weeks to settle my balance. Next time I'll have a clear head, and when I win it back, my father will never know the difference.

"Damn, dude. That's a lot," Teagan says, and for a moment, I forget he's talking about my father's affair.

"Yeah," I mumble as he heads to the mini fridge at the wet bar and grabs a beer. "So, now you see why I called. I need to de-stress after this nightmare."

"Fair enough," Jace says as Teagan tosses him a beer and he cracks it open. "To letting loose and letting go." He holds it up.

I raise my whiskey bottle out in front of me. "To letting loose." We clink bottles, then I tip mine back while Jace does the same before he lowers his beer and belches.

"Classy, bro."

"You know it." Jace grins, then motions to me. "So, what are you gonna do about it?"

"What do you mean what am I gonna do about it?"

"Like"—Jace waves his beer bottle around—"are you going to tell your mom?"

I clench the bottle in my hands, my knuckles turning white. With all the other shit running through my mind and then my loss at poker, I hadn't really thought about it.

"Nah. I don't think so," I say after a moment.

"Yeah. Probably best not to get involved."

I shrug. "I just figure my mother has to know what kind of an asshole she's married to, yet she's stayed with him this long. Besides, with Atlas's mom back in town, he'll probably hang himself. It's only a matter of time before she finds out on her own anyway."

Then who knows what will happen. Maybe she'll leave him.

The thought doesn't bother me nearly as much as it should.

"Man, that's rough," Teagan says. "I can't believe Atlas's mother is back. How's he handling all this shit?"

I shoot him a look that says I don't know and I don't care.

"I mean, it's gotta be rough, right?" Jace adds, and I roll my eyes. Not because I disagree—I'm sure it's fucking with his head—but because I don't want to think about Atlas and I'm annoyed they care as much as they do.

"What about the kid? Have you ever met him?" Teagan asks.

"Nope. Don't plan on it either."

"Really, man?" Jace eyes me, bottle halfway to his mouth.

"Why would I want to? I've got enough shit on my plate. The last thing I need is to further complicate my life. It's already gone to shit since Atlas showed up." I set my whiskey bottle down and pick my pool stick back up before I move toward the table, needing something to do with my hands.

"Speaking of Atlas," Jace says, sharing a look with Teagan, "you share a brother. How weird is that?"

"It's fucked up," Teagan chimes in.

"Took the words right out of my mouth," I say as I smack the cue ball and miss.

"What's fucked up?" Knox asks from behind.

I turn to see Knox and about half a dozen others piling into the room. With a smile, I shoot Jace and Teagan a look that tells them the conversation is over. "Nothing. Just my father, as usual."

"Ah, Cal Scott strikes again?" He offers me a handshake and a fist bump. My father's reputation for giving me a hard time is well known to the guys. "Is this about the MVP award? Or did the old bastard do something else now?"

"Just the same old, same old." I shrug, not wanting to get into it with the rest of the team. Nor do I want to dwell on the MVP award. Hell, it feels like old news at this point. And though I'm tight with all my boys, Teagan and Jace are different. They're my brothers, the ones I can trust with anything.

More than an hour later, music blasts from the stereo system and I move on my feet, dancing with a girl I don't recognize. My hands grip her hips, and I pull her closer, whispering into her hair, "You're a cheerleader, right?"

Dark eyes shift, staring up at me. They're the wrong color. I prefer blue. Ice blue.

My thoughts drift to Mackenzie as the girl in my arms scowls. "It's me, Tiff."

I blink down at her and my vision doubles. "Who?"

"You jackass," she mutters, then storms off.

"Smooth," Jace says, staring after her. Then he turns back to me and reaches for the booze in my hands. "Maybe we should slow down a little, huh?"

I yank the bottle out of his grip, sloshing some of the golden liquid out of the rim. "Why don't *you* slow down?" I say, slurring my words before I tip my head back and laugh.

My phone dings and I fumble as I try to slide it out of my pocket.

"Everything okay?" Teagan asks, his brow pinched, as he sidles up next to Jace.

"Dude's drunk as shit," Jace mutters, but I'm barely paying attention. I'm too busy trying to clear my vision as I read the text from Mackenzie.

She's been trying to call me for hours now, along with my father, but I've sent every one of their calls to voice mail. Apparently, she thinks I'll answer her texts instead.

"Silly girl," I mumble to myself as I sway on my feet.

Kenzie: *I'm worried about you. Please come home so we can talk. I'm here waiting for you.*

My jaw hardens as I cram the phone back in my pocket, then take another sip from the bottle in my left.

"Come on, man," Knox comes around me and clamps a giant paw around the bottle. "Don't you think you've had enough?"

I turn to face him and find the three of them staring at me. "What happened to letting loose?" I ask them. When they say nothing in return, I poke Knox in the chest. "Just having fun, bro. Back off."

Knox rips the bottle out of my hand, and a string of garbled obscenities leave my mouth.

"Shit, man. We've got practice tomorrow," Teagan says, stepping between us. "We're a week away from States, dude. It's time to take it seriously, not fuck things up."

I roll my eyes.

Like I give a shit about States. Or fucking football.

But I don't say that, because I'm supposed to care. I'm the son of the infamous Cal Scott, former quarterback for the Pittsburgh Steelers. Golden boy of Riverside High. And I'm supposed to be pumped—chomping at the bit—to win a state title, even though I'm not.

Instead, I slap Teagan on his muscled back and say, "Relax, man. I'll be fine." But when I try to swipe the bottle back off Knox, he steps out of the way and I stumble, nearly crashing into the end table next to the couch.

I tip my head back in laughter, then right myself again. "You all are a bunch of sellouts anyway."

"What the hell are you talking about?" Jace snaps.

"You kiss Atlas's ass on the field."

Jace grins, but his eyes crease at the corners, and I wonder if he's actually super pissed. In my current state, I can't tell.

"I don't know about the others, but my problem is you're a sloppy drunk," he says.

"Yeah, well, you're a sloppy receiver." I snort at my own joke, but no one joins me.

"I'll tell you what my problem is, man." Teagan steps forward, and I roll my eyes. He's always the serious one. "You've abandoned the team ever since everything with Kenzie went to hell. And I know it hurt, but what about us? We're your brothers, and it's like you don't even care, but the rest of us have been waiting years for our shot."

Jace makes a slashing motion with his hand across his neck, and Teagan stops.

"No, it's okay," I say, getting in Teagan's face. "Please, let me hear what you really think."

He's not wrong. I don't care about winning anymore, but for some reason hearing the truth hurts coming from them.

"What we really think," Jace says, stepping in between us, "is that maybe we should take a walk outside. Get some fresh air, huh?" He motions toward the door, but I'm still too busy glaring at Teagan to pay him much attention.

My lips part, but before I can say anything, my phone rings for the millionth time. I glance down at it and contemplate answering when I see it's not Mackenzie, but my father instead.

I need another drink.

"Who the hell keeps calling you?" Teagan snaps. "I swear, if it's Mackenzie . . ."

"Don't even say her name." I point in his face. "She's too good for you. She's too good for all of us," I say, talking nonsense.

Hell, I'm not even sure why I'm defending her to them. They know what she did—how she ripped my heart out with her bare hands and tore it in two. Still, I can't help but feel protective of her. I can't help but want her even if I shouldn't.

Old habits die hard.

"Whatever, man." Teagan raises his hands in the air and takes a step back.

My phone pings, and I glance down at the screen as my fingers curl around it, expecting it to be a message from my father this time, but it's not. It's Mackenzie. And she's still waiting.

My stomach clenches as I lift my gaze and scan the room, my eyes wild. "I need a drink," I say, and I stumble away from them, heading to the mini fridge where I grab a beer, then make a beeline for the sliding glass doors. "Maybe I'll take that walk, after all," I mumble as I pop the top.

Jace calls after me, but I ignore him. Instead, I push my way through the doors and out into the rapidly cooling night air.

A chill wraps around me, but I'm too numb to care. The events of the day no longer bother me. They feel hazy, like a blurred photograph—grainy and out of focus—which is the way I want to keep it. I barely remember why I was angry. My father has always been a selfish prick, I'm used to it.

But Mackenzie . . . She's one problem I can't forget, no matter how hard I try.

I make my way further into the backyard and find a spot tucked away next to the garden shed where I sit, leaning my back against its solid exterior. Every bone in my body is weary and in need of rest. So, I close my eyes as I take another sip of my beer and do something I rarely allow myself anymore. I imagine what Kenz and I would be like together. How different things would be if she had chosen me.

Most dangerous of all, I remember our kiss. The way she moaned at my touch. The rapid beat of her heart against my chest, like a hummingbird's wings. How soft her lips were. How sweet her mouth was.

I groan from the pain the memories stir to life and blink my eyes open.

Nothing has changed. I can lie to myself and say I'm over her, but I still want her just as much as I always have. I probably always will, which is why loving her from afar is so painful.

I get to my feet and abandon the beer bottle, ambling my way through the backyard and toward the driveway at the side of Jace's house.

I need to go to her, push my wounded pride aside, and tell her how I feel. I've been too afraid to put my heart on the line since she chose Atlas over me. But the booze is working its magic and I don't give a damn if I'm pathetic or sound like an idiot. I just want a chance to get this off my chest. To either claim her or rid her from my heart once and for all.

Digging the keys out of my pocket, I click the unlock button on the key fob and reach for the handle at the same time two arms stretch around me and grapple for the keys.

"No fucking way, man." Jace's voice comes from behind.

"What the hell?" I spin around at the same time he manages to yank them free from my grip and toss them to Teagan behind him.

"I'm all for a good time, but you sure as shit aren't driving like this," he says, slightly out of breath from our tussle as his gaze makes quick work of me. "You're wasted."

"I'm fine," I say, staggering.

Okay, so maybe I had one too many. But I'm still fine to drive, just a little buzzed.

"Listen," he says, calmer now, "we sent everyone home for the night. Why don't you just sleep it off at my place."

"No way, man. Kenzie's waiting on me."

Teagan spins around and curses, pinching the bridge of his nose, before facing me again. "All the more reason to sleep it off here."

"Hell, no. Why is that a good reason?"

"Other than the fact that you can't even stay on your feet?" Teagan arches a brow.

Fucking idiot.

"Come on. I'll make it worth your while. We'll cuddle." Jace wiggles his brows like a jackass.

"Screw you," I spit.

"All right," he sighs dramatically, "I'll let you be big spoon."

I know he's just messing with me. It's Jace being Jace, but right now, he's pissing me the hell off. I run a hand over my face and stare at the ground as if considering it, before I lunge toward Teagan and snatch the keys from his loose grasp, then swing open my car door, hitting him in the shins.

His curse echoes behind me as I slam the door, nearly taking Jace's fingers off in the process, and hit the locks with a wave of triumph. They pound on my window like maniacs, yelling at me through the glass while I fumble with the keys. It takes me several tries, but I finally get it right and the engine roars to life. With a grin, I lift my hand and wiggle my fingers at them in a wave.

"Come on, Graham. We'll drive you home man," Teagan pleads. "Just get out of the car."

"How did we not see he was getting this fucking wasted sooner?" Jace says beside him.

Teagan shakes his head, his expression pinched, while I give them a salute and say, "Peace out."

I begin to back out of the driveway, but Teagan follows, running with the car. "We'll take you to see Kenz, okay? Just let us drive?"

I shake my head, knowing he's just saying that to try and get me to stay. They've been biased against Mackenzie ever since she broke my heart. If I get out now, they'll stop me from leaving. They won't let me outsmart them again.

I make a sharp turn onto the road, curbing it as I do, but I lose Teagan, which is what I wanted. The rubber of my tires squeals on the pavement as I hammer the gas and take off.

Mackenzie's waiting for me, and nothing will get between us.

Not my friends. Or my bruised pride.

And certainly not Atlas.

CHAPTER 18

MACKENZIE

ATLAS DROPPED ME OFF at the Scott residence hours ago and the more time that passes, the more worried I become. I thought he'd be here, but he's not. He isn't answering any of my texts or my calls, and I have no idea where he is. All I know is he's been gone for hours and is hurting and angry.

I pace by the pool, watching as fallen leaves scatter across its covered surface then swirl around my feet on the breeze. Above me, the sky is clear, the moon bright, and I hug my jacket tighter around me to ward off the cold when the sound of an engine draws my attention. I round the house at the same time Graham screeches to a stop and opens his car door. He stumbles as he steps out, bracing himself on the side of the car so he doesn't fall.

I frown, wondering if he's hurt as I call out, "Graham?"

His head whips in my direction and he smiles instantly. "Kenz . . ." he says, voice husky. He pushes off his car and rounds the front of it but he sways on his feet, struggling to stay upright. His hand comes down over the hood of his car and he straightens.

I step closer and my brow pinches as I take him in. "Are you drunk?" I ask, my voice an octave higher than I intend. But when he comes to a stop in front of me, I can smell the sour scent of alcohol on his breath and my stomach sinks.

"I might have had a couple with the boys," he mumbles.

I wrinkle my nose and take a step back, disgusted. "They let you drive like this?"

"Well, not exactly." Graham laughs, his eyes at half-mast.

"What the hell is so funny?"

"Nothing. It's just . . . I kind of tricked them," he slurs. "But I had to get to you." His expression sobers as he reaches out to tuck a lock of hair behind my ear, his green eyes as dark as the forest. "My Mackenzie," he says, his tone soft.

My heart thumps, warring with the anger swirling inside me. "What the heck, Graham?" I shove at his chest with barely enough force to swat a fly, but he stumbles back. "I've been waiting here for hours worrying about you while you're off getting shitfaced? And then you freaking drove like this?" My spine stiffens like a hot rod. "Are you kidding me right now?"

"What's the big deal?" He shrugs.

"The big deal is that a drunk driver killed my mother, remember? It's the reason I laid in the hospital for weeks. Couldn't get out of bed for months. Or have you forgotten?" I snap.

The color drains from his face, and he reaches for my arm. "Mackenzie, I—"

"No." I shrug him off, yanking my arm away. "I can't believe you would be so careless, so reckless."

"I'm here now, though, and no one got hurt. Can we just forget it and focus on us?" He stumbles forward and grabs my forearms in his hands, trying to meet my gaze, but I refuse to look at him. "Mackenzie, I came for you. Do you even know how much I still care? How in love with you I am?"

"Graham, don't." I bite my lip as I try to move out of his grip, but his hands tighten like a vice. "You're drunk. You don't even know what you're saying right now."

"I know I haven't gotten over you. I know I never will."

"Stop." I lift my head, pleading with my eyes for him to stop. "A lot has happened today. You're emotional and understandably upset, which is why I came here. But, Graham, you can get through this. I know what it feels like—"

"Aren't you fucking listening?" he shouts.

I flinch, and he drops my arms then takes a step back, raking a hand through his hair. "I'm trying to tell you how I feel and you wanna talk about my father?"

"Graham . . ."

"No." He raises a hand. "I get it. You're still hung up on *him*, aren't you? Even though he broke your heart."

"This isn't about Atlas."

Graham laughs bitterly. "This is all about Atlas. It has been since the moment he came to town. You're just too damn blind to see he's the problem here."

"Who *are* you?" I narrow my eyes as I stare at him. "I don't even recognize you anymore."

He stiffens, turning to stone as I take a step back.

"One minute you're snapping at me and telling me how much I hurt you. The next, you're acting like the old Graham, like my best friend. And now you're pledging your undying love for me again, but when I don't say exactly what you want to hear, you're screaming and cursing at me. Then you're driving drunk," I say, waving toward his car. "Drinking all the time, and running off with God-knows-who. I don't even recognize you anymore." My voice is thick with the tears I'm trying to hold at bay. "All I know is the old Graham, the Graham I know and love, wouldn't act like this."

"Yeah, well, maybe the old Graham died the moment you slept with my cousin."

My eyes widen and I stumble back, his words hitting me like shrapnel. How did he . . .? My head spins. Though I know he's merely lashing out from a place of pain, I have no idea how to get us back on track. And I'm so pissed he drove while so completely drunk, I'm struggling to find a reason why I should.

Which scares me, maybe more than anything. Because a friendship like ours is supposed to last a lifetime.

"Don't say that." My voice trembles.

Spinning on his feet, Graham slams his fist against the hood of the car with a thunderous boom, leaving a dent. "Fuck!" He kicks the side mirror, smashing it as he falls against the vehicle. "What do you want from me?" he screams. "First, you choose my cousin over me. Then I find out my father screwed his mother and has some secret love child with her. What do you expect, Kenz? Do you want me to be happy that my life is going to shit?"

He pushes off the car and storms toward me, his eye glistening in the moonlight. "You were always the one bright spot. No matter how shitty my father was to me or how much I felt like I needed to prove myself to him, I still had you."

"You still have me," I shout, trying to get through to him. "It's just different than you imagined. But I can't help it that—"

"Screw that!" Graham pulls an elbow forward, ready to smash the passenger side window when two arms come around him in a bear hug, stopping him.

My mouth gapes as I watch Cal Scott grapple with his son, struggling to maintain his hold around him. Graham flails, trying to shake him off. His face is red and angry, and he spits obscenities as they struggle.

"Get the hell off me!" he screams.

"Not until you calm down," his father barks.

Tears pool in my eyes, my anger turning to sorrow as I watch the emotions playing over Graham's face. His pain and rage are eating him alive. It reminds me of someone else when they first came to town.

It reminds me of Atlas.

Finally, Graham manages to push Cal off him, brushing at his arms as if he can remove his touch from his skin. "Put your hands on me again, and I'll tell Mom everything," he snarls. Then he glances at me.

"Fuck you!" he says, before he storms off.

CHAPTER 19

ATLAS

I STARE OUT AT the Riverside middle school football field as I lean against the fence, opposite the bleachers. I can't tell one from the other with their helmets on, but the scoreboard shows thirty seconds left in a tie game. As the little Rebels take the offensive line, I watch as the quarterback snaps the ball, passing it off to the receiver—number twenty-one. He tucks it beneath his arm as his feet move like lightning over the field. Two defensive linemen come straight for him and I wince, preparing for the tackle, but he surprises me. He dodges one, then fakes right and spins left, passing him by and barreling for the end zone.

Once he makes it across the goal line, he slows to a walk and spikes the ball while the small crowd roars with excitement. Ripping his helmet off, he lifts it in the air, and my smile fades. He has dark, shaggy hair, the same color as my own, and when he turns in my direction and catches my gaze, it's like looking in a mirror.

Storm.

His teammates rush him, slapping him on the back and bumping him with their chests, while he stands rooted to his spot on the field as he stares in my direction.

Several days have passed since I promised to take Mackenzie to see my father, and in that time, I've thought a lot about what she said. Despite my feelings about Cal and my mother, she's right about one thing. Storm is innocent. He doesn't deserve the hand he was dealt any more than I do.

For a moment, my chest swells with pride. A pride I have no right to feel. Until a couple of weeks ago, I didn't even know he existed. But that's my brother, and he's a receiver just like me.

A damn good one at that.

I raise one a hand, and he returns the wave, his face instantly splitting into a boyish grin before his head whips in the direction of the bleachers. I know what I'll find when I follow the trajectory of his gaze, but I do so anyway, homing in on my mother quickly.

Even from here, I can see her glancing between us, her hands pressed to her chest over her heart, while mine leaps into my throat.

I inhale, tearing my eyes from hers and shove them in my pockets before I take a step back, unable to take this twisting, churning feeling in the pit of my stomach. When Storm turns his attention back to mine once more, I lift my chin in a nod, acknowledging him before I turn and mount my bike, then throttle the gas.

I move around the parked cars, headed for the exit when someone darts in front of my path. "Shit!" I squeeze my brakes and prepare for impact, but I stop just shy of hitting them.

With the breath rushing from my lungs, I glance up at the person I nearly creamed when I get a good look at their face.

My mother.

You've got to be kidding me.

"Are you completely insane?" I scream. Ripping my helmet off, I stare into her eyes, my breath rattling in my chest.

"I had to talk to you. It was the only way to get you to stop."

I turn my head, muttering a string of obscenities under my breath before I glare at her once more. "I've made it perfectly clear I have no interest in anything you have to say, especially in light of everything between you and Cal."

"I know," she says, her voice shaking. "And I can't even imagine how you or Graham must be feeling, but I'd like the chance to explain."

"No." I shake my head. "No amount of explaining is going to make any of it better. You'll just be wasting your breath."

"Maybe." She crosses her arms over her chest, shifting on her feet. "But I'd like to try. For him." She turns and nods in the direction of the field where the little Rebels celebrate their win.

I exhale, torn between wanting to tell her to fuck off and reminding myself that Storm is innocent. "Fine." I pull my bike off to the side, turn of the engine, and dismount. "You have ten minutes, tops. Then I'm out."

Her dark eyes glitter with hope. "I'll take it."

I follow my mother as she leads me further down the parking lot and away from prying ears. Then she turns to me and says, "It's not exactly as Cal made it seem."

"So, you didn't accept money from him to leave town?"

"I can't deny that," she says, and I fight the urge to roll my eyes. "When your father first started drinking heavily, it was after I got pregnant. His dreams for a career in football went downhill . . ."

"Yeah, I've heard this sob story before," I say, fighting off the surge of irritation. "How about we fast forward the part where my father throws his life away and get to the point. Particularly, the part where you leave me."

Her throat bobs, but she nods. "I had started drinking, too. Nothing like your father. I wasn't an addict or an alcoholic, but one night, I had too many. It was a hot and we'd been at a barbecue with friends," she says, her eyes filling with tears. "I put you in your booster seat in my car because we were supposed to leave at a decent hour to get you home. Your father promised me he wouldn't drink so he could drive, but I couldn't find him anywhere. I went looking, but I got"—her eyes shift, taking on a faraway look—"sidetracked. By the time I remembered you were still in the car, thirty minutes had passed. I rushed back outside to find your father had pulled you out. He was high as a kite, but just so happened to pass by and see you. It was dumb luck he saved you.”

So, she nearly killed me in a hot car?

I frown, waiting to see where she's going with this. “Go on,” I say, anxious to hear the rest.

Her hands shake as she clasps them out in front of herself, her voice thick. “I was so mad at myself. I'd cracked the windows but not enough. I had no idea what might have happened had your father not found you. I decided right then and there that any drinking and drug use needed to stop. Your father was out of control, and clearly my own drinking almost had devastating repercussions, but your father didn't take kindly to my suggestion we quit cold turkey.”

I snort. “Nah, not Dad.”

“So, I threatened to leave him. I even stayed with a friend for a couple weeks to prove my point; show him I'd make good on my promise.” She shakes her head and stares down at her hands. “It was a mistake. When I returned, he filed for custody. He used every picture, every video or text he ever had of me drinking or holding a glass of anything in my hand which could be mistaken for alcohol whether it was or not, citing that I was an alcoholic and a danger to you. I fought for months.” She takes a step toward me, her lip quivering as tears spill from her eyes. “You have to believe that. I fought so hard. But I had no proof to support my counterclaim that he was the problem, and when it came time for the court hearing, he showed me the statement a witness gave the night I left you in the car. One of his friends was willing to testify on his behalf."

Ice water chinks in my veins. I take a step back, trying to make sense of what she's telling me. "Are you saying you lost custody of me to Dad?"

"Not exactly." Her lips quiver and she wrings her hands. "He made me a deal. If I left, he'd drop the custody battle. I knew I had no chance of winning, so I did as he asked, thinking that someday I could come back for you."

My forehead creases. "But Cal . . . he paid you . . ."

Her throat bobs and an emotion flickers in her eyes I know all too well. Guilt. Shame. Embarrassment. Suddenly it hits me. "You said you left me in the hot car because you got side-tracked," I say, my voice tight. "It was with Cal, wasn't it?"

She nods slowly, a sob escaping the back of her throat. "Your father threatened to tell Sheila about the affair, so Cal gave me money and promised he'd watch after you." She covers her mouth with her hand and closes her eyes, the tears coming faster now. "He assured me . . ."

"What about coming back for me?" I snap. "Or was I that easy to forget?"

She blinks her eyes open and reaches out, but I step aside when she starts to explain. "Cal had been in contact with me and off. He knew I'd been wanting to come back for you, and I admit I waited too long, but I didn't know how bad things had gotten. I also didn't know where you and your father went after you moved from the house we had together. So, Cal paid me a visit. He was supposed to tell me where you were. Instead, he fed me a bunch of lies. He told me you had been heartbroken when I first left but finally adjusted. He said you were happy and thriving. That your father had a serious girlfriend who was like a mother to you, and if I came back and tried to take you, I'd only be hurting you more. When I was distraught at the news you no longer needed me, he comforted me"—she covers her face with her hands, her cheeks turning pink—"I found out a couple months after he left that I was pregnant."

She rakes a hand through her hair. "I know now he was feeding me lies, but back then . . . he'd convinced me the best thing for you at that point was to stay put. I believed him when he said it would be cruel to uproot you. Because, Atlas," she says, hand outstretched, pleading, "hurting you further was the last thing I wanted." She hiccups, choking on a sob, and my heart sinks.

So, Uncle Cal is more of a piece of shit than I ever thought.

I clench my teeth so hard I see stars.

When my mother reaches out to me this time, I let her. "I know I don't deserve a second chance, and I'm not trying to place all the blame on your father and Cal. I made mistakes and they cost me dearly. I've paid the price for so many years."

"Why now?" I ask, shoving my hands into my pockets. I barely recognize my own voice when I ask again, "Why did you come back now?"

"When I read about your father's arrest in the papers, I realized Cal was lying, so I tied up my loose ends where I was living in New Albany and came to find you."

I swallow, unsure of what to do with this information. "What do you want from me?" I ask warily, my heart in my throat.

"A chance to make it up to you. But even if you can never forgive me, I'd like the chance for Storm to have a relationship with his brothers. I made a mistake not finding a way to fight harder for you. I won't make that mistake with him. Do you think you could ever give him a chance?"

I stare at the concrete beneath my feet, wondering how two men could be so selfish. Apparently, Cal and my father are more alike than I thought.

All this time I believed my father was the only one who cared enough to stand by me, when all along, he was the whole reason my mother left in the first place.

"I don't know," I whisper, though I do know. Because the minute I watched number twenty-one fly down the field and score the winning touchdown, he had my heart.

Storm, Graham, and I are all collateral damage in our parents' games, and I'll be damned if that kid grows up thinking he's not good enough.

For reasons I can't explain, I want Storm to have more than I did. A man to look up to, one he can be proud of.

Maybe I can be that for him.

MACKENZIE

Anastasia smiles over at me as we pull into the school parking lot. "Here we are."

I catch sight of Graham headed toward the front doors, his mouth drawn down in a frown, and my stomach clenches.

"Are you sure everything's okay?" she asks me. "You've been quiet all week, but especially today."

I nod, tearing my eyes away from him as I force a smile I don't feel. "Yeah, I'm good. I promise."

It's a lie, but I don't feel like talking about it. A week has passed since the incident at Fall Fest and my fight with Graham. Anastasia has been kind enough to drive me to and from school, but everything that happened still plagues me. Graham and I have barely spoken; we're back to ground zero. I thought remembering the crash would fix everything. Instead, everything in my life has just gotten worse.

"Have you had any more panic attacks?" she asks, concern laced in her voice as she reaches out and touches my arm.

I place a hand over hers and shake my head. "No."

"Did you call—"

"I called a therapist, I swear. The earliest she could get me in is two weeks out, but I've scheduled an appointment," I say. After Anastasia witnessed my last panic attack, she gave me the information for a family friend who just so happens to specialize in trauma and post-traumatic stress disorder. Though I'm reluctant to spill my guts to a total stranger, I know it's the right thing to do. I'm beyond the point of self-help.

But first I need closure—vindication. Which is exactly what I'm hoping for with my trip to see Lee Scott.

"Okay, good." Her smile spreads. "And you're sure you don't want to come over my place tonight? A couple of the girls will be there. We're planning on vegging out and binging lousy reality TV with a couple of pizzas and a gallon of cookie dough.

"As amazing as that sounds, I have plans, remember?" I say, realizing I mean it. Part of me yearns for a carefree weekend with my friends so badly I can taste it. But I can't concentrate on anything until I decide what to do about Lee. I need to put the past to rest once and for all. And though I know I'm hanging all my hope on this one interaction, I can't help but feel like it'll give me all the answers I need and solve all my problems. Either Lee's remorse and shame will be enough for me, or it won't. Either way, I'll know what to do and I can put the past to rest. Even if it hurts my father.

"Yeah." She sighs. "Something about a road trip with Atlas. Are you sure that's a good idea after everything that's happened between you?"

Only Graham knows the truth about what happened between Atlas and me. All my other friends just think there was another girl. It's the only plausible explanation I could give them for my meltdown and the reason we broke up.

"I promised him, and I want to go."

"Still . . ." She bites her lip, concern creasing her brow.

"I'll be fine, I swear." I say it so convincingly I almost believe it myself.

"Suit yourself," she says, glancing back out her windshield where she nods toward a brooding Atlas. "Speak of the devil . . ."

My smile fades as I watch his lazy gait. His hands are shoved in the pockets of his black leather jacket while he makes his way up the sidewalk, an unlit cigarette tucked behind his ear.

My heart stutters at the prospect of spending hours pressed against his back as we make the three-hour drive to the rehabilitation center.

Anastasia turns, one brow arched as if she knows what I'm thinking. "If you wanna spend hours with the enemy alone, who am I to stop you?"

Atlas and I barely speak when I meet him by his locker. We say nothing as I walk with him to the student lot and my mind churns with what I'm about to do.

I've thought about this day a million times in the past month. Dreamed about its outcome. And now it's here. Today I will confront his father, Lee Scott, the man who killed my mother. Today, I will get some answers.

We descend the hill toward the student parking lot when he comes to an abrupt stop by a small silver Prius I recognize as Teagan's and unlocks it. "We're not taking your bike?" I ask, glancing over at him for the first time. My brow creases in confusion as I wait for an explanation.

"It's too cold. This time of year, I usually have to retire my bike." He motions toward the graying sky. "Besides, there's a chance of heavy snow further north. It wouldn't be safe, let alone comfortable."

"Oh." I exhale and glance back at the car, feeling stupid. The truth is, I never thought about him needing to retire his motorcycle for the winter, though it should be obvious.

I eye the car warily as he opens his door and waits for me to do the same. Before today, I dreaded getting back on his bike. I fretted endlessly, worrying over the prospect of wrapping myself around him as we drove and the memories being so close to him might stir to life. But now my heart is pounding with the notion of sharing this small space where we'll be able to look at each other head-on and actually converse.

"What did you have to trade him for the car?" I ask, trying to sound lighthearted even though my head is spinning.

Leaning toward me over the roof of the car, he drapes his long muscular arms over the its smooth surface, dark eyes gleaming as he says, "He's always wanted to ride a Harley." His mouth presses into a flat line. "I guess now he'll get his chance."

I nod. Knowing how much Atlas's bike means to him, lending it out is no small feat. But Teagan will be fine. Out of all the boys, he's definitely one of the more responsible ones.

"Well . . . thanks," I say awkwardly.

Atlas nods, and when I can no longer take his eyes on me, I clear my throat and open the passenger side door, then slide inside. My hand moves to the seatbelt with a shaky breath and I snap it on while Atlas joins me. Under normal circumstances, he's a big guy. Muscular with a broad frame, large hands, and long legs but in this matchbox of a car, he's massive.

"Could he have gotten a smaller car?" he grumbles as he settles himself behind the wheel, pushing his seat back as far as it will go and still eating the steering wheel.

I watch as he shifts around, adjusting himself and messing with the seat gears for a whole five minutes until I can no longer help myself. Laughter rumbles inside of my chest, exploding into a burst of giggles.

He scowls, turning to me. "Oh, you find this funny?"

"I mean, your knees are in your chest."

He curses as he glances down at his legs, then breaks out into a smile. "Damn Teagan."

We burst out laughing as he starts the car and pulls out of the lot.

Well, that's one way to break the ice.

After I catch my breath, I marvel at how good it feels to laugh. The way I see it, we have three hours together. Either we can ride in awkward silence, or we can make small talk and act like normal human beings for once instead of being miserable.

"How long have you had your bike?" I ask, making my decision. I've had enough tense interactions the past couple of months to last a lifetime.

He glances over at me, as if surprised we're speaking, before returning his eyes to the road. "I got it shortly after I turned sixteen. By that point, I'd started making decent money with my side gigs doing repairs and car work. One of the women I was working for mentioned her husband was going to get rid of it. The engine was busted, and she asked me about fixing it, but ultimately decided it wasn't worth it. He bought a new one, and I got it for a pittance. It was the first purchase I ever made that was for something I truly wanted, not just something I needed."

"So, if you can't drive it in the winter, what do you do?"

He hesitates, and I can tell by the crease in his brow he's working through something in his head. "Usually by now, I've already put it away until spring. This year, I decided to hang on a little longer, but it's cold as shit and with the roads starting to get icy in the mornings, it's dangerous. Add snow to the forecast, and it's time."

"Okay," I drawl. "But how do you get around if you can't ride your bike?" Somehow, I don't see him relying on anyone else, considering he's made it a habit to be independent.

"Borrow a car, usually. But that isn't an option this year." His throat bobs, his hands tightening on the steering wheel and I'm about to ask him why, when it hits me.

He drives his father's car. And he would borrow it again this year if it weren't for me. If he hadn't discovered it had been used as a murder weapon.

I glance away from him, the lightheartedness from moments ago gone as I try not to think of the accident. A bubble of panic swells inside my chest while my pulse begins to race. It's as if the harder I try not to think of that day, the more the memories press on my consciousness, and I'm one morose thought away from having an episode. But this is the last place I want to break down. Not when I'm beside him and on my way to confront his father.

I close my eyes and lean my head back against the headrest, forcing myself to breathe. I'm safe, I tell myself. I inhale through my nose and out through my mouth, focusing on the rise and fall of my chest and the way my lungs fill with air, until the tightness fades.

"Can I ask you something?"

I blink my eyes open at the sound of his voice to find him watching me. Any questions coming from him seem dangerous, so I'm tempted to say no, but I don't. The more we talk, the less room my mind has to wander to places I don't want it to go. "What is it you want to know?"

"What are you hoping to get out of this today?" He turns his attention back to the road. "What do you hope to gain?"

It's a good question, one I'm not entirely sure I know the answer to. I only know I need to talk to Lee Scott; I need closure.

I stare out the windshield, focusing on the passing mile markers. "I want to tell him I know." I admit. "I want to make him understand what he's done. Explain how it felt to lose my mother. See the look on his face as I do. I want . . . vindication. His remorse and shame instead of mine." I shrug. "I'm not sure I know where to go from here until I have that."

His gaze shifts, watching me for a moment. "You think this will give you direction?"

I nod, relieved he gets it. "The reason I didn't want you confessing everything to my father is because I'm not sure I want to know what he'd do with the information. It would be like making him decide whether or not to turn himself in. Considering he's the chief of police and ignored eyewitness testimony, his job is at risk if he reports the truth now, after all this time. In a small town like Riverside, the news will spread like wildfire, along with the gossip. Everyone will know about my mother's affair, and our family name will be torn to shreds."

I glance down at the closed fists resting in my lap. "Quite frankly, I don't give a damn about what anyone else thinks. I might be furious with him, but I'm not sure I want his entire life turned upside down any more than it already has been. Especially since I don't plan on sticking around after graduation." I stare down at the hands curled in my lap, and I make another confession. "I guess I'm somehow hoping a confrontation might quiet my demons."

I guess I want a lot of things. I'm just not sure I'm going to get any of them.

"Fair enough," he says, his tone even, and I'm relieved to hear no sign of judgment.

"What about you?" I ask in the hopes of diverting the conversation toward him. "Surely, you're going to talk to him. I assume this will be the first time you've seen him since he went to rehab. Is there anything you want out of it?"

The muscle in his jaw flickers as he stares at the stretch of highway before him, taking his time to answer. "I'm not sure I have anything to say."

"He's your father. Surely, there's—"

"He's been hurting me my whole damn life," Atlas cuts me off. "When is it one fuck-up too many? When does he stop getting a pass?"

I swallow at the pain in his voice. I don't want to feel for him; sympathy will make me soft, and Atlas is a bad habit I can't fall back on. "Are you going to tell him your mother is back in town?" I ask, unable to resist.

"I thought about it. I thought about telling him about Storm and Uncle Cal. I mean, talk about poetic justice, right? The man responsible for getting him out of jail and two months sober is the same man who shagged the love of his life and knocked her up. But, if I told him those things, it would be to hurt him. To get even for hurting me. And I'm not sure I wanna be that guy. I want to be better than him, you know? So, no, I won't tell him, and I don't think I'm going to talk to him. At least, not alone, anyway."

My throat tightens as I think about everything he said. He's not the bitter, broken boy I met months ago at Crow's Creek. He's different. Changed. I have no idea what caused this—whether it was me, or Cal, or everything that's happened since he moved to Riverside—but I can't help but admire this side of him. The one without the thick suit of armor weighing him down. But it scares me, too, because this version of Atlas would be so much easier to love.

"Want some music?" he asks, interrupting my thoughts.

I nod, grateful for the change of subject and the levity as he flicks it on and the smooth notes of Mozart come on the stereo. Atlas and I share a look and immediately laugh.

"Who would've taken Teagan for a classical guy?" I say.

"He plays football, drives a Prius, and listens to classical music. The dude's an enigma."

With the tense line of conversation behind us, we make small talk the rest of the way to the rehabilitation center, stopping only once to get gas and grab a drink. The time passes quickly, and I'm almost able to forget I'm spending it with a boy I'm supposed to hate—one that broke my heart only a short time ago. Regardless, the distraction from what I'm about to do is a godsend, because the second we arrive at Rise Rehabilitation Center, my stomach ties in knots.

I stare ahead at the sprawling compound with its sunny yellow siding, large front porch, and massive windows, thinking the man responsible for my mother's death is just inside those walls.

I press a hand to my stomach, hoping to quell the sudden wave of nausea as Atlas guides the car around the lot. He finds an empty spot in visitor parking and twists in his seat, bracing an arm across the back of my headrest as he backs into the space, then puts the car in park.

Once, when I was five, I'd been hiking with my father and we came to a rather large creek, and the only way to get across without wading in the water was this little bridge. It was one of those old rope and plank bridges, and although the water was probably only a few feet deep, for some reason, at the time, I was terrified of falling in.

I remember standing in front of that first wooden plank, my small hands clinging to the weather-beaten rope, knowing that the moment I stepped on that bridge, there was no going back. One of the wooden slats could break or the ropes could snap, but those first couple of steps were a commitment to follow through.

Suddenly, I'm back there again. Only, instead of the rope bridge and the creek, it's stepping through the doors and over the threshold of Rise Rehabilitation that frightens me. I don't know if I have the strength or the courage.

Atlas once said he nicknamed me "doll" because that's how everyone in my life treated me—like porcelain: fragile and prone to breaking—and maybe they're right. Maybe I am that weak. Because now that we're here, all I want to do is put as much distance between me and Lee Scott as possible.

After a moment, Atlas turns to me, and it's like he can sense the war waging inside my head because he searches my gaze and asks, "You ready?"

CHAPTER 20

MACKENZIE

I STARE AT AN abstract painting on the wall across from me. It's awash with bright colors, vibrant and uplifting—the complete opposite of my mood. The plush sofa beneath me belongs to the visitor lounge of the rehabilitation center. Somehow, the entire space is warm and cozy and inviting, which surprises me. Though, I'm not sure what I expected. Somewhere cold and clinical? A stuffy interior every bit as intense as my nerves?

I exhale and rub my sweat-dampened palms over the tops of my thighs. To my right, Atlas fiddles with a magazine from the side table while we wait for his father to join us, and I fight the urge to rip it from his hands and yell at him to stop fidgeting.

"This is the first time I'll see him completely sober," he murmurs, and it reminds me I'm not the only one facing demons today.

I say nothing, at a loss for words. I only hope I can speak when it counts. At this moment, I have no idea how I'm going to start off the conversation. Though I've rehearsed this moment in my head, the reality of it feels different somehow. Surreal.

There's the echo of a door closing in the distance, followed by footsteps.

When I glance toward the entryway, a man approaches with caution, but the light in his eyes tell me he's hopefully optimistic. His hair is lighter than Atlas's, his eyes a muted shade of hazel instead of the rich dark brown I'm used to. He's pale, his body lean and lanky in comparison to the boy at my side, but when Atlas glances up at him and he breaks into a smile, I see the slightest bit of resemblance.

He pauses a few feet in front of us as Atlas stands to greet him, his dark gaze drinking him in as his father moves to pull him into a hug.

Stepping out of reach, Atlas averts his gaze and his father's smile drops. "When they told me you were here, I didn't believe them," he says, his voice thick with emotion. "I knew they sent you that card, but I never thought you'd accept."

My head jerks toward him, and I frown. *What letter?*

"Either way, it's so good to see you, son." This time, instead of trying for a hug, Atlas's father offers him his hand.

I watch as Atlas huffs out a breath and curls his hands into fists, clearly conflicted between holding onto his anger and embracing this new version of him.

A swell of sympathy rises inside of me that I resent. It's so much easier to cling to my anger, but I can't deny what this reunion must be like for them. Atlas can say he hates his dad for all the ways in which he hurt him, but I can see the little boy deep down inside of him. The one that wants acceptance. The one that craves a father's love and affection. The same little boy who knows his father is the only one who's ever stayed.

After a moment, Atlas accepts the handshake, gripping his father's hand with a fierce gleam in his eye I'm not sure I understand. A muscle in the side of his neck pulses, and his throat bobs. "You look good, Pops."

"Yeah. You too, son. You, too." Lee's eyes tear before he clears his throat and pulls his gaze from his son to where I'm sitting. "And who do we have here?" he asks, glancing back at Atlas for an answer.

Atlas rubs a hand over the back of his neck as he turns in my direction. "This is Mackenzie Hart. We're, uh . . ." he pauses, clearly at a loss of words on how to describe what we are, before he decides on what to settle with. "We're friends, I guess."

His father nods and reaches a hand out. "Lee Scott. Nice to meet you."

I stare at his outstretched hand like it's a snake that might bite, appalled by the idea of touching his flesh with mine. Clearly reading the disgust in my expression, his smile fades and he slowly pulls his hand back. Tucking it in his pocket, he hangs his head. "I have to admit, I never thought I'd see the day where you came to visit." A nervous chuckle bubbles from his lips as he moves forward, taking a seat in the chair opposite mine. "So, how is everything going in Riverside? You made it to States, I hear."

Atlas sinks down beside me. "I'm not here for a social visit, Dad." He glances over at me, and I know it's my cue to jump in.

Lee glances between us, a crease between his brows. "Well, what are you here for?"

This is it. My chance.

I swallow as I stare at his face, weathered from years of drug abuse and drinking, and I allow myself to imagine him drunk behind the wheel of the car that killed my mother. I remember the sound of our screams. The jolt when he hit us. The impact when we crashed into the pole. And the pain in the hospital when I woke alone. The choking realization my mother hadn't survived.

Anger grows inside my chest like a fire breathing dragon, scorching me from the inside out, and filling me poison until I taste the bitterness of it in the back of my throat. "Do you know who I am?" I ask, my tone cold. "Do you recognize me at all"

He shakes his head, eyeing me closer. "Should I?"

"On January seventeenth of last year, my life changed. Do you want to know why?"

His brows lift. "Why?"

"I was in a car accident. The person who hit my car sent me spiraling off the road, headfirst into a telephone pole. I spent weeks in the hospital. Doctors had to put me in a medically induced coma. And do you know what I found out the moment I woke up?"

His throat bobs as if finally catching on. "What did you find?" His gaze flickers to Atlas, who can't even look at him, and instead, stares at the ground, his mouth a hard line.

"I found out my mother died," I say when his eyes meet mine once more. "She didn't survive the impact. In fact, they pronounced her dead on the scene. Turns out, a drunk in a rusted blue Ford Fiesta with a yellow bumper sticker and a rabbit's foot hanging from the rearview mirror tried to pass us."

I watch with satisfaction as my words sink in and the color drains from his face. "No . . ." he murmurs, shaking his head as if it couldn't possibly be the truth.

"Yes," I say between clenched teeth. "It most definitely was you."

"It . . . it can't be. I wasn't . . ."

"Dad, you even told me that day on the phone," Atlas snaps. "You knew you hit someone, but you kept driving."

Lee runs a hand over the back of his neck, shaking his head, and my nostrils flare. "Do you remember hitting us? Do you remember the events that led up to that moment? Because I do. I remember all of it, in grave detail. I replay it over and over in my head," I say, thinking about the past month—the flashbacks, the painful memories, the nightmares. "The memories plague me. They strike without notice and bring me to my knees. They make me cry and scream, and every time I remember, it's like it's happening all over again."

"I didn't . . . I . . ." His eyes search around us, as if looking for an escape.

"This is her." I reach into my purse and pull out several photographs before I shove one of her in front of his face. "Here, look," I demand.

In the photograph, my mother is sitting on a park bench, the sun shining down on her as she smiles for the camera. Her sandy hair spills over her shoulders while the corners of her eyes crinkle.

She's vibrant. Full of life. Perfectly happy.

He takes one glance and closes his eyes.

"I said, look at her!" I yell.

He shakes his head, his throat bobbing, hands shaking as he moans and curls in on himself. "I can't do this." His voice catches. "I know I've hurt a lot of people—"

"The least you can do is look at the eyes of the woman whose life you took." I swallow, feeling the swell of emotion tightening the back of my throat. But I must stay strong, because I'm not done here. I'm not even close.

"I said, *look at her*," I say, between clenched teeth. "You owe her that much, at least."

Finally, he heaves out a breath and lifts his head, his gaze landing on my mother's face. A sob rips from the back of his throat as he takes the outstretched photograph from my hands. "What was her name?" he whispers.

"Laura Hart. She was only forty years old." I shove another picture in his hands. "This was our family." It was the last happy memory of us together. We'd gone to pick pumpkins. I remember how we sipped hot cider together and went on a hayride before I bailed on them early to catch a movie with Graham. I think about that night often; if I had known what was in store, I would've gone to dinner. Stayed just a little longer. Made one more memory.

Lee stares at the photo and his lips part. "I'm sorry. I didn't know it was that bad. If I had known—"

"You drove under the influence and you knew you hit someone. You knew," I say, my voice shrill. "Yet you chose to drive away. How can you even sit here for one second and say you didn't know how bad it was, and in the same breath claim you would've helped?"

"I thought . . . I was so out of it, so drunk . . . I knew I hit someone. I heard the crushing of metal and glanced in the mirror. I swerved, nearly going off the road myself. The car was there. I remember it, and I . . . I kept going, told myself it was fine. Whoever it was would be fine. And I believed it because I was in no position to help."

"You killed her, and I—" My voice breaks, and I pause to compose myself. "I blamed myself because I didn't remember what happened, not at first. After the accident, I wished I had died, too, I wondered why I didn't, why I survived. I went more than nine long months thinking her death was because of something I did and hating myself for it."

"I'm sorry. I didn't know—"

"Stop saying that!" I shout, jumping to my feet. Atlas places a hand on my arm, a subtle reminder to maintain my composure, to calm the raging storm inside, but I shake him off. I take a step closer, towering over his father as anger boils in my veins. "You *did* know. You said you remembered hitting someone. You just didn't care enough to find out what happened to us or turn yourself in." My eyes fill with moisture. "Instead of calling the police, you left us to die, all so you wouldn't get in trouble." The dam on my emotions breaks and tears begin to fall down my cheeks.

Lee bends at the waist, covering his face with his hands while he sobs, mumbling, "I've done so many things in my life I regret. So many . . ." He pauses and lifts his face, swiping a hand down his tear-stained face. His eyes are red, his mouth contorted with anguish. "I was a terrible husband, and even worse father. I abused drugs and alcohol. Destroyed the relationships around me. I was a shell of a man. I've learned all of that here, and I'm just starting to try and come to terms with the things I've done, the people I've hurt. I can't take it back. I know I can't, but I wish I could."

He digs his heels into his damp eyes, a keening moan escaping his lips. "Oh, how I wish I could. I'd take it all back. All of it. I'd trade places with her, and I know that doesn't help you, but I have nothing else to give except my shame. My sorrow and regret for the things I've done. All I have is the guilt of everything I've put my loved ones through, and now this." His hand trembles as he reaches out, offering the photos back.

I take them, my own tears drying as I stare at him, watching him fall to pieces.

This is what I wanted. His pain. His remorse. For him to understand how much he hurt my family. To see firsthand the lives he's ruined.

I watch as he sucks in a breath, his tortured gaze finding Atlas, who sits beside me, stony-faced, his face the color of sheetrock. "What would you like me to do?" His voice trembles as he pulls his gaze from his son back to me again. "Say it, and I'll do it. Anything. I don't have any money, nothing to give you, but I'll turn myself in if it's what you want."

I stare at him as a numbness creeps under my skin, sinking into my bones. I no longer know how to feel. All I know is his sins can never be washed away, at least not by me. He should have to live with his guilt, just like I had to live with mine.

"No," I say, my voice even.

He shakes his head. "Then, what? Tell me."

Emotion clogs the back of my throat, and I turn away, confused by the churning inside my gut. When Atlas asked what I hoped to gain from our meeting, I told him I wanted vindication. His father's remorse and shame.

This feels a whole like all of those things, yet it's not nearly as satisfying as I thought it would be. It doesn't bring me peace or joy. I saw the moment he understood, watched as he unraveled and fell apart. The scent of regret lingers in the air between us, the sound of his sobs evidence that my words hit their mark.

In the days to follow, I have no doubt he'll think about this day and hate himself for the choices he's made. The smothering weight of his guilt will threaten to crush him. I know this to be true because I experienced them myself. But none of those things can bring my mother back. None can give me the closure I seek.

My lungs seize at the realization, and the anger I felt moments ago morphs into soul-crushing grief.

I can't be here anymore. I can't spend one more second in this room, breathing the same air as this man.

I stand and hurry from the room, my feet carrying me past the lobby and through the thick glass doors of the building, out into the frigid autumn air where I wrap my arms around myself. A sob rips through my throat. I bite my fist, frantic to stifle the sound, to smother the emotion swelling inside me with enough force to crush me like an ant.

"Mackenzie," Atlas calls out behind me, his voice the breath of fresh air I need.

But I don't turn. I'm too busy falling apart.

Instead, I squeeze my eyes closed and start to walk, needing this time alone. Time to work through this myself.

"Mackenzie, wait!" he calls out, his voice closer. A hand wraps around my arm from behind, but I ignore it and keep up my pace. "Please . . ." he says, but his hand falls away.

"Just, go back. Please. Say whatever you need to say to him for yourself."

"I have nothing to say to him. Dammit, Mackenzie, look at me!" I spin around, unsteady on my feet as my wet gaze meets his. "Are you okay?" He reaches a hand toward my face, but I dodge him, nodding.

"I need a minute alone, okay? I just need to take a walk."

"Not alone. I won't talk. I'll give you your space, but, please, just let me go with you."

"No," I say, my tone firm. "I'll call you in an hour."

"It's cold and supposed to snow," he reasons, but I turn and start to walk away. "It'll be dark soon," he yells after me.

"I'll be fine," I force out, then step onto the sidewalk.

CHAPTER 21

MACKENZIE

NIGHT HAS FALLEN AND my feet begin to ache. Still, I continue forward, head down, eyes trained on the ground, keeping my hands tucked into the pockets of my coat to ward off the cold. The wind stings my damp cheeks, and the snow that has started to fall clings to the strands of my hair.

I have no idea how much time has passed since I left Atlas at the rehabilitation center. All I know is that the tightness in my chest remains but the tears have stopped, leaving in their wake a foreboding sense of hopelessness mingling with the feeling that I'm a fool. I thought I'd feel vindicated, that the anguish inside of me might somehow vanish when I confronted Lee. But it didn't. Instead, I watched a pathetic shell of a man crumble before me, leaving me empty with no sense of direction.

I don't know how far I've walked when I finally lift my head at a two-way stop, but based on my surroundings, I surmise I'm not in the best of neighborhoods. Several of the businesses up ahead are closed, their windows dark and boarded shut. Graffiti and litter cover the sidewalk, blowing in the cracked concrete toward a seedy bar with a half-lit Miller Lite sign.

I cross the intersection quickly, hoping there's a gas station up ahead where I can stop and grab a cup of coffee while I call Atlas and wait for him to pick me up, but I only find myself disappointed. The street in front of me ends at a small convenience store whose claim to fame appears to be lottery tickets and the cheapest beer in town.

With a sigh, I kiss my chances of a good cup of joe goodbye as a muffler backfires somewhere in the distance. A dog barks, punctuating the sound before the streets fall silent again.

I walk a little further, growing closer to the convenience store and pause, unsure of whether I want to go inside. Leaning against an old brick building that appears to be unkempt apartments, I contemplate calling Atlas, then turning around and heading back to meet him partway when I notice a darkened alleyway to my left. Swallowing, I pull my phone from my pocket and dial Atlas's number while a shiver runs through me. I'm unsure whether it's from the cold or my surroundings but I uselessly tug my coat tighter around my neck with my free hand, waiting as my phone rings.

Willing him to answer, I curse when his voice mail picks up, and try him again. I wonder if I pissed him off.

Maybe he was right. I never should've left him. I'm in the middle of nowhere in what appears to be a bad part of town with nothing but my cell phone. I've got no money, no Goliath for protection, not even the pepper spray my father insists I carry in my backpack and on keyring.

Pick up, pick up, I urge.

The sound of gravel crunches behind me to my left, and my heart skips a beat. Swallowing, I lower my phone mid-ring as a creeping sensation slithers up my spine, and I slowly peek over my shoulder.

Two men, maybe in their early twenties, hover in the entryway to the darkened alley. A door opens and another one steps out, making three. I subconsciously take a step back further into the shadows in the hopes they don't notice me, but the movement draws their attention and the two men nod in my direction while the third one glances my way. A slow smile spreads over his cracked lips, revealing yellowed teeth, and he has a glint in his eye that makes my skin crawl.

My mind starts to race. Fear coats my insides like tar.

Turning, I calmly make a beeline toward the front door of the convenience store, telling myself I'm overreacting. They might be creepy, but it doesn't mean they're bad guys. I'll head inside and have a good laugh at myself for getting so freaked out once I'm safe.

"Hey, baby, where you headed in such a hurry?" one of them calls out.

On second thought . . .

I swallow over my fear and pick up the pace. The soles of my sneakers slap over the cracked sidewalk as their laughter carries after me. I ignore them, trying to remain calm despite the frantic beat of my pulse.

Until one of them shouts, "Get her!"

Run.

My heart pounds in my chest, faster than my feet can carry me as I break out into a sprint. The convenience store grows closer, the lights brighter.

I'm in shape and fast, my arms pumping, bringing me closer to the door; it's only twenty-five yards from me. I can make it, I tell myself. I'm almost there.

But I'm wrong.

A hand clamps down on my shoulder, yanking me back. I yelp as I stumble and slap the hand away when a second one grips me by the hair, making it impossible to move.

On instinct, I shift ever so slightly and sink my teeth into the fingers on my shoulder as hard as I can. Until I can taste blood. Until he yanks it away with a howl.

But the other two men take his place before I can escape. So, I open my mouth and scream.

CHAPTER 22

ATLAS

MY FEET EAT THE pavement as I walk, allowing my anger to fuel me as snow starts to fall. Witnessing Mackenzie speak with my father was probably one of the hardest fucking things I've ever had to do for so many reasons.

Reliving her anguish and grief. Seeing the anger in her eyes. Hearing the pain in her voice as she showed my father the pictures of her mother—of her family—and told him who they were and what he did to them, to her.

Then watching my father fall apart.

I'm so fucking mad at him. There's a river of anger between us, a moat that can never be crossed. Part of me hates him for what he did to me, for what he did to her. It makes the sympathy I felt toward him today all that much more difficult. And it pisses me the hell off that I can even feel anything for him after all the grief he's put me through. Sober or not, he doesn't deserve my sympathy. It doesn't matter if he's my father or the fucking King of England. Some things can't be forgiven. And killing Mackenzie's mother is one of them.

I lift my head, chest aching at the thought of Mackenzie alone and hurting, and take in the street ahead.

I lost her in the snow.

Shit.

I curse at myself for not staying closer, for letting her go off on her own in the first place.

She was upset and emotional, definitely not in the right frame of mind to go for a walk in an unfamiliar town.

But what choice did I have? She didn't want me with her, and if she knew I was following her, she would have been pissed. The last thing I want is for her to hate me more than she already does. And though I know I should've respected her wishes and stayed put, something told me to go—to follow.

I walk faster, scanning my surroundings but find no one up ahead, so on instinct, I make a right and climb a small incline toward town. A single set of footprints in the snow on the sidewalk tell me I'm headed in the right direction, but I can't be sure.

Pausing on the walkway, I squint in an effort to see better. In the dark, with the rapid snowfall, visibility is terrible.

A chill shudders through me as the hair on my arms stands to attention.

She could fall.

Get hit by a car.

Some creep could find her and mug her. Or worse.

Any number of things could happen to her in an unfamiliar place, alone, at night.

She's in trouble. I can feel it in the pricking of my skin and the ache in my bones, even though I tell myself I'm probably overreacting.

Where the hell are you, Doll?

I take off in a jog as urgency claws through my veins. Something tells me I need to find her, and find her now.

I plow through a two-way intersection and past an old bar when a shrill scream pierces the quiet. It's quickly followed by another one, and my feet fly.

It's coming from up ahead. Maybe fifty yards, if that.

My lungs burn as I run faster than I've ever ran in my entire life, my feet barely touching the ground. If anything happens to her, I'll never forgive myself. It'll be one more thing I've done to inadvertently hurt her—one more way in which my father and I have brought pain and grief to her life.

The sound of laughter reaches my ears, and I see red.

If someone's hurting her and laughing about it, I'll fucking kill them with my bare hands.

I blink through the thick tufts of snow as several shadows fall into view. Three men. They have her cornered and one is reaching for her.

A roar escapes past my lips as I barrel toward him. My shoulder connects with his side and I tackle him to the ground. His head smacks the concrete and he moans, but that doesn't stop me from pounding my fist into his face and busting his nose. One of his cronies jumps on my back, but I buck him off, turning with fists swinging wildly.

Adrenaline fills my bloodstream. I'm so wired, I could lift a fucking bus; tear down walls with my bare hands.

My limbs shake as I jump to my feet and deliver a right hook to the mouth of the guy who tried to jump me, not at all satisfied when he screams like a girl and falls back on his ass. He spits on the ground and sneers at me with blood-stained, yellowed teeth. "What the hell, man? We just wanted to talk to her."

Talk to her, my ass.

I ignore him as I eye the jerk still hovering by Mackenzie, noting the rapid rise and fall of her chest, the fear in her wide, blue eyes.

There's only one of me and three of them. I need to make sure they leave, and stopping to think about what might have happened had I not found her won't help anyone.

"I suggest all of you get the hell out of here before I rip your arms from their sockets," I say, my tone menacingly calm.

The dude takes a step back, raising his hands in surrender while the guy beside me snorts.

"The police are already on their way," I lie.

Fear brightens his soulless eyes, telling me this hit the mark. "Shit," he mutters and glances at his friends with a knowing expression. Taking his cue, they tear off down a darkened alleyway a few yards off.

Mackenzie slumps against the brick of the building, catching her breath while my heart splits in two. After the day she's had, having the crap scared out of her was the last thing she needed.

I approach her slowly and reach out, gently wrapping a hand around her arm. "Doll? Are you okay?"

She falls into my arms, a puff of air escaping her lips while I press her into my chest.

"Nothing happened. It's stupid to be so scared. They were probably just messing with me, but . . ." Her voice trembles as she catches her breath. "I'm so glad you're here."

"Yeah, me too." I smooth a hand down her hair, more than relieved I got here in time, grateful for my instincts to follow. I want to press my forehead to hers. To kiss her lips. Lift my palm and feel the beating of her heart against my flesh.

But I can't. She's no longer mine to hold. The only reason she's even allowing me to care for her now is because those goons frightened her. And that hurts like hell.

Swallowing, I lift my head and glance around us. If possible, the snow is falling even faster now. A blanket of white covers the street, and I can barely see more than a body's length in front of me.

With a sigh, I release her. "We should get out of here. Can you walk?"

She nods, and together, we start down the sidewalk when she reaches out and holds my hand.

CHAPTER 23

ATLAS

Heat blasts through the small car, thawing my bones while I lean my head back against the seat of the Prius. When I imagined my eighteenth birthday, it wasn't like this.

The muscles in my jaw tense as I think about everything that happened today, and I close my eyes. I have half a mind to drive back to where we left those guys and hunt them down, make them pay for ever scaring her at all.

"Are you okay?" Mackenzie asks, breaking the silence.

I clench my teeth harder—any harder and they might crack—but now that we're back and I know she's safe, I'm pissed as hell. At those guys. At my father. Hell, I'm even mad at her for walking off on her own.

But she's the only one that's here, so I open my eyes and glance over at her, my voice tight as I say, "What were you thinking taking off alone like that?"

Her eyes widen, and she points a finger to her chest. "Are you mad at *me*?"

"Hell yes, I'm mad at you."

Her mouth gapes. "For what?"

"For leaving. You're lucky I followed you. Who knows what might have happened—"

"I know, okay?" she snaps. "Trust me, it scared the crap out of me. Lesson learned."

I stare at her, well aware I have no right to be angry. We wouldn't even be here if it weren't for me—or rather, what my father did. If he weren't such a selfish prick, Mackenzie never would've been upset in the first place. She would've had no reason to stalk off the way she did, and if I'm being honest, I can't fault her for wanting a moment alone. But, damn, it feels good to deflect, and my father isn't here, so she's the only available target.

"It doesn't change the fact that it was stupid," I mutter, knowing I'm sulking, but I can't seem to help myself.

Shaking my head, I begin to open the car door.

I need to get out of here—I need an escape—and beating something or someone with my fists sounds pretty good right about now.

She stops me with a hand on my arm. "What are you doing?"

"I don't know. I'm thinking about tracking those guys down and kicking their asses some more. I wasn't quite finished."

"Are you insane?"

I bark out a laugh. "Quite possibly."

I'm being a dick, but I can't help it. Everything that's happened since I moved to Riverside is building up in my bloodstream like some kind of toxic wasteland. Any more and my insides will eviscerate.

"You can't just . . . just go chasing those guys down. They didn't even do anything."

I arch a brow at her, and she shrinks back.

Shrugging, she says, "Well, not really, anyway. All they did was heckle and chase after me. They gave me a little scare, but that's not exactly a punishable crime."

She's right. Sort of. Even though I'm almost certain they would've done more than heckle her had I not shown up, it's insane to track them back down now. Still, I'm not in the habit of conceding, so I purse my lips, then say, "It sounds like a pretty good idea to me."

We stare at each other for a moment, both of us angry and neither one of us wanting to crack until she exhales and reaches out, softly gripping the front of my coat. "Thank you," she murmurs.

I stare down at her hand, and my throat bobs before I shift my gaze to her face, taking in the crystals of snow still clinging to the damp strands of her hair, and my frustration cracks in two. Because it's me I'm mad at. After all these weeks, I'm still pissed at myself for lying to her when I learned about my father and I'm furious with him for ruining the best thing that ever happened to me.

I exhale, reminding myself that she's okay—she's safe—and that's all that matters. Even if she's not mine and never will be.

I run a hand over my face, then slide it to the back of my neck before I close my car door at the same time my phone rings. My gaze shifts to where it sits between us on the center console.

"It's Cal," Mackenzie says, her gaze on the screen.

"Let it go to voice mail," I tell her.

She says nothing as the ringing stops, followed by the pinging of a text message. "Why is he asking where you've been all week? He sounds . . . desperate?" she says.

I bite the inside of my cheek, debating how much to tell her. "I've been staying at my old place since Fall Fest."

"And he doesn't know where you've been?"

"I figured he wouldn't care." I glance at her, hating the pain laced in my voice. "I mean, he only ever took me in out of obligation, right? A promise to my mother?" I shrug. "Anyway, it doesn't matter."

I pull out of the parking spot and exit the lot before taking the main road when my phone pings for the second time. This time, Mackenzie picks it up before I can stop her.

I cut her with a sharp glance. "You know, some might consider it rude to read somebody else's text messages," I say, one brow raised. Not that I actually give a shit. I have nothing to hide from her, at least, not anymore.

But when she glances over at me, I can't quite read her expression. She looks . . . sad?

"Is it your birthday?"

"What?" I ask, gripping the wheel harder.

She lowers the phone. "Cal wished you a happy birthday. Why didn't you tell me?"

I shrug. "Does it matter?"

To that, she says nothing. Instead, she smashes her lips together and falls silent. When it pings again, I curse and take it from her, tossing it into the back seat. I'd get rid of the damn thing if I thought he'd stop trying to contact me. It was bad enough I woke to a message from my mother, asking if she could bring me a cake, like she hasn't missed the last fucking thirteen birthdays in between now and when she left.

"If we're to make it home by midnight, we'd better get moving," I say, effectively closing the conversation. Then I flick on the radio and take the ramp onto the interstate.

"Shit." I lean closer to the windshield as if it will somehow help me see through the snow squall, but it's no use. We surpassed zero visibility an hour ago, and thanks to the glacial speed we're traveling at, it'll take us all night to get home.

A gust of wind shakes the car, and I can see for a split second before I'm blind again.

I hit a patch of ice, and the car jerks, but I hold steady as the snow releases its grip on our tires.

"We could pull over?" Mackenzie offers, clinging to the handle on the passenger door. "Wait for this to pass?"

My palms sweat as I loosen my grip on the wheel. "No way. It's too risky. If anyone's driving in this, they might not see us, and I'd rather not get creamed on the side of the road. What's the weather say? When is the snow supposed to stop?"

"Let me see . . ." She clicks a couple of buttons on her phone and, after a minute, holds it up toward her window. "Crap. There's zero reception."

I grit my teeth. Could this night get any fucking worse?
Happy fucking birthday to me.

I glance over at Mackenzie, her pouty mouth drawn down like a bow, and instantly regret my thoughts. Because I'm with her. And the truth is, even if the circumstances are shitty and we're not together like I want us to be, there's nowhere else I'd rather be. Her presence is the only gift I want.

"I think we need to find somewhere to ride out the snowstorm," I say, focusing back on the road. "It's not safe to pull over and sit on the side of the road, and we can't keep going."

"But what about States?" Her brow creases in concern. "Atlas, your bus leaves early in the morning. You can't miss it."

"I know." My lips thin at the thought of missing what is most certainly the biggest game of my high school career. "But what other choice do we have?"

"You've worked so hard. You . . ." She trails off, biting her lip, likely realizing I'm right. "Where can we go?"

"I don't know. But the next exit, I'm getting off the highway and we'll stop at the first place we find. A gas station. Convenience store. Hell, it doesn't matter as long as it's warm and dry and we can get out of this weather."

"Okay. Yeah, you're right." She nods. "I'm really trying not to freak out right now over the snowpocalypse."

I glance over at her to see she's serious.

"Don't freak out. No freak outs on the road. Please."

She closes her eyes, pressing her head into the back of the seat, while her knuckles turn white, her grip on the seat deathly.

"Tell me what I can do to help?" I ask.

She inhales through her nose, about to answer, when a car going way too fast for the road conditions, flies by us. I open my mouth to cuss them out, but I never get the chance. When they jerk back into our lane, their tires catch on a patch of ice and they slide off the road as Mackenzie screams beside me.

Shit.

My stomach drops. Mackenzie presses her palms into her eyes. Her body shakes like a palm tree in a hurricane, and when I call her name, she doesn't respond.

Slowly, I pull over onto the berm of the highway, praying to God no one hits us, then put my emergency flashers on before I turn to her. A keening noise comes from the back of her throat as she cowers into the car door. Her trembling reaches a crescendo, and her breath comes in sharp, short gasps. Much more and she'll hyperventilate.

I unbuckle my seatbelt and lean toward her, unfolding her arms from where they're covering her face. "Mackenzie, it's Atlas. You're safe. You're okay. It's just in your head. Okay?" I croon. "You just need to breathe."

When she doesn't respond, I think on my feet and hop out of the car. I round it to the passenger side and throw open her door, allowing the cold air to embrace her before I pull her into my arms. "Breathe, doll," I murmur into her hair as I run my hand down the length of it. "Just breathe. Feel my chest and follow me. *In . . . out*," I instruct in a soothing voice. "*In . . . out.*"

Her hands fall from her face and her breathing slowly begins to match my pace.

"It's Atlas, and you're safe," I remind her. I have no idea what the fuck I'm doing, or if it's the right thing, but I go with my gut. "*In . . . out.*"

After a moment, her arms come around my neck, and she clings to me on a sob. "Atlas," she says.

"Yeah. It's me, baby." I press a kiss to the top of her head. "It's me."

CHAPTER 24

ATLAS

T WENTY MINUTES LATER, WE'RE moving at a slow crawl when the sign of the next exit comes into view.

Thank fuck.

I take the ramp, cursing Teagan for his tinker-toy of a car and say a little prayer the closest place to stop isn't miles from the exit.

Beside me, Mackenzie stares out the window as we round the bend. Color has returned to her cheeks, and she says she's fine, but I can't be sure. She nearly gave me a heart attack earlier, and all I want to do is get her off the road and somewhere warm and dry.

"Which way?" I ask as I come to a stop sign at the end of the ramp.

"I see lights to the right."

"Right it is," I say, thinking about how much easier this would be if we had cell reception.

I turn, and we drive for a couple minutes as the lights grow closer and a sign comes into view for Daybreak Inn & Suites.

Of course it's a hotel. Not that I mind. Both of us could use a good night's sleep after the day we've had, but the last thing I want is to make Doll uncomfortable.

I glance over at her, gauging her reaction and find nothing but mild relief.

Turning into the parking lot, I find an empty space, and together, we head inside without saying anything. The exterior is warm and inviting. The reception desk is straight ahead with a lobby to our right, consisting of several plush couches. I'm not sure how Mackenzie feels about sharing a room with me, so it's my hope they won't mind us camping out for the night, considering the weather.

When the receptionist greets me, I smile and turn on the charm. "We're just passing through and stopped because of the weather. Would you mind if we hang out for a while, wait out the storm."

"You want a room?" she asks in a chipper voice. "You're not the only one stopping for the night." She begins to tap on her keyboard when I stop her.

"Actually, is there any way we can just chill in the lobby?" Based on the way Mackenzie is chewing her lip, I'm 99 percent sure she doesn't want to share a room. "We'll be out as soon as the snow lets up."

The woman's face falls. "Oh. I'm sorry. I'm afraid you can't. It's against policy. Only patrons can use the facilities."

It's a fucking couch, I want to scream.

My face reddens and the hand resting on the desk curls into a fist. "But we can't drive—"

"How much for a room?" Mackenzie interrupts, surprising me with a sweet smile and her hand on my back.

"It's one hundred ten per night, but you have to be twenty-three." The receptionist glances between us, a brow raised.

Mackenzie's face falls before I yank my wallet out of my back pocket and slide out my fake ID, throwing it on the counter along with a handful of cash. "Book us a room. Is your kitchen open?" I ask, desperate for a hot meal.

The woman smiles, typing away in her computer as she says, "I'm sorry. We only open for breakfast."

"Great," I mutter as my stomach growls. Between Mackenzie being attacked by those goons and the shitty weather, I forgot we hadn't eaten anything since we got on the road. We'd been in too much of a hurry to get to the rehabilitation center before visiting hours ended to stop for more than a drink and some chips, and now that we're safe and warm, my stomach remembers.

As if to punctuate my point, it growls, and the receptionist motions to her right. "There are some vending machines at the end of the hall, though, for your convenience."

Well, shit. Thank heavens for conveniences.

"Here you are," the woman says, ignoring the scowl on my face. "You're in room 203. Breakfast is from six-thirty to nine. Let us know if we can do anything, and thank you for choosing Daybreak Inn."

Like we had a fucking choice.

The second we step away from the desk, Mackenzie grins up at me. "A fake ID, huh?"

I shrug. "I'm from Shaker, and there were a couple of clubs . . ." I trail off, waiting for her response, relieved when I see no judgement on her end.

"Well, it served us well tonight. I'll go hunt us down some snacks and meet you at the room," Mackenzie says, and when she places a hand on my arm, my iciness instantly thaws.

"Thanks." The moment she walks away, exhaustion hits me like a freight train. I'm suddenly so tired, I could sleep for a week.

Without another word, I snatch the keycard off the desk and head to our room, wondering how in the hell I'm supposed to behave when I'll be sharing a room with the girl who still holds my heart.

ATLAS

I stare at the massive king-size bed like it's a foreign object. I'd been so exhausted, I forgot to ask for two doubles. I just figured the receptionist would assume that's what we wanted.

Shit.

I run a hand through my hair. This has already been the day from hell for Mackenzie, and now if she wants to sleep, she'll be forced to do so beside me—someone she wasn't even speaking to a week ago.

I think back to the time we left the school until now. We made small talk in the car, but I wouldn't say we were being much more than civil, and with everything that's happened, I might as well kiss my chances of winning her over goodbye. All I've done is make things worse.

I should never have let her go off on her own in an unknown area. In fact, when I saw the weather was supposed to turn sketchy, I should have canceled this whole thing and insisted we wait until next weekend.

She's probably turning everything over in her head as we speak, finding even more reasons to hate me.

A knock on the door behind me interrupts my thoughts, and my stomach twists. I debate my options when I realize I have none. It's not like I can hide the bed or miraculously split it in two.

I turn around and open the door, blocking the entrance to the room. "I didn't realize—" I don't get to finish the sentence as she barrels past and comes to a halt in front of the giant bed.

"Oh." The single word drops from her lips like a bomb.

"I didn't know it was a king room," I rush to say. "I was tired. I just assumed she'd give us doubles, but I can go back down and—"

"No." She shakes her head with a sigh. "You're tired. Just leave it."

"I swear I didn't do this on purpose. I'll just . . . sleep in the chair," I offer, waving to the small wooden chair tucked beneath the desk adjacent to the bed.

Her gaze follows mine. She eyeballs the chair and frowns. "You can't sleep in that."

"I'll be fine—"

"You have the biggest game of your life tomorrow. You need rest. Just . . . can we not make a big deal about it?" she asks, avoiding my gaze. "Listen," she licks her lips and makes her way to the right side of the bed where she takes a seat, dumping the snacks from her purse on the crisp white bedspread. "Now that we're safe and out of the snow, I've had time to think about everything . . ." She swallows and glances up at me, meeting my eyes. "I owe you."

"You don't owe me. If anyone owes someone—" I start to say, but she raises her palm up to stop me.

"I do. You might as well let me say this, and you might want to listen because I'm only going to say this once. You drove me all the way here, so I could confront *your* father. Then you came to my rescue with those jerks. Somehow, you managed to get us here safely without getting creamed on the side of the road. Not to mention you talked me down from my—"

"It was my fault you were upset in the first place," I say, taking a step closer. If she only knew how much I cared. How I'd take on all her pain in a heartbeat if it meant she no longer had to carry it.

"No. It was your father's fault. Yeah, you may have lied to me and hid the truth, and maybe I can't forget that, but it doesn't change the fact that it was your father's actions, and his alone, that killed my mother. Not you."

I swallow, wishing with everything in me I could go back and change how I handled things. Regret is a bitch no one should have to live with.

"You can't control the weather, and as far as those guys are concerned, I never should've taken off on my own at night like that," she continues. "If something had happened, it would've been my fault."

The thought of those punks even laying a hand on her cripples me, and I wonder if she knows I'd gladly give my life to protect her. If those men had been armed, I'd have taken a bullet, no questions asked and without hesitation if it meant sparing her.

But I don't want to scare her. I know how she feels about me now, despite how I feel about her, so I say none of those things. Instead, I keep my mouth shut as hers flattens into a thin line and she clears her throat.

She nudges the junk food in front of her on the bed. "So, I suggest we eat this crappy vending machine food and pretend it's a freaking five-star meal, because I'd like to at least turn one part of this night into something good. Then we're going to try to get some rest before we leave early in the morning, and we're not going to be weird about it. Whatever history we have, and the things that happened in the past, maybe they can't be undone. But just for tonight, we can set them aside. I owe you that much."

I close my eyes, reconciling myself to the fact that I don't want just one night with Mackenzie—I want thousands—but her peace offering is all I'm going to get. If she's willing to set everything aside, I'll take it.

"Does that sound okay to you?" she asks.

I open my eyes and our gazes lock, her eyes earnest on mine. So, I nod, because I'll take this one night. I'll take anything she's willing to give.

CHAPTER 25

MACKENZIE

I SHIVER AND RUB my arms with my hands.

"Cold?" Atlas eyes me for a moment before he slips his hoodie over his head. "Here." He hands it over.

"No. I'm fine, I swear. It was just a chill."

He pushes it closer. "Here. Seriously. I don't need it, and you're cold."

I hesitate a moment before taking it from him and slipping it on, trying my best not to be obvious about the fact that I'm inhaling his scent as I do. "Thank you," I say.

"You're welcome."

I stare over at him as he leans against the headboard of the bed, eating his peanut butter crackers like he's starving. I meant every word I said when I told him I owe him, not only for bringing me down from the episode in the car, but also for coming to my rescue with those creeps in the street. If I'm being honest, it scared me more than I'd like to admit. My mind has conjured up a million ways in which it could've ended if Atlas hadn't been there, and none of them are pretty.

Maybe I can't forget how Atlas lied to me at a time when what I needed most was his honesty. Maybe I can't trust him. But I can forgive him. And I can give him this—a night where we set our differences and the past aside and just be.

"Thanksgiving is only a couple weeks away. What are you doing for it?" I ask, mostly because I'm dreading it this year. It'll be the first one without my mom, and with my father and I barely speaking, I'm not sure how fun it'll be.

He shrugs. "It's been years since I've had a real holiday of any kind, so I'll probably just spend it at my place."

I frown, though I'm not sure what I expected seeing as how he and Cal aren't exactly on the best of terms at the moment. "You'll spend it alone?"

"Most likely." He pops another cracker in his mouth, like it isn't a big deal that at eighteen he has to spend the holidays alone.

I stare at him for a moment while my chest grows tight and I change the subject. "Are you nervous for the game tomorrow?" I ask, staring down at the bag of chips in my hands.

He exhales, his gaze focused on the wall across from him as if thinking. "No. Not really."

"Not at all?"

"I mean, I want to win. It's not that I don't. Part of me feels like everything I've worked hard for over the past four years has led to this moment, but . . ." he trails off, unsure of whether he should continue.

"But what?" I press.

"I dunno." He avoids my eyes as he adds, "A lot of things have been put into perspective in the last month or so, and football is no longer the most important thing to me."

He finally shifts, meeting my gaze, and my throat bobs because I can read his meaning. Football is no longer the most important thing to him; I am.

Clearing my throat, I pull my eyes away. "You're going to get an amazing offer to an incredible school. I just know it."

"That's the goal."

"If you could choose any school, where would you go?" I ask, taking a drink of my water as I try and forget the heat of his gaze on me.

"I've thought a lot about this, actually."

I nod, encouraging him to continue as he stares down at the package of crackers in his hands. "And . . .?"

"It's hard because my answer might have changed?" he says more like a question. "I wouldn't mind somewhere warmer, that's for damn sure."

"You don't enjoy this lovely Ohio weather we're having?"

He snorts out a laugh and shakes his head. "Definitely not my thing."

"You said your answer might have changed. How so?" I ask, realizing that same urge to learn everything about him—to get a rare glimpse inside his head—still exists as much as it did months ago, when we first met.

"Before . . . well, I probably would've followed you." His gaze quickly darts my way while my heart kickstarts in my chest. "I would've gone anywhere you went, even if it meant going to a lesser school and team, but now I don't know."

My stomach sinks at the acknowledgment that things have changed, and I wonder why it hurts so much more hearing it come from him.

"What about you?" he asks, breaking my train of thought. "What do you plan on doing after we graduate?"

I lift a shoulder. "I'm not sure. Before the accident, I wanted to go to college, maybe teach. Afterward, I spent so much time recovering and just trying to find normalcy. Hell, I think I'm still doing that. And now . . ." I trail off, shaking my head. "Sometimes I think about this experience I had in seventh grade. At the time it meant nothing to me, but we were learning about drugs and alcohol in health class, and the DARE program came to speak. You know, the one with the dog?"

"McGruff?" Atlas grins. "I hated it when they came. I always felt like they were pointing the finger, like all my friends knew my dad was a junkie."

My stomach clenches and I marvel at how two kids can have such completely different experiences.

"That's terrible," I say, my voice flat.

"It's fine."

It's not fine, but I get the impression he wants to move on, so I continue, "Well, I remember they had a speaker. It was a mother who lost her son to drunk driving, and she was using her experience to educate others and bring awareness. Lately, my thoughts drift to that woman and I wonder if I might have something to give, too. I mean, if I can weather this storm, maybe I can help others." I huff out a laugh and pick at a thread on the comforter. "I don't know. Maybe that's a stupid idea."

"No. I don't think it's stupid at all," he says so fiercely, it draws my gaze. His eyes are so rich and dark, it's like staring into a black hole I could easily get lost in. After a moment, I force myself to look away, and I glance at the fat snowflakes still falling like tufts of cotton outside our window. "Any fun plans for after graduation?" I ask. "Before you leave and become some college football superstar?"

He rolls his eyes. "Unlikely."

"Very likely. You're amazing." I smile, almost wistfully. "I won't be surprised if you get drafted," I say, part of me wishing I could be there to see it.

"That's a pipe dream." He brushes the crumbs off his lap, then says, "Don't get me wrong, I love football, and I'd be thrilled to get a spot on a team somewhere. But the NFL is the stuff of dreams, so if it doesn't happen for me, I won't be disappointed. I'm just grateful for the chance to play through college and that it will get me a free ride."

"That's very mature of you. What will you do if not football?"

"I think I'd like to do something with kids. Would it be lame if I said I wanted to be a teacher?"

"Not at all," I say. The truth is I can see Atlas being great with kids. In fact, something warm fists inside my chest at the thought.

"And maybe coach somewhere. Not high school but younger." He stares down at his hands for a moment and I wonder what he's thinking. "It would be cool to help shape kids who maybe don't have anyone to look up to at home, ya know? Maybe I could be that person for some of them."

My heart pinches, and I swallow. "Those kids would be lucky to have you. I think you'd be an amazing mentor."

"Yeah?"

"Definitely."

"I went to see my brother," he blurts.

My eyes widen. "You did?"

He nods. "He was playing football, and he was pretty incredible," he says with a half-laugh. Then he sobers, and I can see something flicker in his eyes before he continues. "And I talked to my mom. I wasn't intending to, but she saw me and cornered me. Anyway, long story short, she didn't quite abandon me like I thought she did." He shakes his head. "I mean, she left, obviously, but there was more to it—*a lot* more, actually. And it involves the Scotts, all of them."

My forehead creases. "So, what does this mean for you and your mom?"

He rolls his neck on his shoulders as if thinking. "Hell if I know. Maybe we can find a way to repair our relationship in the future? I don't know. I still have a lot of shit to work through. She made mistakes and I'm still mad about it. But maybe she's not quite the villain I thought she was."

"Wow, that's . . . crazy? Great for you to find out? I don't know . . ." I laugh, feeling self-conscious because I have no idea how to respond to such a significant revelation.

My thoughts drift to my own mother and how angry I am with her, yet I'd give anything to have her back. "Hey, can I ask you something?"

"Shoot."

"How did you know white hydrangeas were my mother's favorite flower?"

He stares at me a moment, his gaze searching mine as if he's debating on telling me the truth. "At Mancetti's . . . that time I took you . . . They were everywhere. In the flower beds surrounding his house. Fresh cut in vases in the living room and kitchen. It was a good guess."

I nod as a stab of pain hits me square in the chest.

I hadn't noticed.

He crumples up his empty snack wrapper, then glances at me. "Anyway, we should probably get some rest, huh?"

"Yeah." I nod, knowing it's the smart thing to do. After the day we've had, we should both be exhausted, and when we first arrived, I was. But now I don't feel so tired. If anything, I'm oddly wired. And besides, I still have the treat I scored for him from the vending machine, so I don't say anything else. Instead, I sit in the same spot, neither of us moving as we glance over at each other.

"Unless, you're not tired yet. We could stay up a little while," he suggests, and I break out into a wide smile.

"Yeah, that sounds good, actually."

CHAPTER 26

MACKENZIE

"**I** think I want to run a marathon," I say as I stare straight ahead.

"Seriously?" He places an arm behind his head as he leans against the headboard, glancing over at me.

"Yeah. Most of them are coming up in the spring. I'd like to do a big one, though. With all those people, I think crossing the finish line would be pretty exciting."

"That's, like, miles, right?"

I laugh, one arm wrapped around my belly. "It's a little over twenty-six."

He whistles, and it makes me feel like a superwoman even though I haven't even done anything yet. "That's fucking awesome. I'd probably die. I hate running."

"Yeah, right." I roll my eyes and shove at his arm. "You're in incredible shape and the fastest one on the team."

"I still hate it. I'm serious," he says at my continued doubt. "I mean, I'm fast. Great with sprints, but shit, I hate running." He crosses a finger over his chest. "Swear. Lifting weights, I like. Cardio, not so much, it kills me. I only run because I have to."

"Well, I love it," I say, blushing at the wistful sound of my own voice. I have Graham to thank for my love of running. I wonder what he's doing right now. I hate how we ended things the last time we spoke.

"What's that look for?" he asks beside me, his voice soft.

"What look?" I ask, trying to wipe away my guilt.

"The one that looks like someone kicked your puppy."

I sigh and shake my head. "Nothing."

"Nope. Not nothing."

"Trust me. You don't wanna hear about it." I bite my lip, knowing he won't let this go but I'm reluctant to tell him.

"Come on," he says, glancing over at me, his arm still tucked behind his head. "After all the shit we've been through, you can't tell me?"

"It's just . . ." I swallow, unsure if this is a good idea. Where Atlas is concerned, Graham is tricky territory. "I'm worried about him. He's been drinking a lot and he's angry all the time," I say leaving out the part where he's still hung up on me. "And now this thing with his father . . . their relationship was bad before. I don't think they'll recover from this, but it's not Cal I'm worried about."

Atlas nods and his brows pull together as if thinking. "Yeah. I've noticed that, too, and I can't imagine the news that he shares a brother with me was well received, either."

I snort. "That's one way to put it."

He shifts, picking his water bottle up off the nightstand to toy with the cap. "Maybe after the dust settles and we're done with football, I'll talk to him."

Hope ignites in my chest. "Really? You'd do that?"

"For you? I'd do anything."

"Worst movie of all time," he deadpans.

I gasp and lean toward him, crossing my legs on the bed. "How can you even say that?

"How can you possibly defend it? Seriously, on behalf of all feminists, I'm appalled. The movie *Grease* sends a terrible message."

"But it's so good, though," I yell.

He eyeballs me. "At the end of the movie, Sandy completely transforms for Danny to be 'cool'"—he makes quotes with his fingers—"instead of just staying the nerdy, good girl she is."

"Yeah, but Danny did the same for her. Remember when he tried to be a jock and joined the track team?"

"Yeah, and that lasted for all of five minutes before Sandy decided that if she wanted to be with him, she'd better loosen up, ignore her own morals, and become a Pink Lady."

I cross my arms over my chest. He has a point, but I refuse to admit it. "I don't care what you say. *Grease* is easily one of the best movies of all time. A total classic."

He scoffs, crossing his arms over his chest as he shakes his head. "Nope. *The Sound of Music* is a classic."

I break out into a huge smile. "You watch *The Sound of Music*?"

He lifts a shoulder. "I like listening to Julie Andrews sing, so sue me."

"Oh my. That is . . ." I splutter out a laugh. "Hearing you, Atlas Scott, macho bad boy and superstar footballer loves *The Sound of Music* has made my whole night." I shake my head, grinning as I bite my thumbnail. "Maybe even my whole year."

\#

ATLAS

I burst out laughing at the sight of Jeff Daniels clinging to Jim Carrey on the back of his moped, then pop a fruit snack in my mouth. I feel Mackenzie's eyes on me and turn. "What?"

"Nothing." She grins. "I'm just not sure I've ever heard you laugh this much before." She reaches out and steals one of the snacks from my hands. "In fact, the last time I saw you this carefree might've been the day we met all your old teammates and I shamed you on the field."

"Shamed me, did you?" I ask, and when she laughs, I chuck a gummy at her head. Turning my attention back to the screen, I motion toward the TV. "It's *Dumb and Dumber*. How can you not laugh?"

Mackenzie chuckles. "It's so stupid."

"Exactly!" I yell, waving toward the television. "That's the whole point. It's completely ridiculous and mindless comedy."

"It's the dumbest thing I've ever seen," she says, eyeing the screen with one brow raised.

"It's fucking funny, that's what it is, which is precisely why it's called comedy. It's much better than watching a girl with purple hair singing about going to beauty school."

"Hey!" She whacks me with a pillow on the side of the arm as she laughs. "I guess comedies are *okay*," she says like she doesn't really mean it.

Atlas rolls his eyes. "What's your favorite movie genre? Let me guess. Romance?"

She narrows her eyes at me, her posture defensive, and I know I have her pegged.

I stifle a laugh as I eat another fruit snack. It's either that or lean forward and tug her extremely cute and sexy pouty lower lip between my teeth.

This is less likely to get me punched.

"There's nothing better than a good old-fashioned romance. After all, love makes the world go round."

"Right. And after love smashes your heart to bits, comedy is what lifts you up." The second the words leave my mouth, I regret them. I squeeze my eyes closed, hoping she doesn't take what I said personally. I mean, shit, she tore my heart to bits when she broke up with me, but I had it coming. It's fair to say, I did the same to her by lying to her.

But when I hear the soft sound of her laughter, I blink them open as she says, "Touché, Atlas Scott. Touché."

God, I've missed this. Missed her.

MACKENZIE

My stomach flutters with anticipation. "Do you still carry that lighter with you all the time?" I ask, nodding toward his jeans.

"This lighter?" His brow furrows as he reaches inside his pocket and pulls out the silver Zippo.

"That's the one. Let me see it." I wiggle my fingers, and he tosses it to me. I take it, ignoring his frown as I snag my purse on the way into the small bathroom and remove one of the Hostess cupcakes I found in the vending machine earlier. With a flick of the wrist, I light the small candle I practically begged the receptionist for. It may not be a personalized birthday cake with his name on it, but it's our only option, so it'll have to do.

I carefully lift the cupcake and start to turn for the door when I catch my reflection in the mirror and pause. Atlas's hoodie swims on me, yet I love the way it looks, let alone the feel of it on my skin and the way it smells of him. My gaze flickers over my rosy cheeks, the hair pulled into a messy bun on the top of my head, and my normally pale blue eyes which have darkened to sapphires.

I look happy. Happier than I've been in weeks, which is saying something considering the day I've had and the fact that I'm currently stranded in a subpar hotel room with the boy who betrayed me.

I know I said we'd put a hold on reality for tonight and we'd forget the past and everything that's happened between us, but if I'm being honest with myself, I'm not just giving Atlas a pass for today. He's thawing my heart; I can feel it. I'm just not sure what to do about it.

"You okay in there?" Atlas calls out, concern laced in his voice, and it's not hard to understand why. First, I ask him to borrow his lighter, then I disappear into the bathroom for five minutes.

I laugh at myself and shake my head, reining my thoughts back in.

For tonight, I won't analyze anything. I won't worry about what happened yesterday, or what might happen tomorrow, or dissect how I'm feeling. For once, I want to live in the moment. After all, if the past has taught me anything, tomorrow isn't guaranteed, and right now, there's nowhere I'd rather be.

I spin on my heel before I can overthink it and emerge with the lit cupcake in hand, pleased when Atlas lifts his gaze to find me and his eyes brighten. "It might not be a birthday cake," I say, "but it'll have to do."

An emotion I can't decipher moves through his gaze as I come to a stop in front of where he sits on the bed, his eyes on me the entire way. "Where'd you get the candle?" he asks, his voice soft.

"It's from the dining room. I had to practically beg the receptionist to let me borrow it."

"I don't know what to say." His throat bobs, and he reaches back to rub his neck.

"What's wrong?" My stomach tightens.

Did I do something wrong?

Nerves jump in my belly as he clears his throat, glances away from me for a moment, then back again. "Nothing. It's just . . . no one has ever really done this for me."

"Done what?" I frown.

"Celebrated me. At least not since . . . when I was four I was obsessed with dinosaurs. My mother bought me this huge cake, just for us. It had blue piping and a giant T. rex in the middle of it. She left two weeks later. It was the last birthday cake I ever got."

The air leaves my lungs as I glance down to the cupcake in my hands, thinking of all the birthday celebrations I had growing up. How special my parents made each and every one. Not a year went by when I didn't have my own cake and at least something to unwrap. No child should have to go a year without at least being acknowledged. "Your father never . . ." I start, almost afraid to ask.

He shakes his head. "No. These last few years, my dad was usually too strung out or drunk to care, and earlier on, he was either busy working or chasing his next fix, so he never remembered." He shrugs. "Or maybe he did and he just didn't care. I don't know."

The thought of Atlas going year after year without so much as a birthday wish tears me up inside. Suddenly, I'm more grateful for this crappy vending machine cupcake than anything in my life, because he's a person worth celebrating. "Well," I say, clearing my throat, "since it's been a while, I guess I'd better sing to you."

He laughs and the storm clouds of his past clear from his eyes. His smile lights up his whole face. "You really don't have to do that."

"I insist. It's tradition and I refuse to let another birthday go by where you don't get sung to. So, here goes . . ." I take a deep breath, then launch into my best rendition of "Happy Birthday", my voice soft and smooth. When I finish, I hold the cupcake out. Thick beads of wax run down the candle as I wait expectantly. "Make a wish," I say.

Atlas's gaze darkens as he leans in, his eyes never leaving mine as he inhales and blows out the candle. My cheeks heat as I hand him the cake, watching as he removes the oversized candle and licks off all of the frosting while my entire body flushes.

"Thank you," he murmurs. "No one has ever done this for me before."

I nod, ignoring the throbbing ache deep inside. The one that yearns to pull him close, hold him in my arms, and promise him he'll never go another birthday alone.

But I can do none of those things because we're not together anymore and I'm not sure we ever will be.

"It was a little thing," I say, because it's true. He deserves a whole lot more, and it saddens me I can't be the one to give it to him.

"Maybe," he says, "but it means a lot, so much more than you'll ever know."

He holds my gaze a moment longer before his eyes drop to my mouth, and a flurry of butterflies erupt inside my chest.

My lips ache for his lips.

My skin yearns for his touch.

I lean forward, closing the gap between us and brush my lips over his—the touch so featherlight, I think I might have imagined it—before I pull away again.

Even if I allowed us to be together tonight, it would only be temporary. It'd never last, and so with deep sorrow, I clear my throat and say, "We should probably try and get some sleep."

CHAPTER 27

GRAHAM

I CLIMB INTO THE driver's seat of my car and slam the door shut. I've tried calling Mackenzie ever since school let out but got no answer. I wanted to talk to her—to apologize for being such a dick. Seeing as how I acted the last time we talked, I assumed she was ignoring my calls. Can't say I blame her if she is. But after climbing into her window and finding her bedroom empty after one a.m., I'm not so sure.

I grab my phone off the center console and give her another call, listening as it rings, unsurprised when there's no answer.

Where the hell is she?

I stare out of my window, afraid I know the answer because coincidentally, Atlas has been MIA all evening, too.

But I can't think about that now, or I'll go crazy.

I need to get out of here. I need a release, some way to get my mind off my father, the pressure of States tomorrow, and the fact that I'm 99 percent sure Mackenzie and Atlas are together.

As if I conjured it myself, my phone rings. I glance at the screen. *Darrell Crenshaw.*

I rub a hand over my face, wondering if he's calling to collect early on my debt. I debate on whether to answer or not, then hit accept and press the phone to my ear. "Hey, man," I say, trying to keep my tone even.

"Graham. Hey, I know it's late, but we have an intense game happening right now."

I frown and lick my lips. "Don't I still owe you from last time?"

"If you want in, we'll put your debt on hold. Hell, maybe you can even win it back. But this is high stakes, so it's not for the faint of heart. If you're in, prepare to bet big."

Which means I can either win big or lose big.

I think about the first night Peters took me to the Play House. I won most hands that night, putting me up nearly a thousand dollars, and I only owe Darrell a thousand bucks now. It's not that much in the grand scheme of things.

Hell, if opening bets are high, I only need a couple of good hands to win my money back and then some.

And damn if I don't need a win tonight, something to make me feel like I haven't completely fucked everything in my life up.

I squeeze the phone in my hand, only debating for a moment before I reply. "Okay, count me in."

I'll figure out where to get the money later.

An orangey glow from the pendant lamps above us illuminate the faces of the men around me. The pudgy one to my right swivels a whiskey in his hands. The one with the mustache sitting opposite me smokes a cigar, the pungent scent filling the air between us, while Darrell taps his ringed fingers over the felt surface of the table.

I sit back in my seat, smug with my four of a kind, ace-high, as I watch person after person show their cards to reveal a lower hand.

The dealer picks my cards back up. "Winner goes to the four of a kind, ace-high."

I croon as I rake in the pot, which has to be close to five grand. When I initially got here and Darrell announced blind bets would start at two hundred bucks, I'd been nervous. I can't afford to lose big tonight when I already owe him. But now, I have enough to pay back my debt, plus a little extra spending cash to get me started.

We play three more rounds, with me winning one. I'm slightly up but my cash is low. Still, I'm optimistic.

Two hours later, I stare at the cards in my hands. They're complete shit; I should've folded. I've got nothing, but was holding out on the last community card, praying for the ten of hearts to give me a straight flush, but it never came.

A bead of sweat rolls down my neck as I watch the guy across from me win a kitty worth twenty thousand dollars. I bet everything I had on that last hand. Or, rather, all the credit Darrell was willing to give. Now, I'm somehow in debt ten thousand fucking dollars. It's so much money, I can't even believe Darrell allowed me to stay in.

"Last hand of the night," the dealer announces.

Shit.

My eyes bug out of my head as I wipe my forehead with the back of my hand, wondering what the hell I'm going to do to get him the money I owe. My only hope is to win it back on this last hand, but I don't even know if he'll let me play, let alone if I'll win.

Blind bet is announced, and I toss in my car keys. The guy beside me scoffs while Darrell shakes his head. "We don't take collateral."

"Not even an electric blue Corvette Stingray?" I arch my brow, trying to play it cool. If I show him how desperate I am, he might not let me in.

"Kid, you better sit this one out." The man next to me chuckles, and his belly shakes like fucking Santa Claus. He's been downing whiskeys all night and folded more than half his hands.

"Yeah, kid," Cigar man chimes in. "Listen to us and go home."

My cheeks heat with embarrassment, and I fight the urge to stand up and flip the table just to piss these guys off, but something tells me I don't want to make an enemy of Darrell.

He eyes me, legs crossed as he plays with a wad of cash in front of him. His lips purse as he lazily swirls the scotch in his glass, his eyes darker than midnight. "Frankie, what do you think?" he asks, glancing back at the muscled bartender, who I've come to learn is his right-hand man.

Frankie leans over the counter, a wall of booze bottles at his back. He swipes once at the gleaming bar with the towel in his hand. "I say let him play."

A shit-eating grin spreads over my face as I glance back at Darrell, waiting for his direction because nothing happens at the Play House without his approval.

"Okay," he says. "You're in. Car counts toward your bet."

Sitting back in my chair, I wait as the dealer passes out the cards, then peek at mine. A ten of clubs and ten of spades.

I blow out a shaky breath. *Looks like I'm going for four of a kind.*

When the dealer turns over the three community cards, he has a jack of hearts, king of hearts, and a ten of diamonds.

I pray for another ten as each player makes their bets. Four of a kind seem to be my magic spot.

When they turn to me, I nod, trying to sound more confident than I feel "I'm in," I tell them.

The dealer turns over the fourth card. Five of spades.

Damn it.

My leg begins to shake under the table.

Darrell frowns, cocking his head as the others place their bets. "What's that sound?"

I stop, pressing a hand to my thigh to keep it steady as I grit my teeth.

It's my turn. I either bow out now and owe him more than ten grand—a huge sum I have no idea how I'll ever pay—or I stay in and risk losing even more.

My palms begin to sweet as all eyes focus on me. It's an impossible choice. I could be fucked either way.

I nod at the dealer, unable to verbalize that I'd like to place a bet to stay in because I'm so fucking terrified my voice won't work.

The dealer turns over the fifth community card, revealing the ten of hearts.

Let's go!

A shiver of anticipation races up my spine. Adrenaline replaces my fear. This time when bets are placed, I feel a little lighter. Until the portly guy next to me, the one that's folded half his hands, raises by three grand.

I blink over at him, unsure of whether I heard correctly, but he's perfectly serious. Another player folds, but three stay in when it's my turn. A tiny voice inside my gut tells me to fold, to cut and run. I owe a shit ton of money, but I stand to lose a lot more.

Then I think of all the times I've won impossible hands, and my head tells me I'm golden. No way could I lose; it's too much money. It's too crazy to even imagine getting myself in that deep.

"Call," I say, and the dealer takes my cards. "A ten of clubs and ten of spades makes four of a kind."

He holds onto my cards and one by one, reveals the other player's. A straight, king high. Four of a kind, five high. Full house.

I close my eyes for a brief moment. I'm still the winning hand and so close I can almost taste it. One more . . .

The dealer turns to the final player. Santa Claus shoves his cards at him, a viscous gleam in his eyes that makes my back sweat.

I swallow, watching as the dealer turns over the first card. "Queen of hearts."

No.

My gaze flickers back over to the community cards, to the jack and king of hearts.

It can't be . . .

Only two things beat four of a kind. A straight flush and royal flush, but a royal flush is so hard to get, it's practically unheard of.

When the dealer turns over his final card to reveal an ace of hearts, my worst fears come to fruition.

My throat instantly turns to sandpaper.

My stomach sinks.

I might be sick as the dealer announces, "Ace of hearts makes a royal flush and wins the pot."

I push back from the table so abruptly, my chair falls to the floor with a thunderous crash. All eyes shift in my direction. I can feel their gazes burning into my skin while my feet itch to run.

What the hell am I going to do?

My mind races as my gaze homes in on the set of cars keys in the middle of the table, and I realize how screwed I am.

Santa starts to rake in his cash as Darrell stops him, plucking my keys from the pot before he whispers something in Kris Kringle's ear.

A momentary wave of relief washes through me. He's going to cut me a break. Give my car back. I'm just a stupid kid that got in too deep.

He chucks them at me, confirming my suspicions. I catch them as they hit me in the chest and open my mouth to express my gratitude when he stands and makes his way toward me. "As I said, we don't take collateral."

Darrell snaps his fingers and Frankie appears at his side, a fresh cigar and lighter in his hand. Pinching the end of the stogie, Frankie flicks the lighter to life, lighting it as Darrell takes a puff and blows a plume of smoke in my face. "You see, the moment you leave here, what you lost will sink in. You'll panic, run home, and tell Daddy Dearest your car was stolen."

"I won't," I say, but he ignores me.

"The next thing you know, we'll have officers at our door. And I can't have that." He shakes his head, his dark eyes on mine. "No. I want cash. Fifteen thousand and your debt is paid in full."

Fifteen grand? Even though my car is worth a lot more, I nearly choke on the sum.

I lick my lips, my forehead creasing with worry as my heart pounds a staccato beat. "I need time."

"And you'll have it." He stares at the cigar in his hand before he flicks ash on my shoes. "Two weeks." He steps forward, his tone lethal as he continues. "And then we're coming to collect."

CHAPTER 28

MACKENZIE

I T'S ALMOST TWO A.M., and I can't sleep.

I curl into a ball on my side and punch my pillow, acutely aware of the boy beside me. I can feel the heat of his body radiating from his side of the bed. Everything about him draws me in. It's as though my body has been finely tuned to sense his presence and no matter what I do, I can't seem to stop thinking about him.

I replay the fire in his eyes when he leaned in to blow out the candle. The way his deep baritone lit me up inside. The warmth of his breath before the soft press of our lips. I turn the conversation we shared over and over in my head until I forget all the reasons we can't be together, only to remember them again with regret.

My mind is a dangerous place; it's full of conflicting thoughts, dead ends, and sharp turns.

I close my eyes and he's all I see, no roadblocks in sight.

I open them, and he's all I think about.

His scent fills my lungs. Any more and I might go insane, so I remove his hoodie. Maybe I can sleep if I'm no longer surrounded by him.

"You can't sleep either?" His voice pierces the quiet, and I freeze.

"No." A shiver racks my body without his jersey to keep me warm. Or maybe it's his voice that has me shaking.

A moment passes, and I can hear him breathing in the silence.

"Do you want to know what I wished for?" he asks, his voice low.

I shake my head, my throat bobbing with the movement. "It's bad luck to tell me," I say, closing my eyes and praying for sleep. No good will come of this conversation.

"I wished for you," he murmurs.

The breath catches in my throat.

"You're all I want, Kenz. Then, now, always. If you ask me fifty years from now, my answer will be the same."

"Atlas . . ." I fist the sheet in front of me to keep myself from rolling over, from saying or doing something I might regret. "You can't say stuff like that."

"Why not? It's true." The mattress dips with the weight of his body, and I can sense he's rolled onto his side. Heat radiates from his skin, warming the length of my back until it feels like he's pressed up against me even though I know he's not. I shudder when he softly whispers, "You're the only thing I've wanted for a long time and I'd do anything, give anything, to have you again."

I inhale, my nostrils flaring. I can't hear this right now—I can't—and I have half a mind to cover my ears to drown him out.

"Give me one good reason we can't be together," he continues.

I blink my eyes open, staring into the dark abyss of the room as I search for words. "You lied." My words are tiny, inadequate to the longing inside.

"You know why I did. It's not like . . ." He reaches out, curling one arm around my waist and pulling me into the hard plains of his chest while his warm, minty breath tickles the side of my face. "I never had any cruel intention of keeping the truth from you. I planned on telling you. I just didn't know how because I was so damn afraid you wouldn't be able to see past it. So, give me another reason because I don't accept. That's not good enough."

"We can't change facts, and the fact of the matter is your father killed my mother. How do we get over that? I don't know how to move forward with that hanging over our heads. It's an impossible bridge to mend."

"So, I was right to fear telling you."

I roll toward him, my chest brushing against his. I know it's a mistake the second I do, because this close—staring into his dark eyes—I want him more than I've ever wanted anything. More than I want air to breathe or food and water to sustain me.

"You act like everything is so simple. Like, the past is the past. But your father is sober now. He's going to want a relationship with you again. We both saw it when we were there, which means he'll be in your life more than ever before. I can't just forget—"

"Fuck him." His eyes harden to stone as he meets my gaze. "He hasn't been a father to me for as long as I can remember, if ever. I don't care what he wants. If it means losing you, I don't want anything to do with him."

I shake my head and stare down at my hands, fisted out in front of myself. They're the only physical barrier between us. Tears clog the back of my throat. "You mean that now, but—"

"No buts. I want *you*. Nothing and no one else. Not my father, football, money, or even a scholarship if I can't have you in my life. Because without you, those things mean nothing. They're meaningless. Until you came along, I was half a man, just living a shell of a life. Going through the motions and being bitter at the world. But you changed me." He fists a hand over his chest. "You fixed holes inside my heart so deep I never thought anyone could mend them. *You,* you did that. And I'll be damned if I'm gonna just give that up without a fight."

I close my eyes.

"You once told me the world and everything in it could be against us, but you'd still love me. Did you mean it?"

"Of course I did, but—"

"Then don't give up and walk away. Right now the world and everything in it *are* against us. Yet I still love you." He brushes a lock of hair from the side of my face, and he's so beautiful, it makes my heart hurt. "Sometimes the best things in life are hard, but it's up to us to fight for them."

"Why are you doing this?" I ask, my voice trembling, ready to crack.

He slides his arms around me, and with them, the last hold I have on my resolve weakens.

"Why are you trying so hard to deny something so right?" he whispers against my chin. Pressing his lips to my jaw, he drags his mouth over my throat while the blood hums in my veins.

I have no answer. My words are lost in the sensation of his touch as his mouth teases, drifting to the shell of my ear, over my cheekbone, down my neck again, and to my clavicle.

The breath rasps in my lungs while the heat of his mouth consumes my thoughts. Every nerve ending comes alive as he lifts himself to hover above me and my skin breaks out in goose-flesh. Exhaling, I feel the moment my composure snaps, and I give in to the fire in my belly, the yearning in my soul. "Loving you scares me," I whisper.

He presses his forehead to mine, his breathing heavy. "That's because love is a leap of faith. And any leap of faith is frightening. But there's so much to gain by jumping."

"And to lose," I say, feeling the weight of my words.

"You won't lose me, doll. You've had my heart from the moment I met you, and I won't hurt you again," he says, smoothing back my hair.

My eyes close. I needed to hear those words, and with them, my remaining willpower eviscerates.

Crushing my mouth to his, my skin heats as a moan rumbles in the back of my throat. His lips are warm and soft. They feel like home.

He drags his hands down my torso until they reach the hem of my shirt and move beneath the soft cotton. I part my mouth as he angles his head, his tongue brushing mine, and I realize with blistering clarity I missed this—missed him, every single part of him.

He cages my body with his own as my hands tangle in his hair, drifting to his strong back, the powerful muscles moving beneath his skin.

When he pauses and stares down at me, the intensity in his gaze melts me. "I love you," he says, his tone so fierce, it gives me chills. And then his mouth is on mine again—the kiss is different this time; a promise of what's to come—as my eyes flutter closed.

His hands move to my body, making me come alive with the sensation of his touch. The air turns heavy, blistering with the heat of our bodies, as he reaches up, intertwining our fingers as the rest of the world fades away, and only we remain.

I prop myself up on my arm, staring down at Atlas's chest and marveling at his chiseled physique. From his muscular pecs to the ripple of muscle over his abdomen, he's utter perfection.

I bite my lip, hiding a grin.

"What's that look for?" He reaches out and uses the pad of his thumb to pull my lower lip from beneath my teeth.

"Nothing. Your body, it's just . . ." I grin, my cheeks going pink with the trajectory of my thoughts.

"It's just what?" He laughs.

"Insane," I whisper, then cover my face with my hands, wondering how I can be so shy after what we just shared.

Atlas reaches out, chuckling as his strong hands remove my own so he can see my face. "Look at me," he whispers, and I listen. "That's better."

Leaning closer, I trail my finger over his bicep, the one with the tattoos. "There are so many."

"They've certainly grown in number since my first one," he says, holding his arm out so I can take a closer look.

I run my fingers over the ink, tracing the intricate designs as I assess each one. "I've never gotten to really look at them like this. Up close . . . intimate." My gaze flickers to his again, almost shyly.

"Look all you want." He props himself up on his pillows while he offers his arm.

I sit up, gripping the inked arm and stare down at it. "Which one was your first"

He groans. "My first one was lame."

I laugh. "Now you really have to show me."

He turns his arm slightly and points to the underside of his bicep.

"A skull?" I say, taking a closer look at the hollowed-out eyes and stark cheekbones.

He nods. "Not exactly original, but I got my first one at sixteen. I was working and making better money, so I viewed it as a celebration of sorts." He shrugs.

"Why a tattoo?"

"You don't like my ink?" he asks, arching a dark brow. He looks so good I want to lean forward and press my lips to his, but I know where it will lead and I want this moment to study him.

"I love it, but why not a pair of new shoes, a new outfit, or a nice dinner? Why *this*?"

"Oh, you mean, like something practical?" He grins. I love this playful side of him. When he's like this, joking and smiling, it's hard to remember that he has such a heavy past.

I nod and smile, waiting for his answer.

"I probably should have used my money more wisely. But I don't know . . . I started to crave the slow torture of the needle. It gave me something to focus on other than the pain inside. Even the meaningless ones, like the skull which meant nothing, worked as a way to distract myself. Getting new ink gave me an outlet, a way to express myself like nothing else."

My heart aches for him as I stare down at his arm. "So which ones are meaningful?" I ask, wanting this little bit of insight into his soul.

"A lot of them, actually."

He's being evasive, so I roll my eyes. "Okay, which are the *most* meaningful. Give me your top three."

He stills, his eyes steady on mine, and for a moment I wonder if he's going to refuse to show me. But then he raises and bends his arm, showing me the back of his tricep where a dagger pierces a prescription bottle. Pills scatter beside it, each marked with an X.

"Your father," I say, breathless as he nods, his jaw tight.

I move my fingers over the bottle and the dagger—slowly, gently—as if I can feel the anguish that evoked the ink. It doesn't take a genius to decipher the meaning behind this particular piece of artwork. When he lowers his arm, offering me the underside of his forearm, my gaze homes in on a date written in decorative script beneath some feathery vines. Suddenly, I'm sure this is the next one he wants to show me. "The date . . . what is it?"

"The day my mother left," he says, his voice a quiet rasp.

My heart pinches, and without thinking, I lower myself and brush my lips against the numbers. His breath hitches while I take my time, kissing each one in the shallow hope it might somehow offer him solace. It's a feeble offering to the heartbreak those numbers caused, but it's all I have. If I could, I'd fold him in my arms, crush my mouth to his and promise him he'll never hurt again. I'd take the pain of his past and bury it with mine. Smother the darkness inside of him with happiness and light.

After I place the last kiss over the date, he inhales a shaky breath as he shows me the side of his arm, right over the curve of his bicep. It takes a moment for me to realize what I'm looking at, but once I do, I see more than one scattered over his arm in varying shapes and sizes. Dandelions. One is barely a flowering bud, roots intact as if someone pulled it straight from the ground. Over the curve of his muscle, another has gone to seed and dandelion snow floats between the other tattoos like little helicopters. Another in full bloom stands tall and proud near the back of his shoulder.

"Dandelions," I say, breathless. "They're beautiful. But what do they mean?"

"A lot of people think of dandelions as a weed, a nuisance to be eradicated. But that couldn't be further from the truth. Did you know they're masters at survival?"

"Tell me," I say, my voice soft as I blink up at him.

"They can root almost anywhere, some in miraculous places. Once they do, they're nearly impossible to get rid of. No matter how many times you cut them down, they keep coming back. They have long roots and can pop up through gravel and cement, thriving in the worst of conditions. Despite their ability to heal and their medicinal properties and uses, they're still overlooked. Yet they survive in spite of their shitty environment. In spite of being unwanted."

"Oh, Atlas . . ." My throat tightens and my eyes grow damp, powerless to stop the press of emotion rising inside of me. If only he knew how wanted he is, how strong, and beautiful. Just like a dandelion.

A tear breaks free and rolls down my cheek, only for Atlas to brush it away with his thumb, then cup my face in his hands and lean toward me for a kiss.

Our lips meet and I allow my mouth to do all the talking, tell him all of my secrets, all of my fears. How strong he is. How admired. How perfectly imperfect. Both of us are broken, but together, we're somehow better. Stronger.

Together, we're perfect in all the ways that count.

CHAPTER 29

MACKENZIE

I WAKE WITH A jolt, startled by the sound of buzzing.

I blink, eyes bleary with sleep, when I glance at the hotel clock to see it's after four in the morning. In another hour we'll have to start our journey back home but, until then, I snuggle into the warmth of Atlas's chest, encased in his arms.

When the buzzing returns, I open my eyes once more and spot my phone on the nightstand beside me, the screen glowing in the dark as it vibrates. Carefully, I move Atlas's arm and reach out, picking up my phone and glancing at the screen.

Graham.

I swallow while my stomach does a nosedive, and I go to put it back when something stops me. Debating, I wait until voice mail picks up, then it starts to ring again. I slowly get out of bed, being careful not to wake Atlas.

Glancing behind me, I take in his peaceful expression, the sharp angles of his face softened by sleep, and my heart flutters.

With a grin, I head into the bathroom and close the door behind me. I reach into the shower and turn the water on, hoping to drown out the sound of my voice when I answer. "Graham?"

"Kenz, thank God."

I note the panicked edge to his voice and move to the sink. "Graham, what is it? What's wrong?"

"I'm sorry I called you so early, but I needed to talk to you. I went to your house, but you weren't there."

He went to my house at this hour?

Frowning, I glance toward the bedroom where Atlas is asleep. "I'm at Anastasia's," I say, my tone flat as the weight of the lie settles in the pit of my stomach like a stone.

"Right, of course. You're probably leaving together in the morning. For a moment, I thought . . . Never mind. It doesn't matter."

I close my eyes, pressing a hand to the churning in my stomach because I know what he thought. And he's right. I *am* with Atlas.

"Okay, so what's up?" I grip the edge of the sink with one hand while I stare at my reflection. "Why couldn't you sleep?"

"I just wanted to apologize for the other day. You were right. I never should've drove, and I was acting crazy. No matter how I feel or what I'm going through, it's no excuse to take it out on you or to drive drunk. It was dumb, really dumb. And with everything that happened with you and your mother, I would've been furious, too, if I was you."

I hang my head and close my eyes. "It's fine."

"It's not."

"It's already forgiven, Graham," I say, pinching the bridge of my nose, frustrated with myself for reasons beyond my understanding. I hurt him. I get it. It's not like I've made it easy on him, either. Ever since things blew up with Atlas, he's been by my side, supporting me while I dump all my problems on his plate. It's natural for him to act out in pain.

My gaze flickers to the closed bathroom door.

And then I ran back into Atlas's arms. All while he has his own heartbreak and family drama he's dealing with.

"I just don't know if I can do it." His voice cracks, and I close my eyes. "I'm not sure I can go today."

"What do you mean? You wanted to make States. This is your chance, Graham, and you led Riverside there. You can't bail on it now."

"They can win without me."

I open my eyes to see the reflection of my frown in the mirror. "Even if that were true, why would you want them to? Is this about your father?"

Silence follows, and I have my answer.

"I know a lot has happened recently," I say, wishing I were there in person so I could look him in the eye, "but don't let him ruin this for you. This is your moment. Who cares if he wanted it, too. Do this for you."

"I just keep thinking about that day at Fall Fest, replaying it over and over again in my head. And out of all the things that have happened between you and me, Atlas, and my father, you know the one thing that I can't get over? The one thing that keeps coming back to me?"

A lump forms in the back of my throat. I'm not sure I've ever heard him so torn up inside. Not even the night I chose Atlas over him when anger fought for precedence over pain. "What?" I ask, almost afraid to hear his answer.

"After we overheard the conversation with Atlas's mother, I thought, well that explains it. My father's been putting Atlas up on a pedestal all these years because of a debt he owes his former lover. But that's not really true, is it? If it was just about a debt to be paid, he never would've brought him here to Riverside. He wouldn't have invited him into our home. Instead, he would have continued to write a check like I suspect he's done for years to keep a roof over their heads—"

Except, I'm unconvinced Cal wrote a check considering Atlas and his father lost their house at one point, forcing them to live out of their van, but I don't say that. Because it won't help. Invalidating the way he feels will change nothing.

"—why not just call his mother when my uncle got locked up? She could've taken him and my mother never had to know. But instead, he brought him here, put him on my team, and invited him into my home. He coached him and helped him. Because he thought he was better than me. He didn't think we could win without him."

"Graham—"

"No one ever chooses me. Not him. Not even my mother who turns a blind eye to the way he constantly tells me I'm not good enough. Hell, not even you."

His words are like a blow to the solar plexus, cutting off the air to my lungs.

"I'm done pretending like it doesn't hurt," he says. "I'm done being the one who constantly gives and gets nothing in return."

I know he's talking about more than just his father. He's talking about me, too, and the worst part of it all is I can see where he's coming from. I can see how it does seem like he puts me and our friendship first, while he gets little in return.

"But if you don't show today, you're not just thumbing your nose at your father," I choke out. "You're letting your whole team down. You're letting yourself down. Graham, this is what you've been waiting for . . ."

"Maybe. But I just want someone to put me first and I'm tired of being hurt at the expense of everyone else's happiness."

My throat tightens as I spin around, staring at the closed door of the bathroom, knowing Atlas is lying in the bed just outside. It kills me that Graham might be right, even a little bit. I pursued Atlas despite Graham's feelings for me. I allowed him to be the strong one when I fell apart and relied on him. And now when he needs me most, I chose Atlas again, even after he hurt me and Graham helped pick up the pieces.

"Graham, you're my best friend in the world. You know that." I close my eyes and press the phone harder against my ear until I can no longer hear the frantic beating of my heart. "Just . . . show up today, okay? I'll be there for you."

"You swear it?"

I pause while my heart splits in two. "Yeah, I swear. You're my ride or die, remember?"

He huffs out a laugh and I can hear the relief in it. "My day one?"

"Yep," I say as a sad smile parts my lips and my stomach sinks. "My day one."

The spray from the shower scorches my skin as I scrub myself raw, hoping to rid myself of thoughts from last night—the feel of Atlas moving against me, the scent of him on my skin, the taste of him on my lips. I have to forget. For once in my life, I need to be there for Graham—put him and our friendship first—just like he was there for me after the accident and when Atlas broke my heart. He deserves that much and more. So, as much as it kills me to step away from Atlas again, it's the least I can give him.

I turn the shower off and wrap a towel around myself before I step out and throw my clothes back on. When I return to the bedroom, Atlas is awake and holding to-go cups in his hands. "Caffeine," he says, holding one out toward me.

Instantly grateful, I accept it and take a sip. "Where did you get these?"

"I managed to charm the cook into giving them to me even though breakfast won't be ready for another hour." He steps forward and reaches for me, a tender look in his eye, but I dodge him, and step away from his grip as his smile falls.

I swallow, pushing aside the guilt coating my insides, thick and bitter like molasses, and when I try for a smile, it wobbles.

"Is everything okay?" he asks, concern laced in his voice.

"Yeah. Yeah, it's fine," I say, unable to look him in the eye.

"Okay . . ." He runs a hand over the back of his neck, and I can feel him watching me.

"Well, if we want to make it, I guess we better get going, right?" I start for my purse on the desk, but he stops me with his hand on my arm.

"Hey," he says, his voice soft. "Is this about last night? You didn't . . . I mean, you don't regret anything, do you?"

I exhale, staring at the honeycomb pattern on the carpet beneath my feet as I shake my head, too much of a coward to even look at him. "Last night was an exception." I can barely get the words out, my throat is so thick.

"What?" He flinches and takes a step back, dropping my arm. I'm grateful because the heat of his skin on mine only serves as a reminder of all I'm losing.

"Yeah, a one-time thing. Emotions were high after everything that happened, and I think we both just sort of . . . lost ourselves."

"Oh, is that what happened?" he snaps, and I finally find my courage to lift my gaze. His mouth flattens into a thin line, his eyes obsidian with his anger.

"Of course it is," I say, breathless.

"What is this really about?" He takes a step forward, jaw clenched. "I heard your phone ring. Who was it that called you?"

"That has nothing to do with this." My heart rate picks up, and I'm not sure he buys it, so I press harder. "It can't happen again, okay?" I push past him, grab my purse, and head for the door, my voice trailing after me as I say, "It just . . . can't."

CHAPTER 30

ATLAS

W E DRIVE THE ONE hundred miles to Riverside in silence. The roads are mostly clear, the snow having stopped sometime during the night. A layer of slush remains, but as the miles pass, it dissipates.

Beside me, my phone buzzes with an incoming text, but I don't bother checking it. I already know what it says because the guys have been blowing my phone up for the last fifteen minutes. The bus leaves in ten and they want to know where the hell I'm at.

I don't bother texting them back because we're almost there. I'll make it in time, even if football is the last thing occupying my mind.

I sigh and run a hand through my hair, knowing full well I need to get my shit together. I can't let the guys down today. They've been waiting for this moment for years, and I owe it to them and to myself to give it my all. But it's pretty damn hard to concentrate on a sport when Doll is sitting beside me, her gaze trained at the passing scenery outside her window as the sun rises, cresting over the trees and blanketing everything in its fiery glow.

Part of me wants to ask her what's so interesting. Just like I want to ask her again who was on the phone this morning, considering she's done a complete one-eighty in the last few hours.

I grip the wheel tighter as I rewind our night together in my head, replaying it in minute detail in an effort to pinpoint where I went wrong. But I can think of nothing. Yes, my father and his past transgressions are a problem, one we'll have to navigate if we're to move forward. But that's not the issue here. Something else happened between the time I held Mackenzie in my arms and made love to her, and when I heard the shower running and I snuck out for coffee.

I'm willing to bet I know exactly what—or who—the problem is. Best believe, I'm going to get to the bottom of it.

GRAHAM

I sit out of sight in my car, parked in the corner of the school parking lot, with a baseball cap pulled down low on my head. I have yet to see Mackenzie arrive and the bus is due to leave any minute, but I'm not going anywhere without her. I can't. Knowing I have at least one person in my corner is the only thing that got me here, and it's the only thing that will get me on the field.

I grip the steering wheel as Teagan's Prius comes into view. I frown, because, if I'm not mistaken, he was one of the first to arrive along with Jace, who is already on the bus.

I lean forward in my seat. I'm too far from the vehicle to see inside, but when the driver's side door opens and Atlas steps out, followed by Mackenzie on the passenger side, my blood boils.

I curse under my breath as I grip the wheel tighter, grinding my molars to dust as my head spins.

She lied to me.

Mackenzie wasn't with Anastasia and the girls; she was with Atlas. Worse yet, she spent the night with him.

ATLAS

My gaze bores into the back of Graham's head.

He boarded the bus shortly after me, which makes me wonder where he was while Mackenzie and I were busting our asses to get back on time. Was he watching as we pulled in? Was he waiting? And why do I have a feeling he knows we spent the night together? I'm willing to bet if I pulled up the recent call log on his phone, I'd see Mackenzie's number at the top. I'm so sure of it, in fact, I'd bet the outcome of today's game on it.

"Dude, what the fuck, man?" Jace slaps me in the bicep. "You've been staring at Scott for the last hour, and he's being a solemn little shit. Not to mention, he has the faint scent of booze on him. If I didn't know any better, I'd think you two were having a lover's quarrel."

He's not far off—it's Mackenzie we're fighting over— so I shift my gaze to him and arch a brow.

"Seriously, again?" Jace moans, his tone exasperated. "What is it with this girl? Is her vagina made of fucking gold? Can't you two, you know, get her out of your system and move on?" My eyes harden on his face and he holds his hands up. "Wrong choice of words." He lowers them along with his voice as he leans closer. "But seriously, man, you guys have to choose right *now* to fight over her?"

"I didn't choose shit. If Graham would mind his own fucking business and stop playing the wounded friend card, everything would be fine."

"Shit. You're pissed." Jace rubs a hand over the scruff on his jaw. "Damn, this won't bode well for the team."

"Nah. It'll be fine," I say, cracking my knuckles. "He and I just need to . . . clear the air," I say and I start to stand, unable to sit here a minute longer with his smug ass only feet away, thinking he's won.

"Oh, we're fucked," Jace mutters under his breath.

I start to exit my seat as the bus jolts and I fly forward, gripping the leather seat in front of me to keep my balance. "What the—"

A loud clunking cuts me off, followed by another shudder before the bus comes to a complete stop this time.

"Oh, no, no, no, no," Jace mutters in front of me, eyes wide. "You hexed us," he hisses in my direction while I scowl in response.

A commotion spreads among the players as Coach Clancy rises from his seat, palms out. "Stay calm, and let me talk to the driver."

A few minutes later, he stands at the front of the aisle, and judging by the tight set of his mouth and the crease in his brow, it's not good news. "We think something in the engine blew."

The voices around me rise, a panicked edge to the tone surrounding me. I glance around the bus, taking in the faces of my teammates who are all in varying states of shock, frustration, panic, and fear. My eyes stop to pause on the one who shows no signs of the despair everyone else does. If anything, judging by his lack of emotion, I'd say he doesn't give a damn. The more I watch Graham, the more it pisses me the fuck off.

Coach whistles, and I wince as the voices die around me. "Listen up!" he yells.

A hush settles over my teammates, as close as we're going to get to calm when he explains, "This is why we leave early. It gives us a buffer. Having said that, we called another bus, but they'll take too long to get to us. It might be okay with the board to delay the game, but we'll see. We've put in a call. In the meantime, we've been given the name of a mechanic who's about five or six miles from here. He's not answering his phone, but his hours are listed as open online, so we're thinking our best bet is for the majority of us to stay here and wait on the new bus, while a few go into town to see if we can get this guy to come back here and work on the engine."

"Are you sure splitting up is a good idea?" Teagan asks, frowning.

"It's better than a possible forfeit if we're late, so I think it's worth the risk," Coach says. "Do I have any volunteers—"

"I'll go," I shoot to my feet, staring daggers at Graham. When he slowly turns his gaze to meet mine, I grin. "I'll take Graham with me."

"Perfect," Coach claps his hands.

"Um, objection!" Jace raises a hand in the air, but Coach ignores him.

"The Scotts will go. The rest will stay," Coach says as he begins to scribble the address down and blabs about making it on foot in under an hour if we can.

"Graham, you stay, I'll go, man," Jace says as he starts to stand.

"Nah, I'll go." Graham's eyes lock on mine, glittering darkly as one corner of his mouth curls.

"Fuck, no," Jace hisses, glancing at Teagan for help. "Am I the only one that sees this as a colossally bad idea?"

But Teagan just shrugs. "Maybe it's not. Maybe they just need a chance to fight it out, get it out of their system."

"And if they kill each other? We kind of need them, bro."

Teagan glances between us, his brows drawn together as if to assess the chances of us ripping each other apart, then he shrugs. "I say, let 'em have at it."

"Shit." Jace throws his hands in the air, then begins muttering about waiting four years for a state championship only for it to go down in flames.

Ignoring him, I step out into the aisle and make a beeline for Graham. "Let's go, *cuz*."

CHAPTER 31

GRAHAM

IT'S FREEZING OUT. THE open road stretches out before us with no end in sight. Up above, the sky is a gloomy gray with no promise of sun. Frost still covers the grass on the side of the road. Bits of gravel and debris crunch under my sneakers as I walk in silence, though it's not for lack of anything to say. In fact, I'd love to have words with my cousin, but I rather enjoy watching him stew. So, I wait and bide my time, knowing he won't be able to keep his mouth shut for long.

And I'm right. We travel nearly an entire mile on foot before he cracks.

"You know, it's funny. Mackenzie and I had a real break-through last night. In fact, it felt like . . . well, a whole lot like we were getting back together. Then all of a sudden out of the blue, she changed her tune after she woke up this morning."

The thought of them together curdles my blood, and I fight the urge to punch him in his stupid face right here. "Sounds like a you problem, not a me problem, bro."

He hums in response. "Except, I have a feeling it is a *you* problem. Isn't it?" he says, scratching the side of his head as he pulls ahead, then turns to block my path. "Because if we're together, that means you have no chance with her."

I stop with only a couple of feet separating us and stare at him. I'm reminded of the new bond we share—a half brother. We already share blood, football, and our affection for the same girl. I hate that we have yet one more thing in common.

"I mean, I'm not gonna lie," I say as my lips spread into a smug smile. "I quite enjoyed your time apart."

"You little shit." He takes a step forward and jabs a finger in my chest. "Just what the hell did you say to make her change her mind? And how did you even know we were together in the first place? What, are you stalking her now?"

I snort and reach up, knocking his hand away from my chest as my eyes harden like steel. "You know, I guessed you were together last night, and when I saw you pull up in Teagan's car, my suspicions were confirmed. But what I don't know for sure was which came first? Did she lie to me about you being together, then promise me she'd put me first? Or did she lie to me and promise to put our friendship first *before* she ran to you?" I bark out a laugh as his expression turns to stone. "I guess I have my answer."

"Friendship is all you'll ever have with her."

I clench my jaw, and the muscles in my cheek flickers. Still, I loosen my shoulders and roll my eyes. The last thing I want is for Atlas to think he's hit a sore spot. "Whatever, man," I say and brush past him. "I'd rather have her friendship than nothing at all, which is exactly what you have."

"She still loves me."

I swallow, hating that I know he's right. I see it in her eyes every time she looks at him, and it kills me. "You don't just get over someone overnight," I say. If anyone is proof of that, it's me. Lord knows I tried to get over Kenz. I tried to get past her feelings for Atlas and the rejection, but I failed time and time again. Yet here I am, once again, hoping for more. "And one day, once she's over you and all your lies, she'll see what's right in front of her."

Atlas laughs behind me. "What, you? The loyal best friend? Shit, you're like a dog, following after her and—"

"Shut the fuck up," I say as I spin and fist his shirt in my hands. "Just shut your mouth."

"She doesn't love you, man. She never will."

"You don't know that." My voice shakes.

"I do." His eyes search mine. "And I think you know it, too. You just don't want to admit it to yourself."

My nostrils flare, my face inches from him as the fist around the cotton of his shirt clenches tighter. "You have no clue what you're talking about."

"Here's what I know," he says, his voice tight. "She and I were together last night. We shared something you and her never have and never will. I know that I make her happy. Just like I know, for reasons unbeknownst to me, that she cherishes your friendship. So, when you fuck with her head and tell her in no uncertain terms the only way to be there for you is to fuck me over and forget me, she'll do it. Because she's so damn afraid of hurting you again. Because she's loyal, and she's trying to be selfless. But I guarantee you," he says, his breath hot on my face, "that if you keep her from me, one day, she'll realize all you've taken from her and resent you for it."

I turn my head away from him as my hand shakes and a bitter laugh bubbles in the back of my throat. Shoving him back, I remove my fist from his shirt before I double back and come at him. My right hook connects with the bottom of his mouth, as if I can eviscerate my feelings with my fists.

His head snaps back and he puts his fists up, licking at the blood seeping from his lower lip before he grins and charges me. His shoulder hits me straight in the stomach. The wind rushes from my lungs as we fall to the ground. Atlas catches my left eye with his fist, and I connect another one to his right cheekbone.

The coppery scent of blood fills the air, and I feel a warm trickle of something down the side of my face. "You split my brow, you dick," I spit.

"Well, you busted my lip, so I guess we're even." He roars and rolls me over.

A branch from a fallen tree pokes into my back and I growl.

"You need to move on, man," he says as he fists my shirt in his hands.

I throw another right hook but his arms block it, and I barely graze his chin. He pushes off me, stumbling to his feet.

I grunt, my throat tight with emotion as I choke out, "I can't do that."

"She doesn't want you."

"You don't know that," I roar, sweeping my leg out and knocking him back to the ground with a thud. "I can give her so much more than you can," I say as I crawl to my knees, my breathing heavy.

"Like your daddy's money?" He sits and shoves at my shoulders.

"Fuck you."

"No, thanks. Kenz took care of that last night."

I roar as I throw myself at him, knocking him back to the hard ground where we roll several times. Stones dig into my ass and back. A hiss escapes the back of his throat as we move further into the tree line, both of us throwing wild punches.

"You pushed her away and have done nothing but place the blame on her ever since," he grinds out. "But the truth of the matter is, it wasn't her fault or mine that the two of you didn't work out." Atlas stops throwing his fists and blocking my punches, leaving himself exposed. He takes another one to the chin and grunts before I stop.

Moving off him, my chest heaves as I lie beside him in the grass and debris and try to catch my breath.

"We never even had a chance," I rasp out.

"She loves you, but not in the way you want her to. She probably never will, and I think you know that. You just don't want to admit it."

"No," I say, my voice breaking on the word. Pressure fills my chest. I'm an overfilled balloon waiting to burst.

"Yes," Atlas murmurs.

I turn my head.

"Just let her go, man," he says, searching my gaze. "If you love her, just let her go."

I fall silent, imagining a world without Mackenzie in it the way I want her to be. One where she belongs to somebody else for good, where there's no hope of us ever having more than friendship. It's so damn hard to imagine, I have to close my eyes and force the images to come.

"What if I can't?" I ask, turning my head to face him.

Atlas does the same, his dark eyes boring into mine. "You might not have a choice." With a groan, he gets to his feet and reaches a hand down to help me up.

I stare at his outstretched palm, knowing my next move determines the course of our future—or at least our relationship—before I slap my hand into his and stand.

By the time we return with the mechanic, more than an hour has passed. Atlas and I pile out of the guy's work truck and head for the bus while he stops to speak with Coach. He brought some tools, oil, and a few parts with him, but without having seen the engine first, there's always the chance he'll need something he doesn't have.

Frankly, it doesn't worry me.

I climb the stairs to the applause of my teammates. "They've returned!" Jace yells, popping up from his seat. "And in one piece. It's a Christmas miracle."

"It's November, jackass." I move closer and sit down in the seat in front of him, not in the mood for his poking.

"Though on closer inspection," he says, glancing from me to Atlas coming down the aisle, "you're both a little busted it up. Did you two come across a wildcat on your journeys?" he asks, a brow raised. When I say nothing, he continues, "A bear? Mongoose? Rabid raccoon. Shit, what happened to your face?"

I groan and sink further down into the seat. I have no idea what kind of bruises I'm sporting. All I know is that Atlas has a busted lip, thanks to me, and I can't say I'm all that sorry. "Don't you ever shut up, Taggart?"

Jace chuckles. "Testy."

Atlas passes by my seat and takes the one behind Jace, close enough I can hear them talking. "I assume the two of you got everything sorted?" Jace asks him.

"Close enough," Atlas says.

"So this shit isn't going to bleed out onto the field today?"

"I said my piece, so I'm good. The rest is up to him."

"We're relying on Graham to be levelheaded? Shit," Jace mutters under his breath.

I think of telling him to fuck off, but I don't. Instead, I close my eyes and block out the sound of his voice. My thoughts drift to Atlas, and I wonder if he's right. If years down the road, Mackenzie will resent me. Just the thought cuts like a knife.

Then I think of my father, the half brother I never knew I had, and the debt I owe Darrell, until it feels like the weight of the world is on my shoulders and at any moment it might crush me. I have no idea what I'm going to do about it all. All I know is the stress of it might kill me first.

CHAPTER 32

GRAHAM

I'M OUT OF BREATH when the time on the clock hits zero.

We drag out asses off the field.

Grass stains cover my pants. My side hurts from a sack I took in the second quarter, and I've pinched something in my shoulder.

We enter a locker room that smells like sweat. It's halftime and the Crestmont Bobcats are up by one touchdown, so I know what's coming. Sure enough, the minute we're all inside, Coach yanks me by the face mask, his mouth an angry line beneath a pinched brow. "I don't know what the hell has gotten into you. I don't care if Scott stole your girlfriend or ran over your fucking cat. If you don't get your head out of your ass and in the game, I swear I'll bench you and put Snyder in."

My gaze flickers to Snyder, our second-string quarterback. His eyes glitter with possibility, and I have half a mind to tell Coach just to put him in. My heart's not in it.

Shit, I don't even know where the hell my heart is.

That's a lie.

I know exactly where it is, back on that sideline wearing a red and white cheer uniform.

My gaze drifts to the boys around me to see a myriad of expressions: Disappointment. Frustration. Anger.

I swallow and lift my chin. "Yes, sir."

Coach turns and addresses the rest of the group with fire in his eyes. "This is your time. I didn't watch you all work your asses off this season only to witness you get them handed to you when it counts." He slams his clipboard on the ground with an ominous *thwack*. "Jace, get open." He points. "Atlas, move faster." He scowls. "Teagan, you better block those assholes, so Graham has time to move."

Coach spins around, his mouth pinched. "You're fast. You're smart. You know how to win games. Now fucking show me. When we walk back out of this locker room and onto that field, I better see a group of men, not pansy-ass-boys who are afraid to get dirty. You're champions. Now act like it."

Half the team hang their heads while the other half murmur their agreement. Either way, the enthusiasm is lacking, and I can't help but feel like I'm to blame.

Jace comes up to me and claps a hand on my back. Sweat drips from his brow, despite the frigid temperature outside this locker room. "You know, man, a lot of people are depending on you. And I'm not blaming you for the scoreboard. We've been sloppy, too. But we need you, man. We need you to be out there with us on the field. Not just here"—he lightly punches my arm—"but here, too." He taps a finger on the side of my head, and my throat bobs. "Someday you're gonna look back on this, and if you don't give it your all, you'll regret it. Not because of a stupid trophy or a title. Not because of a need to win or prove something. But because we're your brothers. Your friends. Teammates. We've been with you every step of the way and I know you don't want to let us down."

I'm quiet as we step back onto the field. The cold air wraps around me like a vice as I suck in a breath to quieten my thoughts. I need my mind straight because Jace is right. I'm so in my head, I'm going to let everyone else down. And that's the last thing I want.

This is my team—my brothers—and until Atlas showed up, I'd have given anything to be here in this time and place with them.

I know what I need to do, though it's easier said than done. Still, I have to push my personal feelings aside, forget everything eating at me, and help them win this.

I need to focus.

I inhale a deep breath into my lungs as my gaze travels the wide expanse of the emerald green field stretched out before me.

I loosen my arms and roll out my shoulders.

Jump up and down.

I envision every throw I'll make, every pass and running play.

Adrenaline spreads through my muscles, warming my chest. A spike of energy pumps through my limbs and I shake out my legs and wiggle my fingers, ready for the ball in my grip.

Everything comes into focus as the teams take the field and my brain homes in on what I have to do to win.

And we will win, I determine.

For me.

For my friends.

For every little boy trying to please their father on the field.

Twenty minutes later, we're down by one touchdown. We huddle together, and I make the call. "George Washington on one. Ready?"

"One!" the others scream, and we jog out of the huddle.

I inhale, sucking air into my lungs before I take my spot on the green.

I slam my hands together and yell, "George Washington!"

The lineman glances around him, while the center yells, "Hike!"

Jace runs to the left, while Teagan charges toward the Bobcat's defensive player who tries to sneak through the hole on a blitz. I bounce to the right, light on my feet just as Teagan takes him down.

I find Jace to my left, but he shakes his head, unable to get open, so I pivot right. My eyes lock on Atlas twenty yards out.

He's open, so I throw the ball. A perfect spiral.

It sails right into his hands as Knox bowls over the defensive player gunning for him, knocking him straight on his ass while Atlas sets out.

His feet fly like lightning over the field. He makes it to the twenty-yard line . . . then ten . . . five . . .

Touchdown!

"That's right, baby!" Jace screams up ahead.

Knox claps and meets my gaze, wiggling his brows. "Tie game, baby."

I grin as I pump an arm in the air and jog off the field.

Another ten minutes later, the score is stagnant. Neither of us have pulled ahead.

Once the ball is hiked, Atlas runs like hell straight down the field, fakes a hard left, then spins right and lifts his hand in the air for the pass.

I throw it at the same time a defensive player comes for him, and I pray he catches it and tightens up.

The ball sails into his arms, and he spins on his feet. Right into another Bobcat.

Shit.

I grip my head in my hands as I watch, praying he can get out of this bind when Jace comes up on his left.

Atlas chucks the ball.

Jace bobbles it, and I hold my breath when he recovers, tucking it in and covering it with his other hand as he runs it into the end zone.

The rest of the game is a blur. My arm holds strong, and though I make a few mistakes, all of us come together as team to win this damn game. I botch a pass-off to Jace and miscalculate a throw to Atlas, who somehow still catches it with one hand, making it look like he has magic hands.

We get two more touchdowns. One interception and a fumble.

And then we win.

When the time on the scoreboard hits zero, the Rebels's fans roar. Reporters take the field, immediately heading for Coach Clancy and grabbing Atlas on their way. One zeros in on me, but I turn toward the bleachers and avoid them.

There's one person I want to see, the only one I want to celebrate with.

My gaze finds Mackenzie instantly at the same time she makes a beeline straight for me. I bypass my father, ignoring his outstretched hand. "Graham? We did it."

I snort and skirt by him. "You had nothing to do with it." My eyes focus only on Mackenzie as she meets me halfway, grinning up at me, breathless as she says, "You were amazing."

I nod. Her dark hair blows in the slight breeze, her cheeks rosy from the cold. She's so beautiful it hurts. Swallowing, I take in the men behind me, all of my teammates, and shake my head. "No. We did it together."

She reaches out and touches my arm, it's not the congratulations I want, but I'm learning it's the kind I have to settle for. "I'm really proud of you," she says, and I can tell she means it.

"Will you come out after? Celebrate with us?" I ask.

Her eyes dart behind me and she shakes her head. "I think I'll sit this one out." Her expression darkens as she turns her eyes back to mine with a frown, and though I know I shouldn't, I turn to see what's caught her eye.

A few yards back, Atlas stands with the reporter and is answering their questions while his gaze drinks her in. In that moment, I know what he said is true. That if I continue to stand between them, Mackenzie will eventually live to resent me. And though everything inside me wants to deny it and hold her close, consequences be damned, maybe it's time to stop wishing for things I'll never have and start working for the things I want.

CHAPTER 33

ATLAS

FTER THE BUS PULLS into the parking lot, I'm the first one to get off before I remember I'm at the mercy of my teammates. Since I drove Teagan's car here, I either need a ride back to my place, or I have to walk. Considering I feel like the walking dead after our battle on the field, my feet aren't a viable option.

I step off the bus and wait. Teagan's the last one to deboard and when he sees me, he slings an arm over my shoulders at the same time Jace and Knox wrestle Graham to the ground amid a string of obscenities.

The hell . . . ?

They awkwardly lift a thrashing Graham by the arms and legs, then throw him into the front of Teagan's Prius, kicking and screaming.

I turn to Teagan with a frown. "Bro, I thought you were giving me a ride home?"

"I am." He grins, and I turn to watch Jace slam the passenger door shut in Graham's face. Knox guards the driver's side while Graham pounds on the glass with his fists, then furiously yanks on the handle.

Jace steps up to the window and cups his ear. "What? I can't hear you. Open the door? Oh, sorry. Child protection locks." Then he shrugs and heads in my direction. "You ladies ready to go?" he asks, coming to a stop in front of me.

"Why are we kidnapping Graham?" I ask, motioning toward his car.

"Because knowing Graham, he's going to celebrate his win tonight," Jace says, by way of explanation.

"Okay . . ."

"And also knowing Graham," Teagan continues, "that means he's getting shitfaced, and he can't be trusted with his keys when he's around booze and Mackenzie's not with us."

"Whatever, man," I say, because I don't wanna know what they're referring to. Besides, Graham and I have already had it out once today. As far as I'm concerned, we're good. "As long as you take me home first, I don't give a damn who else is in the car."

"Sure thing, brother." Teagan slaps a hand on my back and exchanges a look with Jace I can't read but makes me nervous. Whatever they're up to, I don't like it, but I'm also too tired to give a shit. So, I head toward the car, grateful that Graham's temper tantrum seems to have subsided, at least for the time being.

Once Teagan unlocks the car, and Jace ensures Graham doesn't sneak out, we all pile inside his tiny ass Prius. Jace, Knox and I all cram into the back while Graham and Teagan ride in the front. "Why the hell does he get shotgun?" Knox complains. "My nuts are about to be peanut butter back here."

"At least your knees aren't in your throat." I wince as I fold my legs like a pretzel, my knees practically coming up to my chin. "Dude is your hand on my ass?" I glare over at Jace as his hand gropes my left cheek.

"I'm trying to find my seatbelt, bro. Relax."

"Dude, if we get in a car wreck, we're not going anywhere. I'm smashed in here like a fucking sardine," Knox whines.

"Mmhm," Jace hums under his breath. "On second thought, you do have a nice ass, Scott. Very firm."

"Lord help me," I mutter as I close my eyes.

"*Nice*," Teagan says with a grin as he pulls out of the lot.

"Hey," I say, blinking my eyes back open. "I get dropped off first."

Teagan pulls out of the lot and heads for the interstate. "Yeah, about that . . ." Teagan meets Jace's eye in the rearview mirror. "I'm afraid we're not dropping anyone off."

"What? Where the fuck are we going?" Graham asks, his sulking turning to anger.

"Did you really think we were gonna win a state championship and let you get away without celebrating?"

Graham and I both groan.

"I'm not in the mood, man. Just take me home," I say. My mind is too consumed with Mackenzie for anything else.

"No can do," Teagan says, his tone artificially chipper.

"Listen, we won as a team and we're gonna party as a *team*. Like it or not, that includes you, my man," Jace says, draping an arm over my shoulder. "No girls. Just the guys and a night on the town."

I snort. A night on the town in Riverside is about as exciting as a day in the Hundred Acre Woods. More importantly, a night out with the boys means no Mackenzie, which is a big no thank you. The only thing I have an interest in tonight other than passing out on my pillow, is talking to her and figuring our shit out.

"And I know what you're thinking," Jace continues as I shrug him off me. "Right now, your hamster wheels are spinning. Both of you are thinking about how you're gonna get to Mackenzie if you're with the boys and she's not there, but here's the thing . . ." Graham flips him the bird as he continues, "Mackenzie Hart is fine as hell and she's got that whole damaged thing going on, which for some reason appeals to both of you, but maybe it's time she's water under the bridge, you know?" Jace waves his arms, nearly smacking me in the face. "Let bygones be bygones. Put her in your rearview mirror, like days gone by. Move on. Bros before hos and all that."

"Shut the fuck up!" Graham and I say in the unison.

"Harsh," Jace says, unfazed.

"I think they disagree with you," Teagan quips.

"You know, T, I think you're right."

"We already cleared the air before the game," I say, fixing my junk which is currently being smashed like a grape.

"I see that. It's evidenced by your bloody lip and Graham's black eye." Jace grins. "Consider this insurance."

I sigh and lean my head back against the seat as Graham pipes up in the front. "What's the point, anyway? The season's over."

"I agree," I say, elbowing Jace in the ribs.

"Right." Jace coughs. "So, don't you want to end things on a good note?"

I shoot him a glare.

"No." Graham and I say at the same time.

"See? We've only been in the car for ten minutes and already you guys have been in agreement twice now. It's working."

"You're a jackass," I say.

"Maybe. But I'm a smart jackass. Because here's the thing. The season might be over for most of us, but the two of you are blood. More than that, you now share a half brother—"

My nostrils flare and my gaze darts to Graham. *The fucker told them?*

"—and that means you're tied together for life. You need to bury the hatchet, once and for all."

"If we promise we're cool, will you let us go home?" I ask.

"Not a chance," Jace says with a laugh.

I groan and lean my head back on the seat when I feel something touching my thigh. "Fine. But keep your hands the fuck off me," I grump, which only makes Jace laugh harder.

After driving for thirty minutes, we pull up to the curb at a seedy place somewhere outside of Riverside. I have no idea where we are, but when I duck my head and look past Knox's massive shoulders, my eyes home in on the sign at the shop in front of us.

"Pain Express Tattoo Parlor?" I say out loud, then turn, blinking over at Jace. "What the hell are we doing here?"

He grins like an idiot. "You know, there's a stigma against jocks that we're dumb. Don't prove them right."

I roll my eyes when Graham pipes up from the front. "I am not getting a tattoo."

"Yeah, me neither." For once, Graham and I agree.

"Dude!" Jace waves toward my arm with more than a dozen tattoos.

"I sure as shit didn't get them at Pain Express."

"Who gave you them then, huh?" Jace crosses his arms over his chest, elbowing me in the process.

I shove at his side. "A friend."

"Right. And you're afraid to get one from this place." He jerks a thumb toward the shop.

"He didn't use melted chess pieces, lotion, and a used needle, you jackass. It wasn't a prison tattoo. He had his own parlor."

"And how did you get to know this Picasso?" he asks, like he doesn't believe me.

"Our dads were both addicts."

"Damn, Scott. Do you always have to bring the atmosphere down?" He shakes his head and taps Teagan on the back. "Ready to go?"

"Let's do this."

I sit there a moment as Teagan, Knox, and Jace all pile out of the car. Staring at the back of Graham's head, I wait to see what he'll do, but when he doesn't budge, I hop out. The last thing I wanna do is be on the same page as him.

Jace knocks on the passenger's side window and crouches down until he's eye level with a sulking Graham. "Come on, man, you know you want to."

When he doesn't respond, I nod for him to let me at him, and he steps aside. I swing open the door, and just when he opens his mouth to bite my head off, I say, "It'll piss Cal off."

His mouth falls shut and seconds later, he's out of the car, standing beside me and warily staring at the front of the shop. "Bonding over your mutual hate for Cal Scott," Jace says, draping an arm around both our shoulders. "I can get onboard with that."

After Jace and Teagan's failed attempt at convincing me and Graham to get matching Rebels tattoos, they take their turns in the chair. "Damn, that hurt like a bitch," Jace says as he pops up from his seat, a bandage over the fresh ink on his arm in the shape of a Riverside Rebel.

I take my seat in the chair as the tattoo artist cleans up and prepares his tools. Once he's ready, I tell him what I want, and he quickly sketches it out for my approval.

I nod, and he gets started. The sting of the needle bites into my arm, but with so many tattoos, I'm used to it now.

My gaze drifts to Graham, who is still perusing the books. Despite the fight he put up, he's been rather subdued since we got here, and I can't help but wonder if he's thinking about everything I said to him earlier. It takes a lot of introspection to look within yourself and admit you're wrong, but I hope he can for his sake, as well as Mackenzie's. I know how much his friendship means to her. Just like I know she's going to be mine. But things can't carry on the way they have been. They'll never work with him and I constantly feuding over her like King Solomon's baby. We all know how that story ends, and I have no desire to tear Doll in two.

My phone buzzes in my pocket, but I ignore it. With any luck it's Mackenzie, and after this is over, I can go to her. Work everything out.

I wait patiently as he finishes my tattoo. It's far less elaborate than Jace and Teagan's, so it doesn't take very long. Once he finishes, I step out of the chair to check my phone while Graham waits his turn.

I sidestep Teagan, Jace, and Knox, who are being complete assholes and are trying to punch each other in the arm where they just got inked. I shake my head at them with a laugh and zero in on several missed calls. But they're not from Mackenzie. I don't recognize the number, and when I check my voice mail, I see a new message. Instead of listening to it, I ignore it. I'm sure it's nothing that can't wait.

Graham sidles up next to me and clears his throat. "So, uh, all those things you said about Mackenzie eventually resenting me and . . . well, did she tell you that?"

I shake my head, somewhat surprised he brought her up again. "No. But I know her."

"Has she said *anything* about me to you?" he asks, glancing at me out of the corner of his eye, like he doesn't want to admit he's fishing for information.

I'm about to tell him no and end the conversation when I remember my promise to her. Whether he screwed me over or not, I told Mackenzie I'd speak to him.

"She's worried about you, about the drinking, your mood swings, and behavior."

"She told you that?" he asks with a frown and I nod.

"And honestly, it doesn't take much for me to recognize bad patterns when I see them. I lived with an addict my whole life and, like or not, we're related. That disease is in our blood and you're going down a slippery slope right now. One I'd be careful of."

"I'm not that bad. I just—"

"Need something to stay afloat?" I meet his eyes. "Tread lightly. It doesn't take much to drown," I say as my phone rings again.

With a sigh, I check the screen and see the same unknown number from my missed calls. "I should probably take this," I mumble, then take a step away from him.

Pressing the phone to my ear, I watch as Graham takes his seat in the parlor chair, his gaze distant as if he's lost in thought. "Hello?" I say as I answer the call.

"This is Officer Romero from the Greensboro Police Department. We're looking for Atlas Scott, the son of Lee Scott?"

A creeping sensation crawls up my spine. "This is Atlas Scott," I say, a tremor in my voice.

"I'm calling about your father," he says, his tone soft. "Are you available to come in and speak with us?"

"What?" My forehead creases as I glance over at the others. "No. I'm hours away, and even if I weren't I don't have a car or a ride."

"Are you at home?"

"No, and I'm not sure when I will be. Listen, can you just tell me what this is about?" I ask, clenching the phone tighter.

"Well, I hate doing this over the phone, but I'm sorry to say, he passed away this evening. His body has been sent to the Greensboro County morgue for identification."

"What?" I shake my head.

It can't be.

"That's impossible. I just saw him a little over twenty-four hours ago. How . . .?" I say, my throat tight.

"We responded to a call around seven-thirty about an unresponsive man on a park bench outside the Greensboro shopping center. It appears he overdosed. We tried to resuscitate him on the scene and again at the hospital with no luck. I'm sorry, son."

I close my eyes and drop the phone by my side. All the blood drains from my face as my stomach drops out from under me.

I always suspected one day I'd get this call but these last couple of months gave me hope.

I thought maybe it would stick . . .

I think about my father—stiff and cold and lying in a morgue, his body blue—and my stomach pitches. I bend forward at the waist and dry heave.

"If he's gonna get sick in my shop, get him the hell out of here." The tattooist waves in my direction.

"Shit, man, and you said I was the pansy," Jace says, placing a hand on my back.

I open my eyes and straighten, bringing my hands to my temples. I can't be here anymore. I need to be alone where I can think. Where I can breathe.

"What's wrong?" Jace's voice turns serious. "Talk to me, bro."

I shake my head as Teagan and Knox get in my face. "You okay, dude?" Teagan asks.

"I can't . . ." My throat constricts. I can't talk. Can't fucking breathe through the pain in my chest. It feels like someone has their hands around my neck. "My father . . ."

Graham's head jerks up from where he lies on the bench, the tattoo artist working on his side. I meet his eyes, desperate for understanding, for someone who knows this pain. But I'm alone.

"He overdosed tonight," I say, but my voice is not my own. "He's dead."

CHAPTER 34

MACKENZIE

I SIT ON MY bed, curled into a ball as I stare outside the window into a cloudless night sky. My thoughts drift between Atlas and Graham, much like they have all night, and I once again wonder how I got here—in this awful tug-of-war between them.

For the first time since the accident, I wish my mother were here, not because I miss her like I usually do, but because I desperately need her advice. She'd know what to do. She always did.

I grab my phone off the nightstand and debate on calling the girls. I need an ear, and if I can't have my mother, they're the next best thing.

My phone rings before I can dial anyone, startling me.

Jace's number lights up the screen, and I frown before answering. "Hello?"

"Kenz, thank God you answered." Jace's voice fills the phone in a panic.

A shiver of fear runs up my spine as I straighten. "What's wrong? Did something happen?"

"It's Atlas. He got a phone call tonight while we were out. Kenz, his dad died."

A gasp escapes my parted lips. Of all the things I expect him to say, this is the last. "No. That can't be. He's in rehab."

"Well, something must've happened because he got the call from the local PD out that way. I guess he overdosed."

My heart leaps to my throat and I close my eyes. I can only imagine what getting that call must have been like. "Where is he?" I manage.

"He grabbed Teagan's keys and took off. We're waiting on a ride right now, but he didn't tell us where he was going. Graham said he hasn't been staying at his place, though."

"Yeah, no." My mind races as I jump to my feet and slip on my shoes. Grabbing my purse, I head for the door. "He probably went back to his old place. He's been staying there. I'll go to him. Don't worry."

"I figured you would. Listen," he says, his voice thick, "call us if you need anything, okay? I know there's been a lot of drama this year, but Scott's our boy. He's one of us now, and we rally when a brother's down."

"I'll do that," I say, my throat tight. It's nice to know someone else has his back.

I move quickly for the door as I open up my Uber app and book a car. They're only a few minutes out, so it won't take long. When the driver gets here, I give them directions and lean back into the seat, heart pounding in my throat the entire way.

I close my eyes tightly and think about his father as guilt swims in my veins. It can't be a coincidence he broke his two-month sobriety and OD'd only twenty-four hours after I went to visit. The image of him breaking down into sobs plays in my mind like a movie reel I can't escape. I understand with perfect clarity why he relapsed.

I did this.

The guilt and shame I placed on his shoulders was more than he could bear, and though he deserved every bit of the blame and anger directed his way, I'll never forgive myself for being the one to push Lee Scott over the edge.

I'm the reason he's dead.

I'm the reason Atlas no longer has a father.

My heart aches with the passing miles until I think it might explode. I pick up my cell and try his number again, but there's no answer, which only adds to the guilt-anxiety cocktail brewing inside my chest.

We pass the familiar pines that line the entrance to the trailer park and I straighten in anticipation. After another minute the Uber driver finally pulls into Atlas's driveway behind Teagan's Prius. To the right is his father's car, and the sight of it twists my stomach.

I push my nausea back, thank the Uber driver, and get out. I stand in front of the double-wide, the gravel crunching with his exit, and stare up at the house as fear slithers under my skin. *What if Atlas blames me, too?*

I press a hand to my chest. Even though I'm not even sure what we are to each other after last night, the thought of him forever hating me for doing this to his father guts me.

I take a step forward and step onto the front porch, then try the doorknob to find it unlocked. I push it open and step inside. "Atlas?" I call out tentatively.

I get no answer as I move through the empty living room to the kitchen, and then drift toward his bedroom in the back only to find it empty. My pulse picks up its pace as I call out, again with no answer.

A lump forms in the back of my throat when I hear a noise coming from outside.

I hurry for the door and step back out into the frigid November air and round the house. I've never been back here, but my gaze makes quick work of the large oak and the crumbling cement pad I assume was once a patio of sorts when the shattering of glass reaches my ears from above. With a frown I spin around, glancing above me to find the shape of someone on the roof. I recognize the broad shoulders as he raises an arm, a glass bottle gripped in his hands. My stomach sinks, thinking he's raising it up to take a drink, but then he wrenches his arm back and chucks it off the roof where it shatters in thunderous applause against the base of a large oak. "Was it worth it, Pops?" he screams into the night.

I watch as he leans forward and picks something up off the surface of the roof. I expect it to be another booze bottle but when he lifts it in his hands, I can just make out its rectangular shape in the dark. A framed photograph.

"Atlas?" I somehow manage to yell through the lump in my throat.

His head whips up, and I can see by the silvery track marks from his tears, he's been crying. "Doll?"

I nod, my throat tight as he quickly wipes his cheeks.

"You came," he says, his voice a breathy sigh.

Did he really think I wouldn't?

"Jace called me. He told me what happened."

He nods, saying nothing as his throat bobs in the moonlight.

"What are you doing up there? Do you wanna come down and talk?" I ask, nervous with him up there while he's so emotional.

He moves closer to the edge of the roof, and for a moment, I think he's listening. I think he's going to come down. Instead, he sits and tucks his knees into his chest as he stares off into the distance.

"You know, when I was little and my father still held a job, he'd come home half drunk and finish his bender or down whatever pills he had. It scared the shit out of me, so I'd crawl out my bedroom window and climb onto the roof to get away."

So that explains why he's on the roof.

I pull a breath of air into my lungs, imagining a young, scared Atlas alone on the roof. "Why didn't you go to a friend's house, or a neighbor?"

A hiss of air escapes his lips. "Because I was too afraid to leave the house completely. I was always so scared he'd fall and get hurt or use too much and need me. As I got older and I'd come up here it was to escape what I thought was the inevitable, that eventually he'd use too much and I'd have to watch him die."

Oh, Atlas . . .

My heart squeezes against my ribs while I think of something to say, but I'm at a loss for words.

"I came up here tonight, half expecting him to be passed out on the couch like always when I went back inside. But he's not going to be there, is he?"

"No," I whisper.

He smashes his mouth into a thin line. "I can't believe he's really gone. I always knew he'd kill himself. I guess I should be glad I didn't have to be the one to find him."

"Atlas, I'm so sorry," I say, over the lump in my throat.

"You know, when we went to see him, I was so pissed at him for putting us in that situation. For everything he'd done to me and to you and your family," he says, staring off into the distance. "But there was this small, stupid part of me that was hopeful, too. Like maybe he could be different. Turns out, he's the same old piece of shit user he always was."

"Atlas, don't—"

"Don't what?" His dark eyes flash angrily in the moonlight. "Be angry? Don't act like you don't hate him just because he's gone."

I swallow, unsure of what to say when he digs the pack of cigarettes and the lighter he always carries out of his pocket and chucks them, where they land on the edge of the roof. Then, he plucks the cigarette from behind his ear and takes one long look at it, before he snaps it in half and flicks it from his fingers, while I watch him and wonder what this means.

My hands dampen with sweat as I take another step forward and reach a hand up, motioning for him to come down. The roof isn't particularly steep but with him so emotional, I'm not sure it's safe. "Why don't you come down from there, so we can talk where it's warm."

He says nothing, which scares me more than his anger. But then he nods, and he starts toward the edge of the roof while I wonder how he'll get down.

An upturned metal trash can sits on the cracked cement. I start walking toward it, assuming he used it to give him a boost up, and I'm about to suggest he wait until I hold it steady when his foot slips out from under him. With a yelp of surprise, he falls headfirst onto the cement with a sickening crack and lands on his back.

A scream bursts from my lungs as I race toward him, my heart in my throat.

My hands flutter over him, shaking with fear as I check for a pulse in his neck. I close my eyes, focusing until I feel the soft flutter under my fingertips like butterfly wings.

I suck in a breath, pull my phone out of my pocket, and dial 911. My hands tremble so badly, it takes me several tries to get it right but once I do, I focus back on him again.

"Breathe," I murmur. A tear falls down my cheek and drips on his chest while I wait in the vain hope his eyes will open, like some fairytale brought to life. But they don't. "Keep breathing and stay with me," I plead.

The operator answers but the connection is poor and I can hardly hear her. After a few tries, I rattle off Atlas's address and tell her about his fall, but when I get no response, I glance down at my phone. It's still connected but reception is poor. "Hello?" I yell into my cell, but all I get is a garbled response.

"Shit," I hiss, uncertain they heard me.

I debate on what to do, then cut my losses and hang up. I try them again, but I get the same broken connection. This time, I leave the call connected just in case, but I'm not sure it's much use. I toss my cell to the side. I have no idea how long it might take them to send someone to us if they didn't make out what I said.

My vision blurs with my tears. "What do I do?" I cry.

His chest inflates with a ragged breath, and I'm so afraid he might stop breathing all together, it nearly steals the air from my own lungs.

The way I see it, I have two choices: Stay, and pray like hell the dispatcher heard me. Or take him to the hospital myself.

I know enough about traumatic injuries to know he might have a spinal cord injury and I shouldn't move him, but if I don't try to get him to a hospital, I could be sentencing him to death anyway, depending on what his injuries are.

I take his face between my hands, cradling his head while tears fall freely from my face when I notice something warm and sticky on the back of his head. When I pull my hands away, a smear of something scarlet covers my fingers.

"Oh my God," I say, my voice shaking. A sob rips through my throat as I close my eyes and pray for the sound of sirens in the distance, but all I hear is silence, and I know I can no longer wait. My gut tells me I need to move. Now.

I search his pockets for Teagan's keys but come up empty. With a growl of frustration, I stand. "You're going to be okay," I tell him. "I'll be right back. I promise."

I get to my feet and race around the house, hoping to find the keys in the ignition, but when I peer inside Teagan's car, I see nothing. They're not in the ignition or on the seat. My gaze shifts to the house; they're probably on the roof.

Shit.

My heart pounds like a bass drum as I lower my gaze and it lands on the blue Fiesta. Slowly, I make my way toward it like it's a ticking time bomb waiting to blow and open the driver's side door to find the keys in the ignition.

I suck in a deep breath and close my eyes, unsure of whether I'm able to do this when I slide inside. A prickling sensation creeps over my skin. My chest tightens.

Without thinking, I turn the keys and after a couple of tries, the engine rumbles to life.

I think I might be sick.

My stomach roils as I take a deep breath, trying to calm the racehorse galloping in my chest.

I can do this.

I can drive.

In this car.

For him.

A choking noise escapes my lips as I clench the steering wheel in a death grip.

If I don't do this, no one will. Atlas needs a hospital. *Stat.*

A humming noise gurgles from the back of my throat as I force my hands to move and put the car in gear. Lifting my foot, I slam on the gas before I can stop myself. The car jolts forward as I navigate behind the house and toward Atlas's prone form.

Once I'm directly behind him, I slam on the brakes and throw open my door, only to fall onto my knees beside him on the concrete where I expel the contents of my stomach. My body shakes and my head pounds. When I lift my head, the world around me spins.

Inhaling, I take a deep breath and stand on shaky legs. If I pass out now, no one can help him.

Get it together, Kenz.

I throw open the back door before I lift Atlas by the shoulders and begin to drag him toward the backseat of the car, praying I don't do more harm than good.

Adrenaline fuels me, strengthening my muscles as I manage to angle him onto the seat, then round the car and hook my arms underneath his. I yank and pull with all my might until I have him completely inside.

I shut the door, my breathing heavy from the exertion as I get back behind the wheel. Without wasting any time, I drive out of his yard and onto the road.

A bead of sweat rolls down my back as I grip the steering wheel until my knuckles turn white. I glance in the rearview mirror where Atlas's blood is seeping into the upholstery of the back seat and my stomach threatens to revolt again.

A car comes up on my rear, then passes and my pulse goes into fits. The road blurs. My hands go numb, and I gasp for air.

Don't have an episode. Don't have an episode.

"Not right now, damnit!" I cry out.

I clench my jaw until my face aches, then pull a long breath of air into my lungs as I focus on my breathing.

The closest emergency room is only a few more miles. I can do this.

I divert my thoughts from the road and the machine under my control by focusing on Atlas and getting him to the hospital. I think about all the things I want to say to him once he wakes up and I know he's okay.

Because he's going to be okay.

He has to be.

A few minutes later, I pull his father's car to a screeching halt in front of the ER and get out when a wave of familiarity hits me like a freight train.

Not again.

This can't be happening again.

I can't lose someone else.

My stomach clenches, but I exhale a shaky breath and put one foot in front of the other, chasing away my fear.

I move and the heavy glass doors slide open, revealing the ER waiting room with the intake desk straight ahead.

I hurry to the nurse at the desk as my nerves do jumping jacks in my chest. "I need help. My friend fell and hit his head. H–h–he's bleeding and unresponsive."

"Where is he?" the woman stands, her gaze shifting behind me.

"My car."

She calls out to a couple of nurses for help and before I know it, they're getting him out of the back seat and onto a plastic spinal board, then onto a gurney. They wheel him past me. His eyes are still closed and a nurse is giving him oxygen via a face mask while another one is checking his vitals and shouting out orders to the others.

I follow behind until they burst through the double doors at the end of the hall and the woman from registration stops me. "The doctors and nurses have him now," she says, guiding me on rubbery legs to a chair in the waiting room. "Take a seat. All you can do now is wait, but we'll update you when we can."

I want to thank her, but I can't. I'm too numb to say or do much of anything. Instead, I fall back into the chair and stare at the double doors, as if at any second, they might burst open and Atlas will walk out.

A buzzing noise erupts from my pocket. Blinking, I slide it out and glance down to the screen to see it's my father. I press answer, then lift it to my ear, my throat tight and aching with the need to cry.

"Dad?" I rasp. "Dad, I need you. It's Atlas . . ."

CHAPTER 35

GRAHAM

THE SECOND I BURST through the emergency room doors with Jace, Teagan, and Knox beside me, Mackenzie stands and runs to me. She throws herself into my open arms while I wrap myself around her, squeezing her in a hug. "We came as soon as we could get a car," I say into her hair.

Part of me doesn't even believe he's injured. We were just with him hours ago and while he was upset after he got the news about his dad, it didn't seem like he was in such a state that he could do something that would hurt him. Then again, the whole last year has been one big emotional whirlwind.

"How is he?" Jace asks, breaking the silence.

Mackenzie steps back, sniffling at the same time my gaze drifts to the smear of blood on her shirt. Jace must notice at the same time I do because he sucks in sharp breath, and when I glance over at him, he blanches. Beside him, Teagan's eyes bug out of his head.

"Oh, shit." Jace rubs a hand over his mouth. "That can't be good."

Mackenzie glances back up at me. "They took him in as soon as I got here. No one has been out to update us."

"We never should've let him go alone," Teagan says, shaking his head. "We should've stopped him.

"Like we had a choice, dude." Jace turns toward him. "The man's father just died. We couldn't exactly keep him there with us."

"So, what exactly happened?" Teagan asks.

"I went to his place, the one he shared with his father when they moved here. That's where he's been staying," she says, glancing up at me with a knowing look. "But when I got there, he was up on the roof. He was angry, throwing things and yelling. Just . . . venting and grieving, you know? So, I convinced him to come down. The roof isn't very high, but it was cold and slippery, and when he went to step down, he slipped and fell headfirst onto the concrete."

Jace winces. "Shit."

"You should've heard the sound." Mackenzie says, her voice shaking. "It was unlike anything I've ever heard before. This awful, cracking thud."

I swallow, picturing it in my head. Atlas and I have certainly had our differences, but I would never wish something like this on him. "And the blood . . .?" I ask, already knowing and dreading the answer.

"From his head," she croaks.

Teagan groans and closes his eyes, pinching the bridge of his nose while Jace looks like he might puke.

"What did the paramedics say on the way?" I ask.

Kenzie shakes her head and glances over at me, almost guiltily. "He didn't come by ambulance."

"Wait, what do you mean?" I frown, thinking about the text she sent us earlier. I'd been too shocked to give it much thought. I just assumed . . . "If you didn't come by ambulance, how did you come?"

"I drove."

I freeze, unsure of whether I heard her right. "You *drove*?"

She nods, her eyes glistening with tears, and I can tell it won't take much for the dam to break.

"It was the only way," she starts, her voice heavy with emotion. "I tried calling 911, but the connection was bad and I didn't know if they heard me. He was unresponsive, and I was too afraid to wait around for them. I had no choice, so I loaded him in his father's car and drove him here."

My mouth parts, and for a moment I'm too stunned for words. I know how monumental this is. I know what this means for her.

Then something else she said registers. "You drove *his* father's car?"

"I couldn't find Teagan's keys, but his were in the ignition."
She closes her eyes for a moment, as if she can't even believe it
herself, and I can understand why.

I take a step back and drag a hand down my face as I try to
comprehend what she told me. She drove. For the first time in
almost a year, she got behind the wheel of a car and drove. And
not only that, but it was the wheel of the man responsible for
killing her mother.

"Do you think I hurt him? Do you think I made him worse?"
she asks.

I lift my head to see the fear in her eyes. Suddenly, I understand the look of guilt from before and my heart aches for her.
"No, of course not. You likely saved his life, Kenz," I say, pulling
her into my arms again, although I have no idea if that's true.

"Because if I did, I'll never forgive myself," she says, choking
on a sob. "I keep thinking about how I blew him off at the game.
I said nothing to him before I left. This is all my fault."

"Hey, it's not your fault. Not even a little bit. You can't blame
yourself."

"No." She shakes her head. "You don't understand." She
pushes away from me as tears stream down her face. "We were
together last night. He drove me to Rise Rehabilitation where
his father was staying, and I confronted him. I told him about
how he hit us and killed my mother. I was harsh and mean
and made sure he knew the damage he'd done. It can't be a
coincidence he overdosed twenty-four hours later."

Her eyes search mine as if looking for confirmation of this fact, and I have no idea what to say. All I keep thinking about is how that's the reason they were together.

While I was getting shitfaced and losing a poker game, she was confronting her demons, and Atlas was helping her.

I clench my jaw, angry with myself for so many reasons I can no longer tell them apart. Everything Atlas said to me earlier comes back to me in perfect clarity.

He's right.

I've been making her feel like everything that happened between us was her fault—for choosing Atlas over me—but in reality, I've been a shit friend. I pushed the idea of us on her with little regard to how she actually felt about it. Hell, I probably pushed her away with how I acted. I see it now. I see the connection she and Atlas had from the start, and that her fear of losing me is the only thing that made her hesitate. I've taken zero responsibility for my own actions while I placed all the blame at her feet when she had every right to make the choices she did.

Not only that, but I nearly let my team down tonight. I've gambled away money I don't have. And I've been relying on alcohol to ease my emotional turmoil far more than I'd like to admit.

I'm a wreck, and the last thing I want is to drag anyone down with me, especially Mackenzie.

It's time I get my shit together. Starting now.

"Listen to me," I say, taking her by the shoulders and forcing her to meet my gaze, "He chose to use again. He chose to take his shame and guilt and drown it in pills. It was the easy way out. You have zero culpability in it in the same way you didn't force him to get behind the wheel of a car last January and drive under the influence and leave once he hit you like nothing happened. This is all on *him*."

"Atlas . . ."

"Won't blame you either. Not for a second. He's lived with this his whole life."

She closes her mouth and stifles another sob. I wish I could comfort her. More than that, I wish I could've been there for her today when Atlas fell. I wish she hadn't needed to face this alone.

"He's right, Kenz," Jace chimes in, nudging her in the arm.

"This isn't on you," Teagan agrees.

Letting out a shaky breath, Kenz straightens and wipes her damp cheeks with the back of her hand.

"Hey," I reach out and take her fingers in mine. "Can we go for a walk or something, talk for a bit?"

She falls silent, biting her lip as she glances around the waiting room while worry creases her brow.

"One of the guys will call if there's an update," I say and Knox nods.

"We're not going anywhere," Teagan adds.

"Okay," she says, the relief evident in her voice. "Come on." She grabs my arm, guiding me toward the exit. We make our way through the double doors and out into the crisp night air where we take the sidewalk.

Tucking my hands into my pockets, I think about everything I want to say—all the things I *need* to get off my chest. There are so many, I'm not even sure where to start. But I guess starting is the hard part; we should've had this discussion months ago.

I release a long breath and pause, turning to face her. "You really love him, don't you?"

It's something I've known for a while but refused to admit to myself. Still, I need to hear her say it. If I can see it in her eyes, it won't be easy, but I can move on.

She pauses and stares up at me, likely wondering where this is headed and whether it's safe to tell me the truth. I see the moment she makes the decision. The light in her eyes brightens and she nods. "I do. I know I said I'd put you first but I love him, and I want to be your friend Graham, I really do . . . but not at the expense of me and Atlas."

If it came down to it, she'd choose him. I deserve that, and I respect her for having the gal to say so.

She lifts her chin, as if daring me to challenge her.

"Forget what I said about wanting someone to put me first. I was being a dumbass."

She exhales, and I can practically feel her relief.

"I never should have said that. It was a passive aggressive way of giving you an ultimatum, and I'm sorry." I shrug. "I have no excuse, except that I haven't been thinking clearly these last few months. Between Atlas coming to town and moving into my house, what happened with us, my father . . ." The gambling, and the drinking, I want to say. "I haven't been myself. I've been a jerk and I hope you can forgive me."

"Of course I forgive you." She reaches out and pulls me in for a hug. When she releases me, she asks, "Do you really think we can be friends, though, without things being weird?"

"I think we'll probably need to set some boundaries, and it probably be different than what we're used to, but, yeah. You're my day one, right?" I say, with a grin.

"My ride or die." She laughs. "And you're really going to be okay with this? Me and Atlas? For real?"

"Yeah." I exhale and hug my arms to my chest. "I mean, it's going to take a little getting used to, but I think he and I are cool now." I think about tonight and everything that's happened recently, and I wonder if maybe we have more in common than I thought. "Hell, maybe he and I can even help each other out. Maybe we can figure this shit with Cal out together."

Her smile fades. "If he gets through this," she says in a small voice.

"He'll get through this. He's tough. A survivor. If anyone should know that, it's you."

"You're right." She stares into the distance, and I can tell her mind is working overtime.

"Come on. Let's go back." I sling my arm over her shoulders and guide her back toward the hospital entrance, feeling lighter than I have in months. Funny how doing the right thing can have that effect.

We push back through the thick glass doors and pass the registration desk before heading into the waiting room, and I freeze. My father is sitting next to Mr. Hart and at the sound of our entrance, he glances up at us. "What are you doing here?" I growl.

"I called him," Mr. Hart says. "Seeing as how he's Atlas's legal guardian right now and living with him, I thought he should know."

"*Was* his legal guardian," Mackenzie says as she glares a hole through my father. "He hasn't stayed with him all week, and he's eighteen now. He's legally an adult."

Her father frowns, glancing between Mackenzie and my father, and I can see in his eyes he's questioning whether he did the right thing. Either way, he says nothing else, likely afraid to ruin whatever truce he and Kenzie have formed.

"Excuse me," a voice calls out behind us and we all turn. A doctor in a pair of blue scrubs stares back at us. "I'm looking for a parent of Atlas Scott?" He holds a clipboard in his hands and stares expectantly between my father and Mr. Hart. "Are either of you his guardian?"

Cal opens his mouth to speak, but before he can get a word out, another voice from behind calls out.

"That's me."

My head jerks at the sound of the voice, my gaze zeroing in on the woman I recognize from the day at Fall Fest, and my stomach sinks.

"I'm Atlas Scott's mother."

CHAPTER 36

MACKENZIE

MY FINGERS FLY TO my mouth and cover my parted lips as I stare at Atlas's mother in shock. I've only ever seen her once, and that day at Fall Fest, I hadn't gotten a good look. Now that we're standing only feet apart, however, I see the resemblance. The dark hair and equally dark eyes. The smooth, tan skin and full lips. She reminds me so much of Atlas, it hurts.

I sink down into the chair beside me on shaking limbs and pull in a breath. I don't know if Atlas would want her here, but I'm not sure there's anything I can do to keep her from taking charge. After all, she is legally his mother.

"Do you know who brought your son in?" the doctor asks.

"I did," I say, straightening. Fear pumps through my veins as I prepare myself for the worst—that it's my fault he's in the condition he's in.

"You likely saved his life," the doctor says. I can feel eyes on my back as he continues, "Had you waited or wasted any time at all, the damage would've been much more extensive."

I bend at the waist and cover my face with my hands as relief swells inside my chest. "I was so afraid I did the wrong thing," I mumble to myself.

A hand comes down over my shoulder and when I blink my eyes open, I lock eyes with Atlas's mother before she glances back up at the doctor.

"As it is, Mr. Scott has a fracture in his skull and some bleeding. We're doing surgery to drain the blood and relieve any pressure," the doctor continues.

His mother whimpers, covering her mouth with her hands. "Is he going to be okay?"

"Right now, it's anybody's guess. Luckily, the bleeding in his brain is minimal. We're doing everything we can, so his prognosis looks good. But in these instances, I really don't like to make sweeping statements until after the patient wakes. A lot can happen."

"But he will wake, right?" she asks, her voice thick.

"Again, we're extremely optimistic. But we won't know the extent of the damage the bleeding has caused yet."

My limbs go numb as I listen to what the doctor *isn't* saying. "In other words, we won't know if he suffered any brain damage."

The doctor's eyes shift to me. "Precisely."

GRAHAM

I stare at Mackenzie while she sleeps, pressed up against her father's side. It's been six hours since the doctors came and gave us an update. Six hours I watched her cry and worry until sheer exhaustion finally claimed her.

Jace, Teagan and Knox took off on a food run, and Atlas's mother went in search of coffee. I can't sleep. Nor can I eat or sit still.

The truth is, I'm petrified—scared to death Atlas might not pull through. If he doesn't, Mackenzie will never be the same again, and I'm not sure I can hold her together after a second loss, let alone one so soon after her mother.

I glance at the nurses' station where the on-call is talking to a male aid. She's distracted, and the floor is quiet. It would be easy to slip back to Atlas's room. To tell him he has a lot worth fighting for. To remind him he has a room full of people waiting for him to wake.

I step into the hallway, my eyes glued to the nurse the entire time, but she doesn't look over. She doesn't even so much as blink, so I take another step. And another. Until I'm cruising down the hallway like I know what I'm doing, my stride quick as I peek my head into each room, searching for the familiar crop of dark hair, square jaw, and broad shoulders.

Everything is dismal and gray. The walls. The floor. The hospital beds. Even the plastic supply cart in the hallway. Just passing through is depressing, but I'm a man on a mission, and I won't stop until I accomplish my goal.

Finally, I spot him and come to a halt outside his door. Taking a tentative step inside, I brace my hands on the doorframe, taking him in. A mask covers his face. IVs and tubes are hooked to his arm where red, green, and blue squiggles dart across the screen. His skin is pale and his body lifeless. I'm not sure I've ever seen him this vulnerable, and now that I have, I'm not sure I like it.

I swallow and take a step another step inside, hurrying before I lose my nerve or someone finds me and boots me out. I might only have a few minutes, so I better make the most of it.

I stare down at him. He's one hell of a receiver, and tonight, he laid his heart out on that field. I have no doubt in my mind we wouldn't have won State if it weren't for him, not that I'd ever tell him that. The dude is strong as an ox. Quick as a lion. Despite our differences, seeing him like this, doesn't sit right with me.

I suck in a deep breath and move to the other side of the room, where I peer through the blinds to the darkness outside. "The first time I saw you standing with Mackenzie in the hallway at school, I knew," I say, my voice soft. "She loved you from that very first moment."

I close my eyes and the memories press against the back of my lids. The way Kenz looked up at me when I realized they'd already met, like she was caught doing something she shouldn't. She'd been drawn to him from the start. I just didn't want to admit it.

"I'm sorry for the way I treated you. I'm sorry for not giving you a chance or being a better cousin—a friend. But it was like all of a sudden, you showed up, and everything changed. My father started comparing me to you. I've been trying to be good enough for him for years, and you came in and impressed him in a single day. Everyone was talking about you in the halls. And Mackenzie . . . I've spent the better part of the last four years loving her quietly, just waiting for the moment she loved me back so I could tell her how I felt, and then you come along . . ."

I open my eyes and shake my head, then spin on my heel. I go to his side and sit in the chair beside his bed. I stare at his pale face and will him to wake. "This bitter boy with a chip on his shoulder; I thought you had nothing to offer her. I thought your feelings for her were superficial, and that she couldn't possibly love you the same way I love her. But I was wrong."

My voice cracks as I stare at his prone form. Saying these words while he's unconscious should be easier but somehow, it's not. Somehow, it's harder. "You have to wake up, man. She needs you," I croak.

My heart kicks painfully in my chest.

My feelings for Mackenzie consume me; they fill all the empty places inside and I have no idea how to let her go. I only know that I need to. Because she loves someone else. Her heart isn't mine; maybe it never was, and the last thing I want is to stand in her way.

"I promise if you wake up, things will be different. I won't stand in your way again." My chest splits in two, and I exhale a shaky breath. "You're right. I've never seen her look at me the way she looks at you, like you're the earth and she's the moon just orbiting your axis. Mackenzie chose *you*. As much as it pains me to say it, she loves *you*. And she's waiting for you right outside."

I stand and tap my fist gently against the side of his arm before I head for the door with a final glance over my shoulder. "I trust that I'm putting her in good hands. Don't hurt her." A swell of emotion tightens my chest, but I push it back down. "Or I'll have to come after you. And we both know I have one hell of a right hook."

CHAPTER 37

MACKENZIE

NEARLY FORTY-EIGHT HOURS PASS at an excruciatingly slow pace. In that time, mostly everyone has come and gone. Graham, Atlas's mother, and I are the only ones who remain, but I'm not sure how long that will last. Though the surgery went well, the doctors say it could be days until Atlas wakes.

My eyes drift closed as I lean into Graham's side as he snores softly beside me. The steady cadence of it, combined with my own exhaustion, lulls me to sleep and it's some time later, when a nurse appears in front of us for an update, that I wake with a jolt.

"Ms. Scott," she says to Atlas's mom. "He's awake." The nurse smiles while my heart skips a beat. "He's a little groggy and out of it, but he's responding. It looks like we might get the best-case scenario here."

I sigh as a huge weight lifts off me.

"We can see him now?" she asks, and the nurse nods. "Just one at a time and not for long. He needs his rest. When you're ready, I'll be at the desk. I can take you back."

I straighten in my seat, fully expecting her to stand, but she glances over at me, her eyes glossy with tears. "You should go."

"Me?" I ask, pointing to my chest.

She offers me a sad smile. "I think we both know I'm the last visitor he needs. He and I can talk after, but for now, you should go."

I rise to my feet, heart kicking in my chest at the prospect of seeing him. "Thank you," I whisper, anxious to lay eyes on him. To hold his hand. Kiss his lips.

I hurry to the nurse and she wastes no time as she leads me down a long corridor, then to the right, pausing at a room on the end. She motions for me to go in and I take a deep breath, preparing myself for what I'm about to see. I push my way through the door to his room and am assaulted with sounds and sensations that bring me back to the weeks following the car crash. The steady drone of machines. The beep of his monitors. Disinfectant scenting the air.

I suck in a breath at the sight of Atlas in his hospital bed. Several monitors and an IV are hooked up to his arm. His skin is unusually pale. Dark moons shadow his eyes, and when he blinks them open, I nearly cry in relief.

Part of me feared I might never see him again.

"Atlas . . ." I say, hurrying to his side. Gently, I close the remaining gap between us, hating how fragile he looks as I lift his hand. I bring it to my lips and brush a kiss over his knuckles.

"Hey," he says, his voice a violent rasp. "I'm so tired."

Tears fill my eyes, but I refuse to let them fall because he's awake, and I'm here. He's going to be okay. He has to be.

"Go ahead and rest," I say, squeezing his hand in mine.

I watch as he fights to keep his eyes open, but he gives in and they flutter closed. "Don't leave," he whispers.

"I won't leave," I promise. "I'm here now, and I'll be here when you wake."

ATLAS

A subtle pressure on my chest wakes me. I blink my eyes open, and it takes several seconds to acclimate myself before I remember where I am. The hospital. I got hurt. I fell, I think, though the details are fuzzy.

I glance down at my chest to see the source of the pressure and smile at Mackenzie's sleeping form. One arm is draped over my body, while the rest of her is stretched over the edge of my bed from the chair beside me. The position looks so uncomfortable, I can't help but laugh.

She shifts, then opens her eyes, and I watch as the sleep clears from her gaze.

"Atlas?" she says as she jerks her head up.

"Hey, doll." I reach out, a small smile tugging the corner of my lips. I begin to trace the line of her jaw with my thumb while I contemplate her presence here, hoping it means what I think it means.

"How are you feeling?" she asks, sitting straighter now. "Can I get you anything? Should I go fetch the nurse?"

"Not yet." The truth is, my head hurts like a bitch and my throat feels like someone lit it on fire. I need a drink and some painkillers, but not enough to interrupt this moment alone with her. "Just let me look at you for a minute," I rasp out.

"You scared the crap out of me," she says, her voice trembling, and I will her not to cry. My fragile heart can't take it.

"Well, I'm awake now." I brush a lock of hair from her eyes.

"Do you remember anything?"

I frown as I concentrate on the last things I remember. "You came to see me at my house." I wince and bring a hand to my head. It pounds like a jackhammer. "I was upset about my father and I fell. Then everything went black. Well, everything but your voice. I could hear you even though I couldn't wake up, but I couldn't move or answer."

"Really? You could hear me?" she asks, her eyes searching mine.

I nod. "And I think I was dreaming because I swear you drove a car."

She shakes her head, her mouth a thin line, and her eyes shining with emotion. "You didn't dream it."

It takes me a moment to realize what she's saying. "You really did drive?"

"I brought you here," she says, softly.

A puff of air escapes my lips. Part of me can't believe it. "So, that's what it takes to get you behind the wheel? Me nearly dying?"

She fake punches me in the arm before she kisses me on my cheek. "Don't ever scare me like that again."

"No more roofs. I swear," I say as she leans closer.

I reach out and tuck a lock of hair behind her ear and wonder how much sleep she's gotten. Judging by the dark circles around her eyes, not much. "Are we good?" I ask, thinking about before the fall—how she'd gone cold on me after the night we spent together.

"Yeah, we're good," she says, but her tone is weak and completely unconvincing.

"Talk to me," I say, preparing for the worst. If she's gonna rip my heart out, I'd rather have her do it now. Maybe the hospital staff can find a way to put the pieces back together again.

She clears her throat and I can tell she's reluctant to say whatever's on her mind. "If it wasn't for me, he wouldn't have . . ." Her voice cracks, her chin quivering before she tries again. "My visit, everything I said to your father, it's probably what made him relapse."

My father. That's what she's upset about, not the prospect of breaking my heart for the second time.

I shouldn't be relieved, but as I shake my head, I can breathe a little easier. "You're blaming yourself for my father's relapse?"

Her face crumples and a tear rolls down her cheek.

"No. Doll . . ." I place my hands on either side of her face and wince at the pain radiating up my body. "Look at me." I wait until those ice blue eyes meet mine before I continue. "He's been an addict my whole life. This is not on you. You had nothing to do with it. Relapses happen. He had a chance to do the right thing for once in his life, and instead, he chose the easy way out. He screwed up again, and he paid the price."

"But—"

"No more." I press a finger to her lips, silencing her. "I don't want your guilt. If you think for one second I'm going to finally have you forgive me then blame you for this, you're out of your mind. The world and everything in it can be against us and I'll still love you, Mackenzie Hart," I say repeating back the words she once said to me.

She swipes a hand across her face, wiping away another tear. "I love you," she whispers.

"Love you too, doll." I beckon her toward me and press my lips to hers. I could be dying and I'd still want one more kiss from her, one more touch. "Does this mean I finally get to call you my girlfriend again?" I ask when she pulls away.

She chokes out a laugh then stares at me with so much tenderness in her eyes, it takes my breath away.

"Call me whatever you want, Atlas Scott. As long as I'm yours."

Chapter 38

ATLAS

Mackenzie holds my hand as we step out of the whipping wind into the warmth of Roasted. Early December has brought unusually low temperatures, and I rub my hands down Mackenzie's arms to warm her up as my gaze makes quick work of the place.

Everyone is already here, piled onto the sofa and chairs surrounding a coffee table where Jace and Teagan appear to be playing a competitive game of table soccer using their fingers, a wad of notebook paper, and salt and pepper shakers for goals.

I nod toward them, a grin on my face. "Why don't you give me your order and snag us a seat before those buffoons manspread and take up the rest of the available space?"

Mackenzie laughs. "Okay. Surprise me, as long as it's hot."

I step up to the counter and order our drinks. While I wait, I allow my gaze to drift to our group of friends. Mackenzie told me how they'd been there for me. Every single one of them waited until I was out of surgery and in recovery before they even considered going home. They stopped and brought us coffee and fast food over the course of my stay. Jace told me stupid jokes. He, Teagan, and Knox kept me company alongside Kenz when I thought I'd go crazy from lying in a hospital bed. And ever since I was released nearly a week ago, it's been like this. With the season at an end, we hang out almost daily, even if it's just for a cup of coffee or to catch up.

Mackenzie takes a seat in a plush armchair, her dark hair spilling over her shoulders while the others greet her. Every time I look at her, I can't get over how gorgeous she is. How vibrant and sweet. And *mine.*

Graham sits across from her. His smile is friendly and his gaze no longer lingers on her like it used to, though I imagine his indifference takes a lot of restraint on his part.

When the barista hands me our drinks, I thank him and head their way. Mackenzie rises to her feet as I hand her the paper to-go cup with her coffee. "What is it?" she asks, eyes bright.

"S'mores latte. Something sweet for someone sweet," I say as she leans in for a kiss.

Beside us, Jace groans. "Could you be any cheesier, dude? Cut the sappy shit already, will you?"

I brush my lips over Kenzie's one last time, then hold my arms out. "I almost fucking died, bro. Cut me some slack."

Jace rolls his eyes. "Here we go again, always playing the sympathy card. What about those of us who are left to deal with the PDA? That's a special kind of torture."

I grin and sink down into the armchair and pull Mackenzie onto my lap. By now, their razzing doesn't even phase me. Besides, I'm so dang in love with this girl, they can say whatever they want because maybe I am a little sappy these days. How can I not be?

"So, I hear since you and Kenzie were holed up in the hospital over Thanksgiving, you're having some kind of a redo this weekend with Chief Hart." Jace eyes me with a raised brow, a shit-eating grin on his face.

"Yeah. I'll go to Mackenzie's at noon, then we promised to join Graham at five. Apparently Cal can't be overshadowed, not even by the Chief of Police." And though I want zero to do with Uncle Cal, Kenz and I promised we'd go for Graham.

Jace snickers. "Still trying to mend broken fences, huh?"

"Have fun, buddy." Teagan slaps me on the shoulder.

"I'd take your bulletproof vest to Hart's if I were you," Knox chimes in.

Mackenzie picks up a sugar packet and tosses it at him. "My father has come a long way," she says, tipping her chin up, and I stifle a laugh. While it's true her dad doesn't hate me quite so vehemently, she had to threaten not to come at all in order for him to extend the invitation.

Still, baby steps, right?

"All of you at the Scott residence?" Jace whistles. "Are there going to be any more secret baby announcements?" he asks.

Mackenzie gasps. "Jace!"

"What?" He shrugs. "It's a valid question."

"Seriously, bro? You gotta go there," I say.

"You always were an ass," Graham chimes in, and everyone laughs. "I appreciate the backup though. I'm gonna need it," he says with a sigh. "In no way do I want to sit through a holiday dinner alone, let alone one being put on for show."

I remember the last time he, Mackenzie, and I all had dinner at his house. It feels like forever ago and I can only hope this time around, we can get by with a little less tension. Though I'm not holding my breath.

"What about the kid? Did he get an invite?" Teagan asks.

"You mean Storm?" I frown as I think about it. "No. He came to visit me in the hospital, though, and we've been talking some." Glancing at Graham, I gauge his response. Though I've accepted that we share a half brother, he hasn't. Storm is still a sore subject for him, and he avoids talking about it all together.

"Not to change the subject," I say, even though that's my exact intention, "but I heard the coach from Ohio state called." I turn to Jace. "Are you thinking of signing?"

"Hell, yeah. If he makes good on his promise, I'd sign in a heartbeat. But what about you? From what I've heard you have USC, Notre Dame, and Alabama all in a tizzy to garner your hand," he says, batting his eyelashes. "Have you given a verbal yet?"

I shake my head. "USC has been talking for a while, so that's nothing new, but 'Bama and Notre Dame?" I exhale. It gives me chills just thinking about it. "You're talking about the number one and number two schools in the country."

"And?" he asks, eyes wide like I'm crazy.

"That's a lot of pressure."

"Dude!" Jace moans.

"What about this guy?" I say, waving toward Teagan. "He's been awfully tight-lipped about any offers."

All of us turn to Teagan who shrugs. "I'll announce it when I sign."

A collective groan follows before Jace lays into him about brotherhood and solidarity, and before I know what the hell is happening, they start talking about something that happened with a chick at football camp three years ago.

I shake my head and laugh. Who knew I'd move to the stuffy, small town of Riverside and find friends like these. Not once did they judge me for who I was before or where I came from. They couldn't care less about how much money is in my wallet or which side of town I live on. Hell, even Graham seems to be coming around.

My eyes flicker to him and the distant look in his eye. Something is bothering him, but I can't tell what, and for once, I don't think it has anything to do with the girl in my arms.

"What are you so deep in thought about?" Mackenzie murmurs.

I tear my gaze away from Graham to her, and it hits me like it always does how utterly breathtaking she is.

I reach out and tuck a lock of hair behind her ear. "Just about how lucky I am."

"Show me how lucky." She grins and leans into me, brushing her lips over mine once before pulling away again. Despite how much shit the guys give us, we try as hard as we can to behave when Graham's around. If the shoe were on the other foot, I could only imagine how hard it would be.

As we sit and listen to the guys bicker, Mackenzie traces a finger over my bicep, idly tracing the clean lines of the ink I got with the boys the night my father died. It's mostly healed now. The delicate scroll of the word "doll" somehow stands out among the others.

"Have I ever told you this new tattoo is my favorite?" She meets my eyes again and bites her lip.

"You may have mentioned it a time or two." When I showed her in the hospital, she'd been awestruck. She'd stared at for hours, tracing the lines of ink with her finger. It was the cutest fucking reaction I'd ever seen. "And I'd get a thousand more for you," I say.

"But what would you have done if I had told you I didn't want to be together?" She squints as if trying to read the answer on my face.

I shrug. "Nothing. I would've cherished it just the same. Like it or not, you're a part of me that can never be erased. You changed something in me. I'll carry you around forever in here, anyway." I fist my hand over my chest. "Only seems fitting I carry you around with me for all the world to see, too."

"Atlas Scott, who knew you were a romantic?"

"Just for you."

She snuggles closer to me, falling silent for a moment as my thoughts drift. Knox, Teagan and Jace got Rebels tattoos, but I still don't know what Graham got. He's been rather tightlipped about it.

"I'm thinking about getting one," Mackenzie murmurs, drawing me from my thoughts.

"A tattoo?" I eye her and arch a brow. When she only nods, I say, "I could take you if you'd like. Do you know what you want to get?"

She bites her lower lip again, unable to contain the grin curling the corners of her lips as she glances up at me from beneath her lashes. "A dandelion."

CHAPTER 39

ATLAS

MACKENZIE PULLS UP IN front of the squat building. It's small with pale gray siding, shutters, and a large wreath on the door. It looks more like a house than a shrink's office, but that's one of the things she said she likes about it. It feels more personal, she says. Like going to a friend's house to talk, instead of having your head examined.

Ever since the day she rushed me to the hospital, she's been driving again in small amounts, mostly to and from school. Though she hasn't had another episode yet, her therapist warned her she's not past the point of being triggered. Still, she's learning techniques to shut a panic attack down before it explodes into a full-blown PTSD episode, and I couldn't be prouder of her for facing her fears and getting help.

She leaves the car running and sighs, staring out the passenger window toward the front door. Her first couple of sessions were hard, and I'm not sure she expects today to be any easier. "You'll be back to pick me up in an hour?" she asks.

"Yeah. I just want to drop off some stuff for Storm. We're hanging out on Saturday, so I don't need to stay."

"And your mom?"

I roll my head on my neck. "Baby steps. I agreed to lunch before I take Storm out this weekend."

"Good." She smiles. "I think it's nice you're going to spend some time with him."

I shrug. "I never thought I'd admit this, but it's kind of cool having a little brother."

"He's smitten with you. You know that, right?"

I roll my eyes. I met with the kid once in the last week and made the mistake of asking Mackenzie to come along for moral support. Ever since, all she does is remind me of how the boy looked at me with stars in his eyes.

"We literally picked him up from school and treated him to a Coke and he expressed his gratitude. I wouldn't call that smitten."

"Um, he wouldn't shut up about how cool it was that his older brothers were the Scott boys, and how amazing you are at football."

I frown. Okay, maybe he did do that.

"I just wish Graham would consider meeting him." She sighs.

"He will," I say, though I'm not convinced. "He just needs some time. It's easier for me. My mom and I never had a relationship. But to find out your father cheated on your mom and had an illegitimate son with someone else, then covered it up? That's rough. His relationship with Cal is shaky as it is."

"Ugh. You're right. I can't imagine what I'd do if I found out my mother had a son with Anthony Mancetti. It would be rough, for sure."

"We can't fix the world in a day." I wink at her and her cheeks turn pink.

"One thing at a time," she says. Then groans. "Starting with me."

She hops out of the car and pauses by my open window to give me a kiss. When she walks away, I watch her go, wondering how I got so lucky.

MACKENZIE

I fidget with the place settings, then step back, eyeing them one more time. A gold tablecloth covers the table with bronze chargers and a set of china my mother only ever used for special occasions. "Do you think we need something else with the centerpiece?" I ask, staring holes through the basket of mini pumpkins and dried corn. "It looks like we're missing something."

My father places the butter dish on the table, along with a pitcher of water. "If I have to watch you mess with it one more time, I might go crazy."

I sigh and stick my tongue out. "It's just that Atlas hasn't had a real Thanksgiving in years, and I know it's not *really* Thanksgiving, but I still want it to be perfect."

"Won't it be perfect just by being together?" He snorts. "Isn't that what all you young people in love say? That all you need is each other?"

"Like you and mom never felt that way." I roll my eyes before I realize it's the first time I've mentioned Mom around him without getting angry. It's also the first time I've joked with him about anything in a long time.

He and I have a long way to go, but things are slowly getting better between us. The way he stayed at the hospital the night of Atlas's accident and supported me with no questions asked was the olive branch we needed. Not once did he suggest I leave Atlas's side. Afterward, I explained to him how I felt about Atlas and told him in no uncertain terms that if he wanted me in his life, he needed to accept him, too. And he's been trying, he really has. Today is one giant step in the right direction.

"I'm going to check on the turkey," he says as he heads back into the kitchen. It's our first time cooking a holiday meal, and I have no idea how the food will turn out. Thankfully one of his female coworkers let him borrow an electric roaster for the bird because she swore it was foolproof. Something tells me she has a crush on him. I'm not sure how I feel about that.

The doorbell rings and my stomach drops, a ball of nerves fists in my belly. I scold myself for being nervous. After all, it's Atlas. But then, I've never really brought a boy home to dinner. Neither have I brought a boy home to meet my parents, for that matter, and certainly not one they recently disapproved of.

I hurry to the door and swing it open, awestruck at first by the masculine lines of his handsome face before I take in what he's wearing and burst out laughing.

"Who are you and what did you do with my boyfriend?" My gaze travels the length of him and my lips twitch. The blue argyle sweater, navy blue pants, and loafers are a far cry from his usual T-shirt and jeans or hoodie and jogger ensemble.

"Stop laughing," he hisses, but the pink in his cheeks only makes me laugh harder because he's the most adorable thing I've ever seen. "I wanted to impress your father, okay? I know how much today means to you, and I didn't want to show up with my tattoo sleeve on display or in my leather jacket and jeans."

"Right," I drawl. "You do know he's seen your tattoos and the way you normally dress, right? And he'll likely see them again"—I wink—"since you're not getting rid of me that easy."

"I know," he smooths a hand over his sweater. "But for my first time here with you, I didn't want it to be the thing he focuses on. Next time, he can think whatever he wants."

"Well, I kinda like it," I say, reaching out and fisting his sweater in my hand as I pull him closer.

"Yeah?"

I nod and bite my lower lip while his gaze hungrily tracks the movement. "Yeah. You're easily the hottest nerd I've ever seen."

He arches a brow. "You're teasing me, aren't you?"

"Whatever would give you that impression?" I ask innocently.

"Later, when it's just us, you're gonna be in big trouble," he whispers as he moves forward and quickly nips my lower lip before stepping away again.

"Is that a promise?"

"Atlas . . ." My father clears his throat behind me, "Please, come in."

I press my lips together, my eyes wide as I stifle a laugh.

"Ah, thank you, sir." Atlas blanches, looking as if he wishes he could melt into the floorboards. Then, as if remembering himself, he bends down and grabs a paper sack off the porch. "Um, these are for you."

My father takes the bag and peeks inside with a frown. "You got me flowers?" he asks, sounding so confused it's almost comical. Reaching inside, he pulls out a huge cluster of white hydrangeas.

"And a pie for dessert." Atlas motions to the bag. "The flowers are to represent the people who couldn't be with us today. I know they were Mrs. Hart's favorite." He shifts his weight and licks his lips. "Maybe it's stupid, but I just thought . . ."

My eyes well with tears and a lump forms in the back of my throat. I reach out gripping his arm as I stare at him with gratitude shining in my eyes. Beside me, I hear my father swallow and he nods.

"Ah, thank you," he croaks. "These were her favorite," he says, his voice thick.

Atlas knew this, of course, but I don't say so. Instead, I let my father take the gesture at face value, and when he turns to fetch a vase of water, I sink into Atlas's arms. "Thank you," I murmur breathing in the spicy scent of his cologne.

My face presses against the soft material of his sweater, while his heart thumps against my cheek. "Come on." I tug him inside, through the living room into the kitchen where my father is sitting the vase on the table beside the pumpkins. "Perfect," I say, motioning toward it. "That's what was missing."

At my father's insistence, Atlas and I sit while he brings the bowls and platters of food to the table. We begin to eat, making small talk about the weather and Christmas when my father eyes him over his water glass. I stiffen, ready for the inquisition I sense is about to go down. "So, I hear you've gotten a lot of interest. Are you excited for signing day?"

Atlas nods and sits his bread roll back on his plate before he wipes his mouth with his napkin. "Both excited and nervous, I guess. Honestly, though, I'd be honored and lucky to go to any of the division one schools."

"Will you be the first in your family to get a college degree?"

"Dad?" My eyes widen, and I glance over at Atlas, hoping he didn't take it the wrong way.

"It's okay." He waves off my concern. "I guess I would be. I mean, Graham will be going to school, too. But both my father and Uncle Cal played football. Cal was drafted before he finished, and my father, well . . . to my knowledge, my mother never went either."

My father nods. "Do you know who you want to sign with?" he asks.

"I'm leaning toward Alabama or Notre Dame. But"—his gaze flickers to me—"I would follow your daughter if she wanted me to."

I feel a blush rise to my cheeks. It's something he and I have touched on briefly, but we haven't nailed anything down yet.

"As a man I have to say that's pretty stupid," My dad says.

My mouth parts, ready to defend him.

"But as a father," he adds, "I can appreciate that." He meets my eyes and smiles, then rolls his eyes before continuing. "In fact, I'm sure she'd be thrilled to be close to you. Plus, I wouldn't mind her finally deciding what she wants to do with her life."

"Dad!" I throw a wadded napkin at him.

"What?" He shrugs. "I just want you to find your path, pick a direction, something. Isn't that what all parents want for their kids? To see them successful and happy?"

Atlas winks at me, and my insides turn to mush.

"Well, you'll be happy to know that I've been mulling over some things," I say.

Drug counseling, social work, inspirational speaking and advocacy—they're all on the table.

"Glad to hear it," he says, then returns to his plate. "And I have to say, having Atlas around to watch over you when I can't puts the protector in me at ease." His smile grows and I roll my eyes, before we dig back into our food.

Over an hour later we're sitting around the table, stuffed to the brim as I push the last bite of pie around on my plate. "I can't eat any more or I might explode," I say with a moan. Though dinner went better than I ever could have imagined, I'm ready for some time with Atlas out from under the microscope.

I rise from the table and start to clear the dishes when my father shoos me away. "I'll clean up."

"Are you sure?" I ask.

"Positive. Go ahead in the living room and watch a movie or something. I'll load the dishes then get out of your hair."

"Okay, if you're sure." I turn to Atlas. "Let me just use the bathroom and then we'll pick out something to watch before we have to head over to see Graham."

"Sure thing," he says as he starts to help my father clear the table.

I hurry to the powder room, using it as quickly as possible so as not to keep Atlas waiting. I've only been gone a couple of minutes by the time I return, when I hear my father's voice from the kitchen. Creeping closer, I cock my ear and press my lips together to keep quiet as I focus on what he's saying, praying he's not giving Atlas a hard time. Weeks ago, just the prospect of them being in a room alone together would've sent me into fits.

"I'm sure you know Mackenzie and I have had our problems this year," he says, pausing, "but I'm trying to do right by her. I want her in my life, and she's made it very clear how much you mean to her."

"I appreciate that, sir," Atlas says.

"I haven't always done things the right way, but I'm trying to change the way I do them now, and I'm man enough to admit that I might have judged you prematurely. For that, I'm sorry. In my line of work, I see a lot of the bad in people. Sometimes, it's easier to assume the worst and ask questions later. But you seem like a good man despite your circumstances. Not a lot can say the same, and I respect that. I guess part of what I'm trying to say is, I'm sorry."

My chest constricts, and I have to press my lips into a tight line just to contain my emotion.

"No need to apologize," Atlas says, his voice soft. "You were trying to protect your daughter. No one can fault you for that. Heck, I'd do the same in your shoes."

"Doesn't make it right." I peek around the corner and into the kitchen to see him shaking his head. "But maybe we can start over."

"I'd like that," Atlas says, his voice so genuine, the ache in my chest is back with a vengeance.

If I stand here any longer, I'll cry, so I step around the corner and clear my throat as I say, "What are we talking about?"

Atlas shrugs. "Nothing major. Just guy talk." He jerks his head toward the living room. "You ready?"

"Yes. But I get to pick the movie," I say, rubbing my hands together with an evil smile.

He groans, and I laugh as I guide him toward the hallway. As I do, I glance over my shoulder to where my father watches us go, and mouth, *thank you.*

GRAHAM

My father comes up behind my mother and wraps her in a giant bear hug, nuzzling her neck.

It makes me fucking sick.

The things this man has done that she knows nothing about . . .

Turning away from them, I resume staring out the window. Though things are still a little weird between Atlas, Kenz, and me, I can't wait for them to get here. I'd gladly spend an afternoon of watching them make eyes at each other if it means I have a buffer between my father and I.

"Mrs. White is finished in the kitchen," my mother says behind me, "so I told her to go and be with her family. But look at these place settings, Cal. Didn't she do a beautiful job?"

I roll my eyes.

The table is covered in ivory linens, fine china, real crystal and silver, and is overflowing with fresh flowers.

Like it fucking matters.

It's just going to be the five of us. Who the hell are they trying to impress? Why can't we have one family dinner without the pretense? Why can't we eat our turkey and stuffing on paper plates like the rest of America? For once, I'd like to enjoy dinner without flowers and candlelight and cloth napkins.

I want a hunk of pumpkin pie with Cool Whip. Not freaking French lavender macaroons or pavlova with berries.

I rake a hand through my hair. Clearly my sour mood is getting worse by the minute, but I can't seem to help myself. No one wanted this little impromptu holiday but them. The only reason they're evening putting this on is because they caught wind of what Chief Hart was doing for Atlas since he and Kenzie missed it and felt like they should do the same. I'm one step away from bailing altogether when Mackenzie's white sedan pulls into the driveway and I sigh in relief.

The tight muscles in my shoulders relax as I move. I don't even wait for them to come to the door before I'm heading out into the hallway and through the foyer where I throw the door open. Watching as they get out, I shake my head at the sight of Kenz sliding out from behind the wheel. It's nothing short of a miracle she's driving again. But I'm so stinking proud of her. I guess that's the power of love. It makes you do crazy things. It moves mountains and changes lives. Gives you the strength to overcome your fears.

I want that for myself so badly it hurts.

Bitterness burns in the back of my throat, but I swallow it down. Being around them isn't easy. I'm still in love with Kenz, and though I know it's something I need to let go of. I can't just shut off my feelings overnight. It's going to take time. I'm going to have to give myself grace, but I know I can do it. She and I were friends once before I fell for her. We can be friends again, but it starts with me. Until then, I'm faking it until I make it.

I cross my arms over my chest and lean against the doorframe as I watch my cousin take Mackenzie's hand and lead her up the stone sidewalk to the front porch. "Damn, bro. You look like Mr. Fucking Rogers in my sweater and slacks."

Atlas flips me off and a laugh rumbles from my chest.

Damn, that feels good. I haven't done nearly enough of that lately.

"How did lunch go?" I ask once they're both in front of me.

"It went well," Mackenzie says as they glance at each other with a knowing look.

When she turns back to me, her eyes glitter above a wide smile. I can't help but think this is the happiest I've seen her in a long time—since before the accident.

"Well, at least you had one good meal. You ready for this shitshow?" I ask, hooking a thumb behind me.

Atlas exhales as his eyes make quick work of the foyer. I can tell he wants to do this as much as I do—which is not at all. The fact that he's here anyway . . . well, it means a lot.

"How's it going so far?" he asks, meeting my eyes again.

"Oh, you know. They're putting on a show. For who, I have no idea, probably each other. Maybe if they have their fancy catered meal and their designer tablescape they can convince themselves they're happy."

Mackenzie bites her lip, and I can tell she's worried. She probably should be.

"Listen," I say as they step inside and I close the door behind them, "I say we get this over with and then go see a movie. Deal?"

Before they can answer there's a knock on the door behind me, and I nod toward the hallway. "Go ahead. I'll get this," I say, mostly because I'd like to stall as long as possible.

Atlas grumbles as he pulls Mackenzie down the hallway, disappearing into the dining room while I watch, wondering how we'll get through the next hour without choking my father.

I exhale and turn before I wrench open the door and freeze. A cold sweat instantly covers my body as the air stalls in my lungs. Darrell Crenshaw casually leans against the doorframe of my house, feet crossed at the ankles, a cruel smile curling his lips while Frankie towers over me.

My face turns ashen. Bile rises to the back of my throat, but I swallow it down. "Darrell . . . what are you guys doing here?" I ask, even though I know exactly what they're doing here.

Darrell glances out to the street. Dark sunglasses shade his eyes. "Nice neighborhood." His head turns and he stares up at the house beneath the dark lenses and whistles. "Gorgeous place you've got here."

"What do you want?" I hiss through the pulse pounding in my ears.

He gives a little shrug, his gaze sharp on mine. "It's collection time, Scott."

Beside him, Frankie cracks his knuckles while panic beats in my chest, a winged beast ready to break free.

I step out onto the front stoop, closing the door behind me while I pray my father doesn't choose this moment to come looking for me. "I told you. I need time."

He shakes his head and his lips twitch. "Time is up, Scott."

Want to see Graham get his happily-ever-after?
His love story is NEXT!
Catch more Boys of Riverside in book three.

About Gracie

Gracie is a contemporary young adult author who loves romance and writing fictional characters. When she's not busy telling lies for a living, she's likely wrangling her three kids, cooking subpar meals, and procrastinating. Feel free to reach out to her on social media! She loves talking to readers and chatting books!

Gracie's Gang (FB Group)

Facebook Page

TikTok

Instagram

Pinterest

Acknowledgements

I owe a big thanks to my editor, Yvette Rebello. I love all your comments and your enthusiasm, and I'm so grateful to have found someone who can help make my book better while being a cheerleader for my work and my characters.

And most of all, I need to thank God for allowing me to do something I love for a living. I know how very fortunate I am. With this book especially, his guidance and help got me through. I never would have finished this novel on time while struggling with horrendous head colds, my sons' insane sports schedule, allergies, an injured husband, and a toddler if it weren't for miraculous intervention.